Magic
in Her Eyes

by

Donna Dalton

The Gifted, Volume One

This is a work of fiction. Names, characters, places, and incidents are either the product of the author's imagination or are used fictitiously, and any resemblance to actual persons living or dead, business establishments, events, or locales, is entirely coincidental.

Magic in Her Eyes

COPYRIGHT © 2017 by Donna Dalton

Cover Art by *Rae Monet, Inc. Design*

The Wild Rose Press, Inc.
PO Box 708
Adams Basin, NY 14410-0708
Visit us at www.thewildrosepress.com

Publishing History
First American Rose Edition, 2017
Print ISBN 978-1-5092-1504-1
Digital ISBN 978-1-5092-1505-8

The Gifted, Volume One
Published in the United States of America

Praise for Donna Dalton

A partial of this story won first place in the 2015 HERA Show Me the Spark contest and the 2015 VOTS Hot Prospects contest.

~*~

Check out Donna's other historical romances available from The Wild Rose Press, Inc.:
THE CAVALRY WIFE
THE REBEL WIFE
IRISH DESTINY
IRISH CHARM
SEVEN SWANS BRIDE
THE GIFT
LOVING BYRNE

She charged for the house,
grateful for a clear mind and calm stomach. She had all but broken into a run as she rounded the corner and at full speed met a blue wall of chest and arms. The air left her with a whoosh, and she tottered on wobbly legs. Strong hands curled around her upper arms.

"Whoa there," came a deep, commanding voice. "Where's the fire?"

Her hands splayed over the man's chest, the wool of his jacket rough beneath her fingertips. Shiny gold buttons marched upward to a bold chin, firm lips, and a slender nose. Eyes the color of aged tree bark drilled into her, intense and searching.

Her mind went unexpectedly blank, and her mouth dry as a sunbaked pond. Her stomach was dancing again. She must have pushed herself too quickly after the vision. Certainly that was the problem.

She shrugged out of his grasp and took a step back. He wore the blue uniform of the United States Army and had a curved saber strapped to his waist. *A soldier.*

Like the ones from her vision.

"Do you have Anna? Is she all right?"

"Anna? Don't know anyone by that name. I came to speak with Mrs. Mildred Campbell. I was told she ran this place." He swept off his hat, revealing a tanned brow bunched with frown lines. "Are you Mrs. Campbell?"

Some days, especially days like today, she wished she were. "No, I am not Mrs. Campbell."

Dedications

I dedicate this book to
my wonderful group of fellow writers,
Mary Ann Clark,
Alleyne Dickens,
Jo Bourne,
and Pam Roller.
You helped me develop and polish this story
until it turned into the gem it is today.
Thank you for all your help.

~*~

I would also like to thank my beta readers
for their unfiltered feedback.
You are the best.

Chapter One

Indian Territories, May 1872

The oak was tall and grand, nearly one hundred years old, and not doing her a blessed bit of good. Some called it foolish to repeat the same efforts over and over in hopes of a different outcome. Some called it insane. She called it desperate.

Meredith brushed a hand over the rough bark. Brittle edges broke and fell to the ground. She briefly closed her eyes and formed an image in her head. Rosy, rounded cheeks. Red curls pulled back with a pink ribbon. A matching pink pinafore. And little hands holding onto a gray barn kitten.

What do you see of her? Let me see.

Nothing came. Only silence—no rustling of leaves, no groaning of limbs. Even the birds remained mute. It was frustrating, but not unexpected. Her visions had a mind of their own and would appear only when and if they chose.

She sank to her knees, ignoring the bite of gnarled roots pressing through skirt and petticoats. Bruised skin would be a small price to pay if it saved Anna.

Please let me see her.

The silence persisted, and irritation flared inside her. Time was slipping away. Precious time. A child's welfare was at stake. As much as she wanted to scream and rail, harsh demands might anger whatever governed the tree's life-giving force. She needed its cooperation.

Aunt Mildred had coached her to concentrate on the tree, on connecting with it. Push all other thoughts out of her head and focus on pulling forth a vision of what she wanted to see. She rested both hands on the trunk and refocused her mind.

"Please." Out loud this time, yet barely above a whisper. "I must find her. What do you see?"

The oak trembled beneath her fingertips, its tap root rumbling up into its heart. A low hum filled her ears. Warmth seeped through her fingers and spread into her palms. Energy pulsed through her, inviting her, connecting with her.

"Yes. Yes. That's it. Show me what you see."

Her vision swirled with white fog, extinguishing the sunlight. The legs of a horse emerged. Dark brown. Hurrying. More legs appeared. The thud of hooves thundered in her skull. The sensation knotted her stomach, and she swallowed back a bitter taste of bile. She wouldn't pay the price yet. She hadn't seen the prize.

Splashing replaced the drumming in her head. Water sprayed beneath churning hooves. *A creek? River? Where?*

"Show me more." Louder still. "Show me the girl."

The splashing retreated. Darkness reached in and shrouded the image. *No. No. No. There has to be more.* She dug deep within herself and willed every ounce of energy into reviving the vision. The dark cloud refused to budge. Panic caught in her throat. She had to make this work.

"Come back, please. Anna needs this. I need this.

Show me a glimpse of where she will be." Even an hour into the future would be enough to locate the child.

The vision remained obscured. She was going to fail. *Again.* She dug her fingernails into the bark, straining to wrench something out of the darkness. Anything. There was only swirling silence.

Arms frail as seedlings, she slumped forward and pressed her throbbing forehead against the trunk. There was nothing more she could do. Her *gift* refused to be controlled. Aunt Mildred was wrong. No amount of practice or mental focus would entice the trees to cooperate. She would never be able to command the visions as her aunt did. She was utterly unworthy of Mildred's confidence.

The oak shifted beneath her. Waves of energy swirled around her, ebbing and flowing like the tide. The haze withdrew. The galloping horses re-emerged, more distinct this time, and revealing the legs of riders wearing uniform trousers, tall boots, and sheathed swords.

Soldiers.

She pushed upright. "Is Anna with the soldiers? Is she at the fort? Let me see her."

A brilliant explosion of light answered, and the image vanished, leaving behind a thick curtain of blackness. Tears burned in her eyes. All her other visions had ended in a similar flash. This one would be no different. It was over. Yet again, what she wanted to see, what she needed the tree to bring forth, hadn't materialized. And little Anna would suffer the consequences.

Busy preparing the midday meal, she hadn't noticed the child missing until Anna failed to come to the dining hall with the other children. The last anyone had seen of her was when the girl left the schoolroom to use the privy. Meredith had checked the outhouse and the surrounding area. A search of the barn netted the same disheartening result.

Frantic, she'd scoured every nook and cranny of the main house. She had even gone to Anna's favorite playing spot, the base of a willow that overhung the shallow duck pond. The child was nowhere to be found. That was two hours ago, far too long and dangerous for a five-year-old, especially in light of the recent Indian attacks.

Dread rolled in her stomach. Anna was her responsibility, as were the seven other children at the orphanage. Before coming to Seaton House, she had only been responsible for herself—and look how that turned out. She'd been banished from her home in Pennsylvania to the uncivilized Indian Territories. She wouldn't let that happen again. Couldn't. She had nowhere else to go.

Meredith drew in a deep breath and worked to regain her strength and her wits. Aunt Mildred depended on her to look after the children. If she couldn't do that using her visions, she'd have to employ her more *reliable* abilities. Her stepbrother always said she had the eyesight of an eagle and the fleetness of a deer. If necessary, she'd soar over every inch of the property looking for Anna.

A faint clatter snagged her attention. She blinked the haze from her eyes and focused on the barn. What she could see through the open doors was quiet and still. Nothing moved outside the barn or in the nearby fenced paddock. The only movement came from the chickens scavenging in the garden for insects. She turned slowly to avoid upsetting the agreement she and her head had come to. If she didn't move too fast, it wouldn't spin.

The back of the main house remained equally quiet. Nothing stirred on the veranda or in the wide expanse of grass-covered yard. Even the laundry hung motionless on the clothes line. In her disoriented state, perhaps she had imagined the clamor.

A muted rumble drifted around the side of the house. She hadn't imagined that. It sounded like talking. She grabbed a handful of skirt and shot to her feet. *Please let that be Anna returning.*

She charged for the house, grateful for a clear mind and calm stomach. She had all but broken into a run as she rounded the corner and at full speed met a blue wall of chest and arms. The air left her with a whoosh, and she tottered on wobbly legs. Strong hands curled around her upper arms.

"Whoa there," came a deep, commanding voice. "Where's the fire?"

Her hands splayed over the man's chest, the wool of his jacket rough beneath her fingertips. Shiny gold buttons marched upward to a bold chin, firm lips, and a slender nose. Eyes the color of aged tree bark drilled into her, intense and searching.

Her mind went unexpectedly blank, and her mouth dry as a sunbaked pond. Her stomach was dancing again. She must have pushed herself too quickly after the vision. Certainly that was the problem.

She shrugged out of his grasp and took a step back. He wore the blue uniform of the United States Army and had a curved saber strapped to his waist. *A soldier.*

Like the ones from her vision.

"Do you have Anna? Is she all right?"

"Anna? Don't know anyone by that name. I came to speak with Mrs. Mildred Campbell. I was told she ran this place." He swept off his hat, revealing a tanned brow bunched with frown lines. "Are you Mrs. Campbell?"

Some days, especially days like today, she wished she were. "No, I am not Mrs. Campbell."

"Where can I find her?"

"Why? What do you want with her?"

"I have an urgent matter to discuss regarding the children."

It couldn't be any more urgent than finding Anna. She skirted him and headed for the front of the orphanage. "That won't be possible. She's away on a trip."

"When will she return?"

Not soon enough. "I don't know. A month? Two, perhaps."

A mule-drawn wagon and several mounted soldiers occupied the front driveway. In consideration of the recent attacks, the patrol had most likely come to check on the outlying orphanage. As much as she wanted to stop and find out, she couldn't. A child's welfare demanded her time and attention.

The thud of boots followed her up the steps. "I need to speak to whoever oversees the orphanage."

"That would be me."

"Excellent. If you'll give me a minute to explain…"

"I don't have a minute. Or a second, for that matter." She yanked open the door and rushed inside.

Failing was not an option. Not this time.

****

Preston trailed the woman into the orphanage. What a shrew. She'd nearly bowled him over with her headlong charge. And she didn't seem the least bit inclined to slow down and give him an apology or the courtesy of listening. On the other hand, she was definitely a looker. He'd expected the matron to be older and trail-worn. Not this lovely vision with honey-colored hair and violet eyes flashing with challenge. Her flowery scent brought to mind bedrooms and silken sheets; he'd been reluctant to let her wiggle out of his grasp.

He moved into the foyer of Seaton House, a home for orphaned children, and stopped. The fresh aroma of beeswax polish contradicted the clutter. A doll lay discarded on the floor. Several apples and a mound of leaves littered the base of a pedestal table. A child's straw hat dangled from an oil lamp perching precariously at the edge of the tabletop. The disorder didn't speak very highly of the steward.

She stood to his left, retrieving a bonnet and shawl from a coat tree. Oh, no. She wasn't going anywhere until he delivered his message.

He adopted his most commanding stance, one that demanded respect and obedience. "I'm Lieutenant Preston Booth from Fort Dent. I need to speak with you, Miss…Missus? I'm sorry; I don't know your name."

"Miss Talbot. Meredith Talbot." She slipped the bonnet over her head and tucked in several stray curls that had escaped the bun coiled at her neck. "And I don't have time to talk with you right now."

She would have to make time. "This isn't something that can wait, Miss Talbot."

"It has to. One of my children is missing."

Damn. An unexpected and most ill-timed impediment. "Is there anything I can do to help?"

A door on the far side of the room blasted open, and a flood of young people rushed into the foyer. They surrounded Miss Talbot, tugging at her skirts and peppering her with questions. Their high-pitched voices grated on his ears like fingernails on slate.

Children should be seen and not heard. His father's customary admonishment seemed quite fitting.

"Quiet," he bellowed, the sound bouncing off the walls and grabbing attentions. Astonished eyes rounded on him, yet instead of subsiding, the din grew louder and more insistent.

Miss Talbot raised her hand. "Quiet now, children. Quiet."

Her tone was much lower than his and spiced with sweetness. Good luck with that. To his surprise, the racket dimmed and finally abated. The piercing gazes, however, continued to hold onto him, slicing him with their wariness.

"There's nothing to worry about." Miss Talbot rested a hand on a small shoulder. "Anna is going to be just fine. She most likely took her kitten into the woods for an adventure and lost track of time."

"But Miss Talbot," a girl whined. "She missed the noon meal. Anna never misses a meal. She must be hurt."

"Or maybe the Indians got her," an older boy insisted.

Miss Talbot speared the youngster with a quelling

look. "Don't be scaring the little ones with talk of Indians, Gabe."

"But what about the soldiers?" The boy cut him a mistrustful glare. "Why are *they* here?"

"The soldiers are just checking on us. They will be leaving soon." She shooed the children with a flick of her hand. "Now all of you…back into the schoolroom. I know you couldn't have finished your lessons already."

"But Miss Talbot—"

"Go on now. All these questions will only delay my search for Anna."

With grumbles and dragging feet, the children finally filed back through the doorway. Preston let go a relieved breath. Good. Now, he could hear his own thoughts.

Miss Talbot slung a thin shawl around her shoulders and angled toward him. "If you did come to check on us, Lieutenant, I'm glad for it. As it turns out, I could use your help."

"Tell me what you need." The sooner he got this task over and done with, the sooner he could get back to his regular duties.

"Since my housekeeper had to go into town, I need you to watch the children while I expand my search over the property and into the next."

He'd rather thrust hot pokers into his eyes. "My men and I will conduct the search."

Rosy lips pulled reed thin. "Strange men will only frighten the child. She won't come to you. I need to be the one looking for her."

Damnation. A run-in with the quartermaster over ammunition had already turned his day sour. Now this. His plan to weather his assignment at Fort Dent until

General Pope came through with the promised transfer to a post worthy of his education and training teetered on unstable legs.

He shoved on his hat and retreated to the porch. "Private Greene, dismount and come inside. Watch over the children and don't let them leave the house for any reason. You other two men, set up sentry posts at the front and rear."

As his troopers rushed to do his bidding, Miss Talbot brushed past him and clattered down the steps. He jogged to catch up. For a tiny sprite of a woman, she sure moved fast. Though he preferred his women more refined, this one, with her boldness and single-minded determination, had lassoed his attention.

"Why did you order your men to set up sentry posts?" She spiked him with an anxious glance. "Are the rogue Indians that close?"

"We didn't see any signs of them, but their attacks are moving nearer to this area. I don't want to take any chances."

"Then we have to hurry."

"Agreed. The sooner we find your missing child, the sooner we can all be on our way."

"*All* be on our way?" Lacy lines furrowed her brow. "Whatever do you mean by that?"

"It's the reason my men and I are here. My commander feels it's best if the surrounding homesteaders shelter at the fort until the renegades are captured. I'm here to offer my assistance in moving you and the children."

She stopped at the edge of the woods and cupped her hands to her mouth. "Anna, where are you? Are you out there? Please answer me."

Only a protesting squirrel responded. She muttered something under her breath and dove into the woods. He plunged after her, pushing through the overgrowth invading the footpath. A wily vine ambushed his legs. Another attempted to lynch him. He crushed a curse beneath his teeth. This was the very reason he'd elected to be a mounted trooper and not a foot soldier.

Just ahead, Miss Talbot slowed. A prickly runner had captured the bottom of her skirt. Her struggles gave him a chance to close the distance between them.

"Is the situation with the Indians so dire," she said over her shoulder, "that we must move to the fort?"

"Yes, it is that dire. They have already torched several outlying farms south of here and killed nearly a dozen people, including women and children." That ought to impart the seriousness of the situation.

Silky white calves showed above the tops of her boots, and her backside swayed in delightful wiggles as she worked to liberate her skirt. A gentleman would lend a hand. But he wasn't in a gentlemanly mood. Not with the way his sweat-drenched uniform chafed his skin, not to mention the growing bulge in his trousers.

"Can't you just…" She gave a soft grunt and yanked her skirt free. "There. Can't you just order your soldiers to stay and protect us?"

"We don't have the resources for that. Most of our men are out searching for the renegades. The rest are guarding the fort." He'd trade his last bottle of prime Kentucky whiskey for command of one of *those* patrols.

"If I agree to this move, where will we stay? I won't have the children separated. The disruption will be stressful enough."

"Unfortunately, we have a number of civilians already quartered at the fort and many more arriving daily. I cannot guarantee you will be housed together."

"Do you have children, Lieutenant?"

No, thank the Lord. One day perhaps when…make that *if*…he decided to settle down and marry. He wouldn't want any offspring of his growing up as he had, craving the attention of a father who was rarely home and when he was, had no time or energy to entertain a lonely child. For now and the foreseeable future, his career would remain his focus.

"I don't have any children or a wife for that matter," he said. "The army is my life."

"Then you don't understand how traumatic uprooting a child can be. They require familiarity and consistency." Her voice quivered with intensity. "These children have been through more than most, losing homes and families."

"I was taught that children should do as they are told." Taught by his father's stern voice and heavy hand.

"Thankfully, the children's welfare is *my* responsibility. I won't move them to the fort unless you can guarantee we won't be separated."

Some battles had to be forfeited to win the war. Major Allen would not be happy with this added complication, but he'd cross that trench when he got there. "Very well, we will do our best to see you are provided quarters where you can all be together."

"I shall hold you to that promise, Lieutenant." She gave him a pointed look and then resumed her breakneck advance into the woods.

He swiped sweat from his brow and lunged after

her. Damn fool woman. If the vines didn't kill them, heat apoplexy would.

A few minutes later, the path opened onto a clearing sliced by a shallow creek. The crystal-clear water burbled over submerged rocks, the soothing sound beckoning him to indulge. With his body smoldering beneath the cocoon of wool, a cool dip sounded quite inviting, especially if it included a blonde-haired nymph with flashing violet eyes. He envisioned discarded footwear on the bank and the two of them wading in the water where more of her creamy calves would be visible.

He shook off the image. What was he doing? He should be focusing on the task at hand, not fantasizing about foolish romps with a woman who set his mind and body whirling out of control.

Miss Talbot paced at the water's edge. "I don't see any footprints. I do hope Anna hasn't gone down to where the creek widens and becomes deeper. She hasn't yet learned to swim."

Her comment sparked a memory. "Does this Anna child have reddish-colored hair?"

"Yes, why?"

"When riding up to the property, we spotted a young girl sitting near the creek bank. She had red hair and wore a pink dress."

Miss Talbot reeled to face him, her eyes blasting at him like the barrels of a derringer. "Why didn't you say so before?"

"It didn't occur to me until now. Besides, she didn't appear to be in any distress. She sat calmly as we rode by. I assumed she was being looked after."

"How could you leave a child all alone?"

Her tone poked bayonet sharp. He couldn't stop from thrusting back. "How could you let her out of your sight? You are the steward of this place. As you said, her welfare is *your* responsibility."

A slap to the face couldn't have produced more astonishment. Or hurt. Tears brimmed in her eyes. Damn. What was wrong with him? He knew better than to give free rein to his anger.

Before he could tender an apology, she swiped at her tears and charged past him. "Show me where you saw her."

Thirty minutes and a fiery tromp later, they arrived at the creek where he and his men had spotted the child. Nothing moved in the glade. No hint of pink, no reddish curls. The child had vanished. Of course she had. He didn't expect anything less on a day that had turned foul as a festering bullet wound. He wouldn't let his thoughts drift to the possibility that renegades were the cause of the girl's disappearance.

He approached a cluster of rocks bunched at the creek's edge. "She was sitting right here."

Miss Talbot cupped her mouth and called out, "Anna? Anna, are you here? Please come out."

Only a squawking blue jay replied as it took flight. Preston squinted at the sun just visible through the leafy canopy. The day was wasting away. He needed to find this child and get her and all the others to the fort before the sun set and the predators, both two-legged and four-legged, came out of the hills to hunt.

Tiny, water-filled craters stamped the creek bank, most of them disappearing in the mire. Tracking the child would be nearly impossible. "We'll find her faster if we split up." He pointed eastward. "You go upstream.

I'll go down."

A mutinous glint steeled her eyes. She opened her mouth as if to challenge his suggestion and then just as quickly snapped her lips shut. "Fine," she pushed out. "But, if you locate her, don't touch her. Just call for me."

Like hell he would. This search had already cost him valuable time. The urchin would have to deal with her fear of strangers.

He followed the creek, slipping and sliding on the flood-cratered bank. Sand and mud clotted his boots. Private Greene would have a devil of a time removing the grime and buffing scratches from the boot leather. On the next furlough, he'd give the hard-working striker an extra day, especially after assigning him the onerous duty of looking after Miss Talbot's imps.

As he rounded a bend, a smudge of pink peeked through a patch of bushes overhanging the creek bed. He scaled the small incline and pushed the branches aside. A red-haired girl huddled in the hidey-hole with a kitten clutched against her chest. *Finally*.

He held out his hand. "Here, let me help you out of there."

Her eyes grew wide, and she thrust back against the wall of brush.

"Come now, Anna is it? Be a good little girl and take my hand."

Red curls whipped around pudgy cheeks. He bit down on a curse. *Children should obey their elders*. Another sage dictum Miss Talbot's flock inclined to ignore.

He reached down and plucked the girl from her nest. "There. Now grab hold of my neck."

The child went stiff as a board. The kitten clasped under her arm began mewling in protest. What the hell? He didn't have time for this. He snagged the girl's hand and set it on his neck so she could hang on while he navigated the treacherous creek bed. The last thing he needed was to drop the child on her head and give the pretty, but shrewish, Miss Talbot more ammunition to fire at him.

A moan started low in the girl's throat and grew louder. She started howling and thrashing in his arms. He tightened his grip. Was the creature possessed?

"Stop flailing or you're going to make me drop you."

The child screeched louder. The kitten joined in. His ears rang with the cacophony. The kitten struggled in the child's embrace. Not getting anywhere, it twisted and sank its teeth into his forearm. He let go a yelp and jerked away. The momentum sent him stumbling down the incline. His boot heel caught on a root. He scrambled to regain his balance but lost the battle.

He clasped the child against him as he fell backward. His backside met the creek, and water sprayed around him. He managed to right himself. The fall had dislodged the girl's hand from his neck. She sat on his lap, thankfully silent, holding onto her kitten and glaring up at him as if the entire incident was his fault. Creek water rushed over his legs and lapped at his waist. Not the soothing dip or the nymph he'd envisioned.

Miss Talbot appeared on the path and ran toward them. She wadded into the water and snatched the child from his lap. Violet eyes snapped at him. "Are you daft? I told you not to touch her."

He swiped mud from his face. If he made it back to Fort Dent without ending his misery with a bullet, it would be a miracle.

Chapter Two

Lieutenant Booth's soldiers loaded the last of the luggage onto the wagon. The children crowded around her at the bottom of the porch steps, quiet now after the chaos of Anna's return and the packing of their belongings. While upsetting, the relocation to Fort Dent was necessary for their safety. Yet the fort could very well hold just as much danger as the rogue Indians.

"Are you angry with me, Miss Talbot? Your mouth is tilted down. It does that when people are mad." Anna's chin trembled. "I didn't mean to upset you. Daisy ran off, and once I found her, we decided to play by the creek for a while."

Their neighbor Mr. Pryor had presented the kitten to the orphanage once it was old enough to be weaned from its mother. Anna had immediately adopted the cat and was rarely seen without her playmate. Even now, she had Daisy cradled in her arms.

Meredith smoothed bedraggled red curls. "No, sweetling. I'm not angry with you. I'm just feeling a bit overwhelmed by this sudden need to leave."

"I wish Mrs. Campbell was here."

The child's woeful words echoed her own thoughts. Aunt Mildred would know the right thing to do. During the eight months since her arrival at Seaton House, she had discovered her aunt was a force unto herself. Mildred had left Pennsylvania with her husband well before Meredith had been born. When Mr. Campbell died in a mining accident, Mildred had fended for herself and quite successfully. She turned their tiny silver mine into a profitable business and used the proceeds from its sale to purchase a farmhouse which she ultimately turned into the orphanage. Meredith sighed. If only she could be half as successful and self-assured.

"Everything is going to be just fine, Anna. You'll see."

Lily moved closer, her fingers choking a satchel handle. "Do we *have* to go, Miss Talbot? From what the soldiers are saying, it sounds as if there are a lot of people staying at the fort."

Before being rescued by Mildred, twelve-year-old Lily Kendrick had suffered greatly at the hands of ignorance. She'd been labeled a liar and a witch. No one believed in reading tarot cards or seeing auras. It was understandable that the girl would be reluctant to leave the seclusion and safety of the orphanage.

Meredith pasted on her most encouraging smile, although reassured was the last thing she felt. "I'm afraid we do, Lily. But it will only be temporarily. Just until the renegades are captured."

"Can't the soldiers stay here and protect us?"

She wished. However, as Mildred often said, *if wishes were horses, beggars would ride*. She shook her head. "Lieutenant Booth says most of the soldiers are out looking for the Indians or protecting the garrison. There aren't enough to spare for guarding Seaton House. We'll just have to manage at Fort Dent as best we can until we are able to return."

"What about Mrs. Clement and Mr. Hoggard?"

Worry pinched Anna's face. "What will they do?"

The housekeeper and handyman had left earlier that morning for their monthly trip to purchase goods and supplies. The town of Mineral sat just outside of Fort Dent, some twelve miles west of Seaton House. Mildred wanted the orphanage to be as far from prying eyes as possible, but still have the outside world easily accessible. Unfortunately, it might not be far enough. In anticipation of negotiations between the railway and the Creek Indians, the small mining town had already begun expanding. Privacy would soon be a hard commodity to come by.

"If Mrs. Clement and Mr. Hoggard have already started back, then we should cross paths on the way. They can turn around and join us. Otherwise we'll catch up to them in town." In the distance, dark clouds bruised the skyline. A shiver poured down her spine. Provided that storm held off.

"We're ready for the children now," one of the soldiers called out.

Perfect. Any longer and her doubts and the weather might get the better of her.

"Me first," little Robbie shouted as he broke into a run.

Always the adventurer, the six-year-old wasn't about to let uncertainties hold him back. "Go on, children," she urged the others. "Get into the wagon."

She started to follow, but a tug stopped her. Anna held onto the bottom of her skirt, her little mouth sagging, her eyes wide and ringed with dark circles. The trauma with Lieutenant Booth had drained the child of all vitality.

"Come, sweetling." Meredith gave the girl a nudge.

"You can sit on my lap during the ride if you'd like."

Anna remained rooted in place, clutching her kitten and eyeing the other children being lifted into the wagon. Her lips pulled into a taut line, and she shoved her shoulders back in a mulish pose. "I won't get in the wagon. Not with *them* there."

Meredith called on her last reserves of patience, which after the day she'd had, wasn't much. "I won't let the soldiers touch you, I promise."

Soulful brown eyes lifted and poured over her as if weighing the reliability of her guardian's claim.

"Please, Anna. It's getting late. We don't want to be on the road when the sun sets. You know how frightened Becky is of the dark."

Anna glanced at the wagon and back. Her chin tilted higher. "Only *you* can touch me."

Meredith squeezed Anna's shoulder. "Only me. Now, let's get into the wagon, shall we? Before Robbie and Gabe toss out all the straw the nice soldiers spread in the bed to cushion our ride."

As they started for the wagon, a stiff gust kicked up. Dirt stung her eyes and blasted her exposed skin. Meredith clamped a hand on her bonnet and bent into the squall. Springtime storms in the Indian Territories seemed to be much fiercer than back east. Mildred had told her about the great whirlwinds that could spawn with no warning and cause massive destruction. The good Lord willing, no such beast would lurk within the approaching storm.

The gust thankfully let up as she and Anna reached the wagon. Meredith held out a hand. "Let Lily hold Daisy while you get in."

The girl relinquished the kitten but not her grip on

21

Meredith's skirts. The soldiers were still too close for comfort. Meredith shooed them with a wave of her hand. "Thank you, but we don't require any assistance. You men can go about your other duties."

They stood immobile, blinking at her as if she had invited them to jump over the moon. Daft men. Just like their commander.

As if hearing her thoughts, Lieutenant Booth abandoned the soldier he was talking with and strode toward them. Squishing sounds salted his steps. His trousers and most of his uniform jacket were damp with creek water. Though his expression remained unreadable, he had to be uncomfortable. Wet wool tended to chafe most unpleasantly. She smiled inwardly. Served him right for not listening. Maybe next time, he would heed her counsel.

"What's the delay?" He glanced at Anna, submerged now in the safety of wide skirts. "Oh, I see."

"I told these soldiers we didn't require any assistance getting into the wagon. But they don't seem to grasp my words." She put on her most puzzled frown, the one she adopted when prompting the children during their lessons. "I understand hearing loss can be a consequence of constant exposure to gun fire. Is that what's wrong with them?"

The skin covering the lieutenant's jaw twitched, and his penetrating gaze drilled into her. A poked hornet couldn't look more agitated.

"My men hear just fine." He shifted his glare to the soldiers. "You two mount up and scout ahead. Private Greene, check the mules and then bring me my horse."

The soldiers gave brisk salutes and rushed to carry out his orders. Clearly they had no difficulties with hearing.

The lieutenant took a step back and treated her to a brief bow. "Please proceed with your boarding, Miss Talbot."

That was more like it. She clasped Anna by the arms and swung her up and into the wagon. The child scurried to the middle and turned, giving the lieutenant a wary stare. It would be a long time, if ever, before the officer earned her trust.

Meredith braced her hands on the edge of the wagon and hopped. It wasn't enough to get her rear end anywhere near the bed. She moved closer and tried again. Still short. She might as well be trying to mount an elephant.

"You might be more comfortable sitting on the bench seat with Private Greene."

Comfort was a relative term. "I prefer to ride back here with the children." She gathered her skirts and gave another try. With little luck. She thumped back to the ground, heels stinging from the impact.

"Do you need any assistance?"

His sugary tone chafed, and she bit back an unladylike retort. "No. I do not require any assistance."

"We don't have all day, Miss Talbot."

"I can do this on my own, thank you very much." She didn't need his hands on her, making her stomach dance again. Worry over the move already had her insides roiling.

"Do you also have an aversion to being touched?"

She looked up and met his taunting gaze. It was a challenge she couldn't ignore. She hefted her chin. "Not if I have given permission to be touched."

One corner of his mouth twitched. Surely that

wasn't a smile. From what she'd seen, the most his lips could manage were frowns.

He held out his hand. "May I help you into the wagon, Miss Talbot? In the name of expediency?"

Straw rustled behind her. One child hummed. Another thrummed on the wagon boards. The children were getting restless. She could contain herself long enough to be lifted onto the wagon.

"Very well. I give my permission."

His hands curled around her waist. Heat seeped through her blouse and branded her skin. Her stomach started doing odd little summersaults like the ones she'd seen Chinese acrobats perform at a local fair. So much for containing herself.

His grip tightened, and he lifted her up and onto the wagon bed as if she weighed no more than a rag doll. His hands lingered a moment before he released her. Gray-brown eyes fused with hers. A strange connection churned between them like the rush crowding the air before a storm.

She broke the contact and busied herself with settling in the wagon and placing Anna on her lap. *Such silly nonsense.* She should have better control over herself. The last thing she needed was to arouse thoughts that there could be something between them. A romantic entanglement would only add more kinks to her already matted life.

A soldier approached, leading a bay gelding marked with dark stockings. It reminded her of her earlier attempt to bring forth a vision. She had been close to summoning an image of Anna. The vision just needed a little more guidance; a little more focus. All her life, things came easily to her: riding, cooking, and even tedious needlework. But this...this *gift* seemed beyond her grasp. It was quite maddening.

Lieutenant Booth accepted the horse's reins and turned. His intense gaze fastened on her. Fire rushed through her veins. If she were a stove, her ears would spout smoke.

"Is there anything you or the children need before we leave, Miss Talbot?"

A bucket of cold water? She shook her head. "No. Thank you, Lieutenant. We're as ready as we'll ever be."

"Very well. Have everyone secure a firm handhold. I've ordered Private Greene to set the mules to a fast clip. We're going to have to hurry if we want to beat the darkness and that approaching storm."

"I'll make certain everyone holds tight."

"Be sure you do. We don't have time to stop and retrieve any misplaced children."

Was that a jab? Given their brief but bellicose history, it was. He swung into the saddle and rode away, back straight, seat easy and controlled. He was clearly a seasoned horseman and a most striking man. Any woman on the hunt for a husband might find him the perfect quarry. But she wasn't in the market for a husband. Not now. Probably not ever. Witch hunts, even in these enlightened times, were still quite common. If uncovered, her secret could place her and those she loved in danger.

Mildred had informed her that the gift of *sight* passed along the female line of their family. Her mother had it. Mildred had it. So had her grandmother and great-grandmother. The talent lay dormant until the monthly courses began. Meredith grunted under breath.

Just an added bane of entering womanhood, and another reason she refused to marry. She wasn't about to burden a child with such a curse.

The squeak of springs pulled her back from her thoughts. Private Greene settled on the wagon seat and took up the reins. He clucked to the mules, and the wagon jolted forward. Meredith gripped the rail behind her. Best to keep her mind on the things she *could* control.

"Hold tight, children," she urged. "Just like the lieutenant instructed."

Anna tilted her head back, her little brow puckering. "The lieutenant doesn't like children, Miss Talbot. I heard it in his thoughts."

Like Meredith, the orphans at Seaton House were all gifted with extraordinary abilities. Mildred rescued them from neglect and persecution and coached them on controlling and concealing their talents so they could eventually fit into society. Little Anna's *gift* allowed her to hear other people's thoughts when she touched them. Good, bad, it didn't matter. She heard them all. And it frightened her. She avoided laying hands on anyone at all costs.

Meredith brushed a wayward curl from the girl's forehead. "The lieutenant doesn't have children of his own. I suspect he just doesn't know how to relate to you. He's used to giving orders and having them obeyed without question."

"His horse said he's a nice man," Robbie chirped. "Said the lieutenant gives him special treats and doesn't use spurs like the others do."

Robbie Edmunds had the gift of gab with animals. He could hear their thoughts, and they could hear his.

His twin sister Becky had the same talent. Meredith couldn't imagine having all that clamoring going on inside her head. Her own thoughts were noisy enough.

Anna hefted her chin. "I don't care what his dumb horse said. I didn't want to touch him, but he made me anyway. He's a mean man. I don't like him."

"I don't think he was being intentionally cruel, Anna. He just didn't know what handling would do to you."

"He thought I was possessed. What is possessed?"

Gabe shifted closer and adopted a sinister tone. "It means a demon has taken over your body."

Anna's eyes grew big as saucers. "D-Does a demon have me, Miss Talbot?"

"No, sweetling. A demon does not have you, I promise." Meredith glared at the older boy. At nine years of age, he knew better than to employ unnecessary dramatics.

Gabe heeded her warning and slunk back to the other side of the wagon. She glanced at Private Greene. To her relief, the soldier appeared to be more focused with handling the mules than with listening to his passengers, but better to be safe than sorry.

She lowered her voice. "People who don't understand our abilities will say we are demons or possessed by demons. They may call us witches. They are frightened by what we can do. That fright will push them into being cruel and often hostile. It's why we have to keep our talents concealed."

A small white sack skimmed over the ground, rushing headlong toward the wagon. Only one person could give life to an inanimate object.

"Gabe," she hissed. "Stop that."

The sack hopped over the back of the wagon and landed with a thump in the straw. Gabe snatched up the sack and dangled it by the draw strings. "I forgot my jacks. You know I need them."

Jacks to Gabriel Hunt was like a sugar teat to a teething infant. Instant calm. They were worth their weight in gold, but not at the expense of exposing his secret.

"You could have asked the driver to stop the wagon and retrieved them in a normal manner." She gestured at Private Greene. "What if he or the other soldiers had seen such a display?"

Gabe shrugged. "They didn't. I made sure none of them were looking."

"All of you listen to me." She made eye contact with each of her eight charges. "We must restrain ourselves while outside the orphanage. We cannot risk anyone finding out about us. Do you understand?"

At their nods, she added, "Once we return to Seaton House, you can resume practicing your skills. Until then, there will be no use of our talents."

"What about Petunia?" Robbie patted his breast pocket. "Can I still talk with her?"

A little pink nose sprinkled with whiskers peeked over the top of the boy's pocket. He'd brought his pet mouse. Not a surprise.

"You can talk with Petunia, but only in the privacy of our quarters."

Anna squirmed and clutched her kitten against her chest. "Where will we live? Will we be together?" Her little voice quivered. "I don't want to live with anyone else but you."

"There's no need to fret. Lieutenant Booth

promised he would find a place where we can all stay together." He'd best make good on his promise, or he'd deal with her wrath.

"He's quite handsome," Nel said. "You should set your cap for him, Miss Talbot."

Having turned fourteen the month before, Nelda Sawyer was discovering that boys were not just playmates for hide-and-seek. She had developed a shine for the neighbor's son and devised every excuse to visit the nearby Pryor homestead.

"I am not in the market for a husband." Meredith plucked a sliver of chaff from Anna's hair. "You children keep me occupied enough."

Lily joined the volley. "The lieutenant likes you. His aura turned pink when he handed you into the wagon. Then both your auras melded together and turned purple, as if you were soulmates."

She had blossomed into pink and red and all manner of hot shades beneath the lieutenant's touch. But that didn't mean she should set her cap for him. More fittingly, it should send her running in the other direction.

"Lieutenant Booth is dedicated to the army. He's not looking for a wife."

"He thought you were pretty," Anna said. "Pretty, but shrewish. What is shrewish?"

Meredith stiffened. She might be impulsive and a bit short-tempered, but never shrewish. And pretty? Did he really find her appealing? She always thought her nose was too stubby. And her neck resembled that of a giraffe. Not in the least bit pretty.

She shifted for a more comfortable position. "It means someone who is irritable and quarrelsome."

"But you're neither of those."

"Of course not. The lieutenant just caught me during a stressful time. He doesn't know me like the rest of you do."

"I can brew up a love potion if you'd like," ten-year-old Maddie offered. "Make it extra strong with owl droppings."

Robbie nodded. "Me and Becky can help you find the owls, Maddie. I bet there's lots of 'em in the stable lofts."

Meredith heaved a sigh. Why Aunt Mildred thought she would be able to oversee these children was beyond her. She had about as much sway over them as she did over her *gift*. Not to mention teaching them to fit into society. She didn't even believe such a thing was possible for herself.

****

Meredith swayed with the motion of the wagon. After miles of bumping and jolting, her entire body ached. A hot bath sounded particularly appealing. But according to Nel, who had made the trip to Mineral numerous times, they still had at least another half hour of torture to endure. Besides, once they reached the fort, she had no idea what type of housing would be provided or even if there would *be* bathing tubs.

Her only solace—the children appeared to have heeded her warning. They contentedly watched the passing countryside, pointing out various plants and animals they spied along the way. Hopefully this *normal* behavior would last until they were safely ensconced in private quarters beyond prying eyes and sensitive ears.

The roadway rolled over the landscape, cutting

through short expanses of forests in between broad patches of cleared land. She could almost taste the pungent aroma of freshly turned earth riding the air. Earlier in the week, Mr. Hoggard had informed her that the local farmers were preparing their fields for summer crops. The milder climate allowed plants to grow well into the fall months—a boon to living in the Indian territories, if one survived the unpredictable renegade uprisings.

Situated between Texas and Kansas, the territories had been distributed to each of the five major Indian tribes. While closed to white settlers, the center of the region contained a large tract of unallocated land where many legitimate settlements had sprung up. The town of Mineral had formed around Fort Dent, an army outpost assigned to maintain the peace and protect homesteaders—not an easy task considering the volatility of their neighbors.

The territories started as flat plains in the east and rose to rolling hills and low mountains to the west. Seaton House sat in the south-central portion, just east of the Shoehorn Mountain range. While mostly serene and beautiful, there were pockets of harsh land that showed no mercy for weakness.

One of the wheels dipped into a rut, giving the wagon a hard jolt. Her elbow rammed into the side railing, and she let go a pained yelp. Anna grabbed a handful of her skirt to keep from tumbling off. Squeals and shuffling rang out as the other children scrambled to regain their places. Little Robbie barely clung to the travelling trunk he'd been perched on. At this rate, the wagon would make it to the fort in one piece, but the passengers wouldn't.

"Private Greene," she called out. "Is there anything you can do to avoid the ruts? The jolting is quite painful, even with the straw bedding."

The soldier glanced over his shoulder, his sun-browned face furrowed with wrinkles. "I'm sorry, ma'am. The road is full of runnels and pits from the recent rains. No way to avoid them. All I can suggest is that y'all hunker down until we get through this rough patch."

"Very well." She tightened her grip on the railing. "Children, do as Private Greene says. Find a firm handhold and stay low. Robbie, come down off that trunk and sit next to Gabe."

Frightened by his near unseating, the boy didn't tender any argument. He slid off the trunk and onto the wagon bed quicker than a rabbit entered a burrow.

Anna wriggled in her lap. "All this bumping is making my tummy hurt."

"Mine, too, sweetling." Meredith gave the girl a consoling pat. "Just hold on for a little while longer. The ride should get smoother." So her aching bottom hoped.

Despite her optimistic words, the ride didn't get any smoother. It only got worse. The wagon jounced and juddered so hard it felt as if her teeth were going to shake loose. Each dip brought forth more yelps and groans from the children. Once they got settled at the fort, she'd have Maddie prepare a batch of herbal tea to soothe the aches of the demanding trip.

As she shifted for a more comfortable position, the front wheel plunged into another rut, deeper and more forceful this time. A loud splintering pealed out. The wagon stopped abruptly and pitched to one side.

Meredith lost her grip on the railing and slid across the bed. Lily careened into her. She twisted to keep from squashing Anna, and her back met the pointed corner of a trunk. A poker-hot pang stabbed her spine. She clamped her teeth around a curse. This trip was taking a toll on her—mentally *and* physically.

Her tumble arrested, she pushed back her bonnet knocked askew by the fall. The straw bedding had shifted and mounded around them. Arms and feet stuck out from the jumbled mass.

"Is everyone all right? Did anyone get hurt?"

Lily rolled upright on the steeply canted wagon bed. "I'm all right. I think."

"Gabe? Robbie?"

The two boys bounced to their knees. Bits of straw salted their hair and clothes. "We're fine," they said in unison.

Across from the boys, Nel held a teary-eyed Becky on her lap. The younger girl clutched her arm and grimaced in pain. Meredith's heart took a nose dive. "What's wrong, Becky? Is your arm hurt?"

"It got twisted under her during the fall." Nel cuddled the girl closer. "But I think she's going to be all right. It's not broken. Probably just a sprain."

"Keep your arm still as you can, Becky. We'll put some cold cloths on it when we get to the fort. It will feel better soon, I promise." That was seven children. Where was the eighth? Fear crept up her throat. Surely she hadn't lost yet another child. "Does anyone see Sally? Sally, where are you?"

Straw rustled, and brown curls spiked with chaff emerged from the mound. Meredith's pounding heart slowed to normal. "There you are. Are you all right?"

Sally nodded, eyes twinkling and face glowing. Leave it to a child to find amusement in a calamity.

"Where is Private Greene?" Gabe motioned to the wagon seat. "He ain't there no more."

Meredith turned to the front of the wagon. The mules stood patiently in their traces, but there was no sign of the driver. She craned her head over the side. A dislodged wheel rested in the ditch. A few feet away, Private Greene sprawled face-first on the ground, still as a toppled statue.

She scooted Anna off her lap. "Nel, help the children out of the wagon. I need to see to Private Greene. He's fallen into the ditch."

"Is he hurt?" Nel asked.

"I don't know. He's not moving." She slung a leg over the side, preparing to slide out.

The thunder of hooves stilled her. Lieutenant Booth reined to a stop behind the wagon, followed by his other two soldiers. He dismounted and raced to her side.

"Is everyone all right?"

"Everyone except for Private Greene." She gestured at the ditch. "He was thrown from the wagon. I was just about to go check on him."

He stepped closer and reached for her. "Let me help you out."

The way her muscles smarted, she wasn't about to argue. Besides, the injured soldier's welfare took precedence over keeping Lieutenant Booth at arm's length. She slid over the side and into his grasp. He handed her to the ground, and she hurried to the unmoving soldier.

His sides rose and fell in a steady rhythm. He was

alive. But not unscathed. A small puddle of red stained the ground near his temple.

She dropped to her knees. "Help me roll him over so I can see how badly he's hurt."

The lieutenant removed his hat and squatted beside her. Together they turned Private Greene onto his back. Blood oozed from a two-inch gash slashing his temple. A blood-stained rock submerged in the ground appeared to be the perpetrator.

She rubbed her knuckles over the soldier's breastbone, a technique she'd observed Doctor Winters employ to rouse one of the field hands who had been kicked unconscious by a mule. "Private Greene, can you hear me? Open your eyes."

Eyelids fluttered open. He blinked and blinked again. Dazed brown eyes rolled and tumbled until they finally managed to settle on her.

"Wh-what happened?"

"One of the wagon wheels broke loose," she said. "The force threw you from the wagon."

"The children... Are they...?" A strangled cough choked off his words.

What a considerate man. Thinking of the children before himself. She undid the top button of his jacket to ease his breathing. "The children are just fine. You, on the other hand, hit your head on a rock. There's a good-sized gash that will need bandaging, possibly stitching."

He grimaced and reached for his head. Meredith stopped him with an outstretched hand. "Don't. You'll only make it bleed more."

His face sagged, and he dropped his hand with a sigh. "I'm sorry, Lieutenant. I should have been more careful. Should have slowed the mules or gotten down and led them past the deeper ruts."

"You were only following orders to maintain a quick pace. If anyone is to blame, it's me. Now lie still and let us see to your wound." The lieutenant unwound a yellow handkerchief from his neck. "This should do for a bandage until we can get him to the doctor. Are you squeamish around blood, Miss Talbot? Do you want me to take care of the bandaging?"

"I can do it. You just hold his head steady while I wrap." On a cattle farm, there was almost a daily incident of some sort of injury. She had helped the local physician dress many a gash, some deep enough to expose bone. She had long ago gotten over any squeamishness.

Lieutenant Booth handed her the neckerchief and then shifted until he crouched above Private Greene. He cradled the soldier's head and slowly lifted. His gentleness and concern surprised her. He seemed to be more of the type who would require his men to bite down and bear their pain.

She placed the handkerchief over the gash and began wrapping the tails around the soldier's head. Her fingers brushed the lieutenant's as she maneuvered around his hands. Flutters danced up her arm. Her head reeled as if she'd stolen sips of her father's favorite corn whiskey. Blood might not make her lightheaded, but touching the lieutenant definitely did.

"Remarkable."

Lieutenant Booth's whispered remark wafted over her. She tied off the bandage ends and looked up. "What is?"

His gaze surged over her, slow and sensual, like the waves of a lake caressing the shoreline. More quivers spilled down her spine. Undoubtedly he was gifted with the ability to mesmerize. She was firmly under his sway.

Footfalls approached, and the moment burst like a fragile soap bubble.

"Lieutenant," one of the other soldiers called out. "We inspected the wagon. It looks like the front axle snapped and sheared off that wheel."

"Is it repairable?"

The soldier shook his head. "Not without smithy tools and a lot more daylight."

Private Greene tried to rise up on his elbows. "Let me help, sir. I'll be all right. It's just a little bump on the head. Nothing I can't handle."

The lieutenant restrained him with a hand to his shoulder. "That's no little bump, Private. You stay right here and rest. That's an order."

Private Greene mumbled a dejected "yes, sir," and wobbled back to the ground. Her heart went out to the wounded soldier. She knew all about wanting to help, but being physically incapable of doing so. Several months ago, she'd been bedridden with a twisted ankle and was unable to assist Mildred with the children when they came down with the croup. Watching her aunt work herself to near exhaustion and unable to ease her burden had been very frustrating.

Something brushed her arm, jarring her back to the present. Lieutenant Booth leaned close as he reached for his hat. He was so near his heat breached her dress and warmed her skin. Her mouth went dry, and her heart started racing. What was it about this man that had her reacting so intensely to a mere touch?

He rolled away and pushed upright, taking his

unnerving heat with him. She busied herself with cleaning her bloodied fingers on the grass. If only she could wipe away her reactions so easily.

"Let's get those mules unhitched, Private Briggs," the lieutenant said, his voice even and steady and showing no evidence being affected by their intimate closeness. "There's no sense in keeping them harnessed to a crippled wagon."

As the soldier left to carry out his orders, Meredith rose to her feet. Worry for the children and for Private Greene overrode any annoyance she held for herself.

"What are we going to do, Lieutenant?"

"We walk."

"To the fort? It's almost dusk." The horizon stewed with thick, black clouds. "And that storm is drawing uncomfortably close."

"We don't have a choice."

"But the children…it's too dangerous."

"It's even more dangerous if we stay out here. There's no protection from the elements or from—" He broke off with a scowl.

"Say it. You mean there's no protection from the renegades." She clamped hands on her hips, anchoring herself against the ache to pummel his chest. His dogged campaign to move her and the children to the fort had placed them in this perilous predicament. "I knew this would be a fool's errand. I knew it."

He opened his mouth to respond but instead of speaking, he shifted his attention to a point beyond her. A muffled clattering spanked the air. Someone was coming. She spun on her heels. In the distance, a mule-drawn farm wagon rounded a bend in the road and headed toward them. A weight lifted from her shoulders. It was Mr. Hoggard and Mrs. Clement returning from Mineral. Thank the Lord. Maybe this debacle could be salvaged after all.

She climbed out of the ditch and moved to the middle of the road. The children crowded around her as Mr. Hoggard pulled the mule to a stop.

Mrs. Clement scrambled off the seat, fast for a woman of her girth. A frown plowed through her plump cheeks. "Oh dearie me. 'Twas anyone hurt?"

"Just the driver," Meredith said. "He was tossed from the wagon when the axle broke and hit his head. I applied a makeshift bandage to the gash until he can see a doctor. The bleeding has stopped for now."

"'Tis fortunate it wasna worse. Why are you and the children out here with these soldiers anyhow?"

Why indeed. It was a question she'd been asking herself ever since the soldiers had appeared on the orphanage doorstep.

The lieutenant stepped beside her. "I'm Lieutenant Booth, ma'am. My commander suggested we move everyone in the outlying homesteads to Fort Dent until the rogue Indians are contained. Since our wagon is out of commission, we'll need to use yours to haul everyone the rest of the way to the fort."

Lightning flashed, followed by a boom of thunder that rumbled across the boiling sky. Mr. Hoggard shook his head. "That storm is just about on us, Lieutenant. We won't make it to the fort before it hits. Best to go back to Seaton House and wait until morning."

Chapter Three

Rain thrummed on the darkened window panes, loud and incessant, demanding to enter. A flash lit the parlor, and then came a resounding clap of thunder that rattled the wall hangings and the nerves.

Becky ran over and burrowed in Meredith's skirts. "I don't like this storm," the child whined. "It's too loud."

Meredith rested a hand on the girl's head. "It will be all right, Becky. It's just nature's way of releasing pent-up energy."

Becky peeked from beneath the folds. "Like when Robbie races around the yard after lesson time is over?"

"Exactly so. There's nothing to fear. How is your arm? Did the cold compress help any?"

"It doesn't hurt anymore." The girl eased out of her hiding spot and wiggled her arm. "See, I can move it without hurting."

"Good." She handed the girl a corner of the blanket she'd retrieved from the linen closet. "Then help me spread this near the hearth so everyone can get warm and dry."

There hadn't been enough room in the smaller farm wagon to haul the children, the dry goods, and the wounded soldier. Their luggage had to be left behind. Unfortunately, the storm unleashed before they could make it to Seaton House. Everyone had gotten soaked.

With no spare clothing to change into, they had to remain in their wet garments. God willing, no one would become ill from being damp and chilled.

"I'm hungry," Robbie wailed. "When are we going to eat?"

Not even close to being ill. "Very soon. Mrs. Clement is slicing bread and cheese for supper." She smoothed the blanket onto the floor. "We'll have our own little picnic right here in the parlor."

"Goody." Anna plopped down in the middle. "I like picnics."

Becky released her corner of the blanket and joined Anna, her fear of the storm apparently appeased. "We should play a game. How about The Minister's Cat? I like that one."

The suggestion of an indoor picnic was definitely a winner. Maybe they could get through the night without any mishaps. "That's a good idea, Becky. All of you find a spot on the blanket and play Minister's Cat while I help Mrs. Clement."

As the children settled on the blanket, Meredith left the parlor. Halfway down the hall, a boom of thunder roared through the house, making her jump. She'd never been nervous around storms, but this one seemed especially fierce. She hoped it wasn't a sign of bad things to come.

In the kitchen, Mrs. Clement stood at the work table, carving bread and setting the pieces on a platter already stacked with sliced cheese. The crocheted hairpiece at her nape sagged with the weight of wet braids. A damp towel draped her shoulders. Her skirt and blouse were dark with rain water. Instead of changing, the housekeeper had seen to the children's needs first. There was no one more dedicated than Ida Clement.

Mildred had taken in the destitute widow when both their husbands perished in the same mining accident. They had been together ever since. While the only *gift* Mrs. Clement exhibited was her outstanding cooking ability, she knew the secrets of Seaton House and held them close. An immigrant from the Scottish Highlands, she understood that the survival of the family, or clan as she called them, depended on loyalty and trust.

Meredith unhooked an apron from a wall peg and tied it around her waist. "Why don't you change out of those wet clothes, Mrs. Clement? I can finish up here."

The housekeeper didn't miss a beat with her slicing. "No need, dearie. I'm almost done. Just have to pour the milk Mr. Hoggard brought in from the barn."

"Let me do that for you." She crossed to the table and picked up the pitcher of milk. "I'm surprised Mr. Hoggard was able to get a drop from Bessy, considering the fierceness of that storm. It seems to have the children on edge. I can't imagine how the animals are faring."

"Mr. Hoggard has a way with people and with animals. Always has."

Before retiring and coming to work for Mildred, Joseph Hoggard had ministered God's word to a tiny parish in Kentucky. His *gift* was of the heavenly sort—full of kindness and understanding. Never judgmental. From her first day at Seaton House, he'd accepted her into his flock.

"I wish I could handle the children with as much ease and confidence as he does." She poured milk into the glasses arranged on a serving tray. "Every time I think I have them in hand, it all goes awry."

"Don't be so hard on yerself. Ye are doing a wonderful job. Mrs. Campbell would be proud."

Proud? She wouldn't go that far. Her aunt had welcomed her into the close-knit family at the orphanage and worked tirelessly to help her understand and govern her visions. For all the good *that* did. She'd be more likely to jump over a mountain as to control her gift.

"I worry that I'm not making the right decision about moving everyone to Fort Dent. What if I put the children in more danger by exposing them to those who are less understanding? The little ones are so young. They just don't realize the consequences of exposing their abilities."

"I dinna see any way around it. The threat from the Indians is much more immediate and far more deadly."

"I suppose you are right." She poured milk into the last of the glasses. "But I still worry."

"As would any caring person."

A sharp clap of thunder rapped the air. Pots hanging on the overhead rack rattled against one another. Her hand shook, and milk spilled from the porcelain lip. A white puddle spread across the tabletop like blood from a wound.

Meredith thumped the pitcher onto the table. "Good heavens. Now look what I've done."

Mrs. Clement snatched up the wiping cloth quicker than a duck jumping on a June bug. "Dinna fash yerself. 'Tis just a little spilt milk."

Her heart sagged. "Is this an omen, Mrs. Clement? Should I take greater care with the children as I should have with pouring the milk?"

"An omen?" The housekeeper shook her head as she mopped up the spill. "My Henry used to say, 'There are no such things as omens. Destiny is too wise or too cruel to send heralds.' Just trust in yer heart, dearie. It won't lead you astray."

"Your Henry sounds like a fascinating man. I wish I could have known him."

"I wish ye could have, too. The man was bigger than a bear, but gentle as a lamb. He was the love of my life, even if he were an Englishman."

"When did you know he was the one?"

The housekeeper's mouth curled up at the corners, the smile snuggling into pink, rounded cheeks. Her gaze took on a soft, dreamy look. This was a woman who had loved and had been loved.

"I knew when he put a smile not only on my face but also on my heart. I wanted to spend every waking moment by his side." Mrs. Clement heaved a sigh and cocked her head. "Is there someone special who has ye wondering about such a thing?"

She waved a dismissive hand. "Oh no. I was simply curious about Mr. Clement. Nothing more."

"Yer certain? I've seen the way ye look at the handsome lieutenant." Gray eyebrows arched in speculation. "Henry put that same glow on my face."

Rooster's teeth. Clearly she wasn't as adept at containing her emotions as she thought. "I'm certain. I have no interest in Lieutenant Booth. Besides, he emphatically stated the army is his life."

Mrs. Clement merely broadened her smile and gathered the platter of cheese and bread. "Let's go feed the wee darlings, shall we? Before they start gnawing on the furniture."

Yes, let's. The conversation had strayed well beyond comfortable. Meredith picked up the tray of glasses and followed the housekeeper to the parlor.

The storm seemed to have abated, the lightning and thunder coming less frequently and less sharply. Expectant faces greeted them as they entered the parlor. They set the trays on the blanket amid a chorus of excited chirps. Robbie reached for a slice of bread, and Meredith stilled him with a harsh look. He pulled his hands back and adopted a pious pose, head tucked and hands folded. The little imp.

"Whose turn is it? Nel?" At the girl's nod, she added, "Go on then."

As Nel delivered the blessing, a shuffling noise sounded in the doorway. Lieutenant Booth filled the opening, hat in hand, studying her with those prowling eyes. Her insides heated with a warmth that had nothing to do with the blazing fire. She yanked her gaze away and murmured an earnest "amen" with the others. She'd need all the heavenly help she could get to keep her thoughts virtuous.

As the children dove into the food, her feet moved toward the lieutenant as if being impelled by Gabe's mental machinations. A quick glance confirmed the boy was occupied with stuffing his mouth with bread and cheese.

She laced her fingers together in front of her, mimicking Robbie's pious pose. "Good evening, Lieutenant. How is Private Greene? Did you get him settled into the boys' bedroom?"

"He's doing fine. I appreciate you making room for him. I'm sure Mrs. Clement's tonic and a good night's rest in a comfortable bed will help speed his recovery."

It was actually one of Maddie's tonics, but he didn't need to know who had brewed the elixir. It would only prompt questions she couldn't answer. "We're happy to help. Besides, the boys will consider bunking in the parlor an adventure."

"I imagine they will."

She motioned to the blanket. "Would you like to join us for supper? It's just bread and cheese, but there's plenty."

"Thank you for the offer, but I'll find something later. Just came to let you know my troopers and I will be keeping watch on the house. Didn't want you or the children to become frightened if you hear noises during the night."

Troopers, not soldiers. She'd remember to refer to them that way from now on. "I'll be sure to let everyone know. We'll leave out some food in case you or your men get hungry during your patrols."

A frown pleated his brow. "You might want to reconsider leaving out any food."

"Why?"

He stepped around her. "Because you have a mouse."

He darted into the parlor, stomping the floor as he moved. A gray ball of fur squealed and scurried just out of reach. Robbie shrieked and shot from the blanket.

Meredith grabbed for the officer. "Stop, Lieutenant. It's just a pe—"

Lightning flashed, accompanied by a loud bellow of thunder. Amid the bedlam, a footstool zipped across the floor. The lieutenant's feet tangled with the stool and lost the scuffle. He fell forward and landed with a thump on the floorboards.

No. No. No. She rushed across the floor and bent over him. "Lieutenant, are you all right?"

Red splotches stained his cheeks and flushed his ears. Heaving a strangled grunt, he rolled away and pushed to his feet. He towered over her, his mouth folded into a rigid line. She let go the breath she'd been holding. Not injured then. Just mad as a wet hen.

His scowl lit on the stool. "Where in tarnation did that stool come from? It wasn't there before."

She gave Gabe a quick glare. She'd deal with the miscreant later. For now, she had to convince the lieutenant he didn't see what he saw. She nudged the stool with her toe. "You must be mistaken. The footstool was there. The lightning must have blinded you for a second, and you didn't see it."

"I'm certain my path was clear. Blasted storm." He gave another exasperated grunt and looked around the room. "Where is my hat?"

Robbie popped from behind the chair with the lieutenant's uniform hat wobbling on his head. "It's right here, sir."

Lieutenant Booth reached the child in two strides. He snatched up the hat and brushed the brim. "Look here. You've soiled it with your grubby hands."

Robbie's eyes went wide as wagon wheels. His bottom lip dipped into a pout. He didn't expect such a harsh reaction from the officer. Neither did she.

Meredith scooted between the two and gave the boy a gentle nudge. "Go on back to the blanket, Robbie."

"But, Miss Talbot, I only wanted to—"

"I know." She squeezed his shoulder. "It's all right.

Go back to the blanket."

Robbie glowered at the lieutenant, clearly wanting to say more. She couldn't blame him; she wanted to give the officer a good tongue-lashing for his brutish behavior. But doing so might make things worse. Best to just remain silent and avoid fanning any flames.

As the boy wheeled around, the lieutenant stopped him with an outthrust hand. "Wait. Is that a mouse in your pocket?"

Meredith stuffed down a groan. She couldn't explain away the long tail dangling from the boy's trouser pocket. "Yes. That is a mouse. It's Robbie's pet."

"His pet? It's a filthy rodent."

Robbie shoved up his chin. "Petunia is not filthy. She washes for supper just like we do. You shouldn't have tried to squash her."

"Was it you? Did you push that stool in front of me to protect that creature? Someone ought to take a strap to you."

Robbie stiffened, eyes brimming with tears. Anger climbed inside her. No one treated her children in such a harsh manner. No one. She prodded the boy forward. "Go and finish your supper, Robbie. I'll handle this."

The boy tossed the lieutenant a hurtful glare and shuffled to the blanket. Meredith rounded on the officer, unable to hold back her wrath. "There was no reason to threaten the boy like that. He had no hand in your clumsiness."

Lieutenant Booth turned his glower on her. "Miss Talbot, you run the most unorthodox establishment I have ever encountered."

"It may appear that way to someone not

accustomed to children, but I assure you, they are happy and thriving."

"Such anarchy will only lead to trouble; I can *assure* you of that." He shoved on his hat. "I'll leave you to your…whatever it is you are doing. Good night."

She stared at his retreating back. She was right to keep her desire for him in check. He didn't understand her or the children. Even if she did entertain the idea of having a relationship, he was entirely the wrong man.

Why then did her stomach feel as if it had been stomped?

****

A tiny heel dug into her thigh. An elbow poked her ribs. Meredith groaned upright. The bed was barely wide enough for one person. Add two more bodies, small though they were, and sleep was nearly impossible. It didn't help that her mind churned with thoughts of the impending move and of the handsome officer who had brought all that turmoil to her doorstep. Perhaps if she stretched her legs and took in a breath of fresh air, it might help her to relax. Then she could find some rest before the sun and the children wakened.

She pushed aside the sheet and slowly swung her legs over the side of the bed. The last thing she wanted was to disturb Anna or Becky. The girls had insisted on sleeping with her, claiming the storm was too scary. It had taken nearly an hour for the two twitchy magpies to settle down and fall asleep. This getaway required stealth and silence.

She gathered her robe and padded barefoot to the door. Shoes would only clunk noisily on the floorboards. She would be fine without them.

The door thankfully opened without a squeak.

Once in the hallway, she tugged on her robe and sailed for the stairs. A single gong of the parlor clock drifted up the staircase. Not much of the night left. She'd have to hurry with her relaxing.

She made it to the main floor and out the front door without incident. Moonlight shimmered on the glistening puddles dotting the front yard. Stars winked in the broad, black sky. Against that soothing backdrop, the night insects played their courting songs. She leaned against the porch railing and drew in several deep breaths of cool, refreshing air. Perfect. Just what she needed. She closed her eyes and savored the peacefulness.

"Couldn't sleep?"

She whirled toward the sound, a gasp escaping her lips. Though the shadows obscured him, the owner of that commanding voice was unmistakable. Her heart pounded against her ribs. Not because of him—because he had frightened her.

"Lieutenant Booth." She clutched the robe tighter against her. "You startled me."

"My apologies. I should have made my presence known."

Why hadn't he? Surely he'd seen her come out onto the porch. Had he been appraising her? The mere thought of his intimate inspection set her blood to simmering. Heat climbed up her neck and flamed in her face. She turned away, not wanting him to see her reaction to him. She didn't want to encourage any boldness. Not when they were alone and under the intimacy of darkness.

"It appears the storm has moved on." A silly thing to say. It was obvious the storm had abated. But her flustered mind couldn't think of anything more suitable.

Boot heels thudded softly across the porch and stopped just shy of the railing. Her senses tingled, aware of his presence without the need for touching.

"Weather cleared off about an hour ago. If you're worried about the renegades, don't. My men and I have the house well guarded. Besides, the storm has most likely put a damper on any attacks tonight."

His deep voice rumbled through her. She stiffened against a responding shiver of delight. "A blessing in disguise, my Aunt Mildred would say."

"Mrs. Campbell is your aunt?"

"Yes, my mother's sister." Though her father would never claim Mildred as any type of kin. He had never talked about his sister-in-law. Never even acknowledged she existed until Mildred's existence halfway across the country provided a solution to a thorny problem with his afflicted daughter.

"Why did she build an orphanage in the middle of the Indian Territories? And why call it Seaton House? We aren't anywhere near the sea."

"From what she tells me, she was able to get the place at a reasonable price. Until now, she's had no problem with the location. As for the name, it comes from one of our ancestors who lived in England centuries ago. Mistress Seaton began taking in orphans and cast-offs and providing them with food and shelter. It was a tradition that continued generation after generation." He didn't need to know that Martha Seaton was the first in their line to be gifted with the power of visions and that the children she took in were anything but normal.

"Is that why you came to Mineral? To carry on the

tradition?"

"Partly. The orphanage was growing too much for Mildred to handle alone. My father sent me to help." Not quite the truth, but it would have to suffice.

"I don't recall seeing you in town before. Have you been here for very long?"

Some days, it felt like decades. "I arrived about eight months ago. And you? How long have you been at Fort Dent?"

"Almost a year. I came from Fort Leavenworth where I'd been stationed after graduating from West Point."

She had passed through Leavenworth on her way west. The frontier town was much larger and more civilized than she had expected. Hundreds of buildings lined the streets, from haberdasheries to theatres to elegant hotels. And the people. Thousands of them— soldiers, civilians, and immigrants from all corners of the world. It was a soup pot of humanity.

"That must have been quite an adjustment, going from the comforts of Leavenworth to the wilds of the Indian territories."

"I go where the army sends me."

The barest hint of bitterness spiked his tone. His fingers tightened around the porch railing, knuckles whitening. Was he unhappy with his assignment? Life in the territories did require an adjustment. It had taken her weeks to become accustomed to the lack of amenities. Now, she preferred the seclusion and simplicity to lavish comforts.

"What made you decide on the military, Lieutenant?"

"My father was a career officer...as was my

grandfather and his father before that."

"A family tradition, then. Like mine." Although one aspect of her family heritage wasn't at all voluntary. "Are any of them still serving?"

"My grandfather passed on years ago. My father retired after the War Between the States. He and my mother live in a small seaside town in Connecticut."

"Is that where you're from, Connecticut?"

"I'm from all over the country. We moved from garrison to garrison, wherever my father was stationed." He released the railing and turned, head tilted and eyes shadowed by his hat brim. "From the lack of any distinctive accent, I'm guessing you come from the East as well. Maryland or possibly Pennsylvania?"

A night beetle buzzed around her head, no less pesky than his questions. She waved the insect away. The lieutenant wouldn't be so easy to brush off.

"How perceptive you are. I grew up on my family's estate in Pennsylvania." Thoughts surfaced of the tall, columned mansion overlooking vast fields dotted with white-faced cattle—of the barns and the flower gardens and the family cemetery that held her mother, her grandparents, and more recently her stepbrother. A cloud passed over her heart. His death had been the reason for her exile from Hickory Hills. Not that she could blame her father for sending her away. She blamed herself just as much. If she had just kept the details of her vision to herself, Charles might still be alive.

"You must have left many a broken heart behind."

His softly spoken comment knifed into her. She hadn't left behind any broken hearts. Her father's stony expression as her train left the station house had been quite clear. She was dead to him.

She spun for the door. His questions had unearthed memories better left in their coffins. "It's getting late. I should go back inside."

"Wait." His hand shot out and closed around her arm. "That was far too personal. I apologize."

Moonlight played across his face. His mouth parted, and her mind exploded with thoughts of those lips capturing hers. She'd only been kissed once when she was sixteen. The stable master's son's fumbling efforts hadn't brought on the knee-melting response her maid went on and on about. Perhaps she hadn't been kissed by the right man.

Instead of kissing her, he stiffened, his expression hardening to steel. Before she could ask what was wrong, he tugged her behind him.

"Keep still," he whispered as he drew his pistol from its holster.

"What is it?"

"Something moved out in the shadows."

The click of a cocking hammer crawled over her skin. She risked a peep around him. Nothing moved in the yard or on the long stretch of driveway. Yet the night insects had stopped their singing, a sure sign of an intruder. "Is it the renegades?"

"I don't know. Be quiet now."

She buttoned her mouth and huddled against him. His breaths were even and measured—his muscles taut and steady. Not a panicked bone in his body. She felt safe, protected. She didn't want to think about what *else* she felt around him.

After a few minutes, he relaxed and lowered his

pistol. "It's all right. It's just a mangy dog."

She let go a relieved breath and stepped from behind him. A big shaggy brute trotted out of the gloom and headed toward the house. She smiled and moved to the top of the steps. "It's Buster. My neighbor's herding dog. He often comes to visit, though not usually this late at night."

The dog clambered up the stairs, and she bent to rub his ears. "What are you doing out and about, big fella?"

Buster nuzzled her palm and slopped a tongue over her fingers. He peered up at her through his good eye, the other one permanently sealed shut.

"That's an ugly scar. What happened to him?" asked the lieutenant.

"He was injured chasing off a coyote that tried to attack his owner's sheep."

"Humph. The beast nearly lost his other eye. He should stay home where he belongs."

"He's a good, boy. Aren't you, Buster?" She gave the dog one final pat and prodded him off the steps. "Go on now. It's time for you to go home."

As the dog loped away, she straightened. "He shouldn't bother you any more tonight."

"For his sake, I hope not."

He couldn't be that hard-hearted. Surely some softness lurked beneath that armor. She wouldn't be so drawn to him otherwise. And that concerned her. She didn't want to be drawn to him. It would only cause problems, and she already had enough of those to fill a bottomless lake.

She turned for the door. "I should go back to bed. The sun and the children will be up soon."

"Good night, Miss Talbot. Sleep well."

Sleep? Well? Neither was likely. His silky voice and fiery touch had awakened both her mind and her body. So much for finding relaxation.

Chapter Four

His assignment was plagued. From the missing child to the broken axle to the ill-timed weather, moving the inhabitants of Seaton House was like trying to forge a thaw-swollen river. For every step forward, the currents pushed him back two.

And now this.

Sometime during the night, vandals had tossed the orphans' trunks out of the crippled wagon and destroyed their contents. Though the storm had been gusty, the winds weren't strong enough to shred cotton garments into ribbons. Only a knife could render such damage.

He squatted and ran a finger over a depression in the dirt. Unshod pony tracks. Renegades most likely. They had probably come upon the abandoned wagon and decided to vent their anger. That meant they were close. Too close. He had to get Miss Talbot and the children to the safety of the fort—fast.

He rose and mounted his horse. Miss Talbot stood near the side of the road, plucking clothes from the bushes. Her gown stretched across her curves. Nicely shaped curves. And soft. He'd felt every gentle slope, every valley, when he'd pulled her behind him on the porch. As pleasant as that felt, it couldn't be repeated. The last thing he needed was a romantic entanglement. He wasn't ready to settle down just yet. And when he was, it would be to an obedient, disciplined woman. Willfulness was not a favorable attribute for an officer's wife.

He reined in his lust and his mount. "Find anything salvageable?"

She straightened and swiped a stray curl with the back of her hand, leaving a smudge trailing across her forehead. "I'm afraid not. Most of the clothes are damaged beyond repair."

"That's unfortunate. If I had any idea this was going to happen, I would have sent the men back to collect the trunks."

"Surely the storm couldn't have done all this."

A frown puckered her mouth. He wanted to kiss it away. He shifted for a less restricting position in the saddle instead. "It wasn't entirely the storm. I found unshod pony tracks stamping the ground around the wagon. My best guess is the renegade Indians are the culprits."

Her anxious gaze swept the surrounding woods. "I didn't realize they were this close."

"No need to worry. My men scouted the area before our arrival. It's safe." *For now.*

"That's a relief." She held up a shirt that could have passed for a battle-tattered guidon. "Though it doesn't help our situation any. I suppose we'll just have to make do with the clothes we have until more can be procured."

On her, a burlap sack would look like a ball gown. "I'm sure my commander will assist you with that. Major Allen has been quite generous to those in need."

A dirt clod thumped the ground near her feet. She turned and glared at the two boys huddled in the ditches lining the roadway. "Gabe, Robbie, stop throwing dirt. If you're finished gathering the clothes, go and get in the wagon."

The two mischief-makers stopped their battling and raced for the wagon. Good. It was time they started for the fort anyway—before some other calamity befell this ill-fated band of misfits.

"We've lingered longer than we should have. I instructed my men to get you all back on the road and heading for the fort as soon as possible." He nestled his hat tighter on his head. "I'm going to ride ahead. Let Major Allen know you are on the way so preparations can be made and housing located."

"A place for all of us...together."

"I am well aware of your conditions, Miss Talbot."

"Just making certain." The hard lines around her mouth softened. "This is important to us—to me."

He wanted her to have it too. Damn if she hadn't gotten under his skin. But she was an itch he couldn't scratch. His father had warned him to *keep his eye on the prize*. His career should be paramount to all else. Miss Talbot, with her unrestrained spirit and inviting curves, was a distraction he couldn't afford.

He nudged his mount forward. Once he delivered his report, his assignment would be complete. The Seaton House evacuees would become Major Allen's headache. And his hunger for the intriguing Meredith Talbot would shrivel and die.

Thirty minutes later, he arrived at Fort Dent. Civilians and military personnel swarmed around the garrison like bees in a hive. The fort was smaller than Leavenworth and much cruder. The buildings were made of thin wood planks that held onto the heat in the summer and let in the blustery weather of winter. There were few amenities. But he could handle the coarse conditions. It was the poorly equipped troops that had him discouraged and frustrated.

The rifles were antiquated and barely operational. Many jammed at the least provocation. Requisitions for new arms had been ignored or just plain denied— probably because it wasn't warranted for such a small fighting force that saw little action. He couldn't wait for his request for reassignment to be approved. Then he could put his four years of military education and training to better use.

He dismounted in front of Commander Allen's headquarters and tied his horse to the hitching post. As he pushed through the door, the major's adjutant rose from behind a desk and snapped to attention. The soldier was lean and leggy, like a yearling colt, with little facial hair. The army appeared to take them straight out of the schoolroom these days.

"Lieutenant Booth, sir. The major has been looking for you. Go right in."

He removed his hat and crossed to the open doorway on the other side of the room. No sound came from within. A good sign or bad? Major William Allen was known for his mood swings, made worse by an unexplained and painful stomach ailment that hit out of nowhere. He supposed that kind of suffering would make anyone surly. Unfortunately, the report he had to deliver would only toss oil onto any belly fire.

Steeling himself for the worst, he entered the office and stood at attention in front of a desk behind which sat the commander of Fort Dent. The major looked fit enough, no sweating, no grayish pallor that usually accompanied his ailment. His neatly arranged jacket was fully buttoned. Maybe he'd lucked out and had arrived between bouts.

Preston delivered a brisk salute. "Major Allen, sir."

The major grunted and peered at him over the rims of his spectacles. "Where the hell have you been, Lieutenant? You were expected yesterday evening."

Definitely not between bouts. "We were delayed by a broken wagon axle, sir. And then the weather turned on us. We had to wait out the night at the orphanage."

"But they are here now."

"They are on the way. There was a problem with their belongings." He explained the situation with the trunks and Miss Talbot's request for housing.

"Who is this Miss Talbot? I thought Mildred Campbell was the steward."

"Mrs. Campbell is away on an extended trip. She left her niece, Miss Meredith Talbot, in charge of the orphanage."

The mention of her name conjured images of flashing violet eyes and beckoning lips. It would take some time to get thoughts of her out of his head. What he needed was a long, bone-tiring patrol to cleanse his mind…the sooner, the better.

The major leaned back in his chair and rubbed his belly. A second later, he grimaced and let go a rumbling belch. His scowl eased. "Pardon me. Stomach is acting up again. So this Miss Talbot wants housing where they can all be together?"

"She insisted on it, sir. It was the only way she would agree to move everyone to the fort."

"Well, I suppose there's nothing for it. We'll have

to accommodate the niece's wishes."

For all his surliness, Major Allen retained a clear, rational head. Tension rolled out of Preston's shoulders. He didn't want Miss Talbot to think he'd spoken in bad faith about attaining quarters where she and the children could stay together. He could hand over their care to the major with a clear conscience.

The adjutant appeared in the doorway. "Excuse me, sir, but Mayor Wood is here. For a tour of the fort."

"Yes, yes," Major Allen said with a flick of his hand. "Tell the mayor I'll be right there."

As the soldier left the room, Major Allen unhooked his spectacles and set them on top of the desk. He stood and straightened his jacket with a tug on the bottom. "Delicate business these orphans. We don't want to appear hard-hearted, especially with most of the townsfolk watching."

In his opinion, the orphans and the townsfolk ought to be grateful for the military's help in whatever form that came. But then, he wasn't the commander.

"With that in mind," Major Allen continued. "I'm assigning you to look after them from the moment they arrive until they leave. Anything they or their caretakers need, housing, clothing, or food, you will do your best to provide. I don't want any complications, is that understood?"

Damn. Damn. Damn. Overseeing latrine maintenance couldn't be a worse assignment. "Yes, sir. I understand perfectly."

"And one other thing, Lieutenant."

Of course there was more. How could there not be?

"I have requisitioned the officers' barracks for the arriving civilians. You will need to make other arrangements for your quartering. For convenience sake, I suggest you have your striker pitch a tent near the orphan's quarters. That will facilitate the administering of their needs."

Wonderful. Now he'd be living near the noisy, unruly urchins day and night—not to mention their bewitching guardian.

****

"I don't like it here. There's too many people, and the fence is too big. I wanna go back to Seaton House."

Meredith contained a grumble of agreement. The ten-foot tall stockade walls *were* intimidating, as were the dozens of soldiers and civilians swarming around the gaping maw at the gate. As much as she wanted to tell the driver to take them back to the orphanage, they had to stay until the threat from the Indians was allayed.

"It will be all right, Anna. The big fence and all these soldiers are here to protect us. Besides, once we settle into our new quarters, you won't even notice them." She hoped.

"Those people are staring," Lily whispered. "And they have black auras. I don't like this, Miss Talbot. Not one bit."

A group of civilians gathered near the gate watched as the wagon rolled past. There were no smiles, no gestures of welcome, just cold, disapproving stares. A chill scuttled down her spine. This did not bode well for their stay. Yet, however unnerved it made her feel, she couldn't let the children see her misgivings.

"They are merely curious," she offered in a positive tone. "Considering all the folks that live outside the fort, we are probably just the latest in a long string of arrivals."

"Do you think they know about us? About what we can do?"

"I sincerely doubt it. Mrs. Campbell has worked hard to keep Seaton House sheltered from the outside world."

Lily's face remained pinched with uncertainty. Meredith supplied her with an encouraging smile. "Everything will be just fine, Lily. You'll see."

"They don't look happy to see us," Anna said. "They have tilted down lips."

Out of the mouths of babes. "The situation doesn't lend itself to happiness. They are probably just as unhappy as we are about leaving their homes."

In a large clearing ahead, troopers rode in formation while putting their horses through a series of exercises. Perhaps shifting the children's attention to something more fascinating would take their minds off the frosty reception.

"Look, children. The troopers are practicing their riding skills."

"Just like we practice ours," Anna chimed in.

"Well, somewhat. And look over there." She pointed to a large building where troopers were leading horses into and out of a pair of wide doors. "That must be the stables."

Robbie bounced in the straw, his eyes dancing with excitement. "Can we go visit the horses? Please, Miss Talbot? I bet they have lots to say about the goings-on at the fort."

"No, Robbie. The stables are off limits. We need to keep to ourselves, remember?"

The boy's face and shoulders fell. Meredith's heart went out to him. She didn't want to dampen his spirits, but they had to keep the danger of their talents being discovered in the forefront of their thoughts.

A bugle blared, and Mrs. Clement jerked her head upright, eyelids springing open and mouth snapping closed, putting an abrupt end to the snoring that had serenaded them for the past half hour. The housekeeper had somehow found the discipline to nap. How she managed with the noise and the jolting was unfathomable.

"Have we arrived then?"

Meredith nodded. "About five minutes ago."

The housekeeper grimaced and rolled her shoulders, working out the kinks like a magician escaping from a small locked box. "Ach. It feels as if I've been riding in this wagon for a week. Quite exhausting, you ken. 'Tis a relief to finally be here."

The entire ordeal had been exhausting. Mr. Hoggard had the right of it. He'd decided to stay behind and watch after the animals. Rogue Indians or not, she had half a mind to join him.

Gabe rose up on his knees. "There's the lieutenant over by that little white building. And he don't look none too happy to see us either."

"He doesn't look happy," she corrected.

"Nope. But he ain't ever happy, so it's all the same."

Private Greene, his head still swathed in bandages, gave a strangled cough and slowed the mules. The trooper had insisted on driving. Said he wasn't going to let a little bump on the head keep him from his duties. Hopefully that dedication wouldn't cause any permanent damage.

The wagon stopped in front of a wood-planked

building that had been slathered with whitewash. A small window flanked a plain wooden door, over which hung a sign that read, *Headquarters*. An American flag fluttered atop a tall pole stuck in the ground. If their assigned housing was half this quaint, their stay would be bearable.

Lieutenant Booth stepped off the stoop and crossed toward them. Whatever Gabe had seen on the officer's face had been wiped clean. Stubble darkened his jaw, making him appear rakish and unrestrained—a pirate of the prairie. Her pulse stuttered just as it always seemed to do at the sight of him. If she wasn't careful, he might find her easy plunder.

He climbed aboard the wagon and sat next to Private Greene. He twisted around and tipped his hat. "Mrs. Clement. Miss Talbot. I'm glad to see you made it to the fort without incident."

Meredith returned his greeting. "As are we. The only attack we suffered was from an irritable wasp. Unfortunately, Sally's arm took the brunt of the assault."

"I can have Doctor Troutman have a look at the child if you'd like. His temporary office is not far from here."

The less contact they had with others, the better. "That won't be necessary. Mrs. Clement applied a plaster of mud and grass. The swelling has gone down, and Sally is feeling much better. Aren't you, sweetling?"

Sally smiled and nodded. A piece of peppermint also went a long way to helping a whimpering child get over her pains.

"Very well. I have two possible locations for your

quartering. I'll show you each of them, and you can decide which will suit." He spoke to Private Greene who bobbed his head and then slapped leather to the mules.

As the wagon rattled forward, the lieutenant faced her again. "Is this your first visit inside Fort Dent, Miss Talbot?"

She had only caught a glimpse of the garrison when she arrived on the stagecoach. Ever since then, she'd remained secluded behind the walls of Seaton House—by choice. "This is the first I've seen of it. The orphanage keeps me quite busy. I have little time for seeing the sights."

He pointed to the whitewashed building. "That is the headquarters of Major William Allen, commander of the garrison. He assigned me to look after you and the children during your stay. Whatever you need, I am to do my best to provide it."

Having someone at hand who was familiar with the fort and its operation would make their stay easier. But that meant she'd be seeing more of him—a lot more. She'd have to redouble her efforts to keep a firm hand on her body's fascination with him.

The wagon approached a long rectangular building with a wide veranda stretching across its length. The open porch would be an ideal spot to socialize and to catch an evening breeze during the hot summer months. Doors of the same height and width paraded from one end to the other. The walls appeared to be constructed of wood planks, unpainted and wafer thin. No doubt sounds and chilly weather would find easy entry into the apartments.

"This is the officers' barracks," the lieutenant said

as the wagon rattled to a stop. "It's one of the places where we're currently housing civilians."

"And what of the officers?"

"We've been ordered to find other accommodations."

That was a relief. While she didn't wish any hardship on him, having him living within earshot and eyeshot would only add to her strain.

"This is one of the options for you to consider," he continued. "Unfortunately, most of the units have been taken. There's only one left. It has a bedroom and a larger living space which includes a cooking and eating section. With ten of you, it will be cramped."

A door opened and then another. Two women and several children surged onto the veranda. The ladies eyed them warily, while the children stared with open curiosity. One boy started for the wagon but was pulled back by a stern-faced woman. Meredith's stomach bunched. Cramped conditions she could handle. Being under the scrutiny of so many eyes she could not. It would be a calamity waiting to happen.

"Would you like to have a look at the unit, Miss Talbot?"

The living quarters could be grand as the *Taj Mahal,* and she wouldn't accept it. "This other place you have in mind, is there more room?"

"It is larger and a bit more isolated than the barracks, but…"

Uncertainty scampered across his face. Whatever reservations he had about the other housing, it couldn't be nearly as bad as living in a fish bowl.

She nodded. "It sounds perfect. Take us there."

After wending around the stables and passing a

building the lieutenant called the *Sutler's Store*, Private Greene stopped the wagon in front of a one-story structure made of hewn logs chinked with mud. It was indeed set off from the rest of the fort. However, instead of glass panes, vertical bars adorned the windows. There was only one reason for such trimmings.

"You want us to live in a *jailhouse*?" She couldn't keep incredulity from staining her voice.

"It's either here or the barracks."

Neither was particularly appealing. "Surely there is some other place we could stay."

"All of the larger accommodations have already been commandeered. What I've shown you are the only choices where you can all stay together."

She didn't think this misadventure could get any worse, yet it had. Meredith climbed out of the wagon and crossed to the jailhouse. A thin layer of moss coated the logs near the ground. Holes pocked the mud chinking. Worst of all were the cobwebs. They hung in the windows like macabre curtains. A shudder bucked through her. Moss and mud she could deal with. Spiders made her skin crawl. They creeped about on spindly, stealthy legs, and their bites itched for days. The beasts would have to go before she called this place home.

"What about the prisoners?"

"We moved the only detainee to a secure room at the stables." He pushed the door open amidst a squeal of hinges. "The place is all yours."

She hefted her skirts and went inside. A rank, sour smell that would offend even a skunk nearly bowled her over. Dirt and grime covered every surface. The filth didn't deter the bugs. Ants marched in perfect formation across the floor. Flies buzzed near the window. She'd bet her last dollar there were spiders lurking in the shadows.

"How could you allow your prisoners to live in such wretched conditions?"

"They're not incarcerated for their enjoyment."

"Nor their health, it appears."

She went up on tiptoe and crept toward the opening on the far side of the room. Beyond the archway, jail cells lined either side of a narrow aisle. The smaller space smelled much worse than the main chamber, if that was even possible. The odor scorched her nostrils and settled in a curdling hollow in her stomach. She sucked air through her mouth to avoid losing her lunch.

Two places to stay—both of them ghastly. Yet of the two, this reeking hovel seemed the lesser evil.

She sailed for the front door, and once outside, drew in several deep gulps of clean air. It would take weeks to get the noxious stench out of her lungs.

"Well, Miss Talbot," the lieutenant said as he joined her. "What do you say? This jailhouse or the barracks?"

Eight pairs of eyes latched onto her. If they all pitched in, they could make this place work. They had to. The children's safety trumped a little dirt and odor.

"The jailhouse will have to do, though it will take a lot of work and supplies to make it livable."

He pulled a small notepad and pencil from his pocket. "I can have some buckets and mops sent over. Just write down a list of items you need, and I'll make sure you get them."

"Thank you, Lieutenant. That will help

tremendously."

"Meals are served twice a day at the fort mess hall or dining hall as you would call it. I'll have Private Greene show you where that is and explain the various bugle calls which announce the meals and other activities." He gestured to a large tree about fifty yards from the jailhouse. "If you need anything, I'll be billeting in a tent over there for the duration of your stay."

Just her luck. Not only would she be living in a house for criminals, she would have a neighbor—a handsome officer who had her imagining all sorts of sinful misconduct.

****

Meredith squeezed the sponge and dribbled water over her bare legs. Soapy lather rolled off and gathered on top of the bathwater. The wood tub Lieutenant Booth sent with the rest of the supplies wasn't nearly as large or luxurious as her copper bath at Hickory Hills, but it would do. After two days of sweeping and scrubbing and hauling water from the community well, she reeked. Her stepmother would be beside herself with horror. But then Cordelia always found outrage at the least little transgression. According to the fractious woman, instead of Meredith, her name should be *Disgrace*.

She dropped the sponge in the water and leaned back against the rim. She wouldn't think about Cordelia's hatefulness. She would enjoy this little slice of heaven for as long as it lasted. Mrs. Clement had taken the children to the dining hall for supper. Meredith elected to stay behind and enjoy a nice, quiet bath with no interruptions—a treat for all her back-breaking work. Besides, Anna had promised to bring her some food…as had Becky and Robbie and Lily. She would have more than enough to sate her hunger.

The children had used the tub earlier to bathe. One after the other, they had scrubbed, rinsed, and rinsed again. The tub had to be emptied three times to refresh the dirtied water. Afterward, they had dressed in the clothes that also came with the supplies Lieutenant Booth had procured. She would have to thank him for his promptness in filling her list and also for the few extra items he'd unexpectedly included. The children had enjoyed the peppermint sticks, and Daisy dozed contentedly in her little wooden box lined with blanket scraps. This excursion to the fort wasn't turning out as bad as she imagined. Perhaps they would survive after all.

Tepid, lavender-scented water lapped at her aching muscles. She moaned and slunk down as far as the small tub would allow. Some of the bath water sloshed over the sides and puddled on the floor. Let it. It had taken three scrubbings to remove the grime caked on the boards. A little more water wouldn't hurt.

The logs that formed the interior walls gleamed in the lamplight, polished now to a soft luster. Cobbled remnants of their shredded clothes hung at the windows, replacing the disgusting webbed curtains. A vase of wildflowers sat on a table surrounded by chairs. All their hard work had been worth the effort. The place looked much homier and inviting. Only a slight, nose-prickling stench remained. Hopefully the lavender possets Maddie had scattered throughout the jailhouse would soon tame the smell.

Speaking of children…they would be returning

before long. She should dry off and dress. She groaned to her feet and stepped out of the tub. After toweling dry, she pulled on her undergarments—frilly bits from her more genteel life in Pennsylvania that had somehow managed to survive the renegade's defilement. They were as fit for the harsh territories as shoes on a pig. Yet they would have to do until she could wash and dry her more serviceable underthings.

As she reached for her dressing gown, a hairy, spindly-legged creature the size of a half dollar darted from under the tub. She backed away, a screech spilling up from her lungs.

The squeal of hinges rang out, and the front door careened open. Lieutenant Booth rushed through the opening with his pistol drawn. She froze. A spider was nothing compared to being alone and half-naked with a man whose mere presence set her body on fire.

He pulled up, nostrils flaring like a stallion scenting a ready mare. "I heard...you screamed. I thought..."

Unlike him, she found her wits and snatched up her dressing gown, holding it in front of her. For what little good it did. She didn't feel the least bit shielded. More like stripped bare and vulnerable beneath his heated stare.

"Lieutenant Booth. Wh-what are you doing here?"

His gaze raked over her, hard and fast. He let go what sounded like a frustrated groan and spun on his heels. He leaned against the door jamb, his back rigid as a tree trunk.

"My apologies," he rasped. "I didn't intend to intrude. I spoke with Mrs. Clement at the mess hall. She said you weren't feeling up to going out and remained behind. I came to see if you were all right. Heard you scream and thought something had happened."

"I'm perfectly fine." Or she would be once her heart stopped racing and her blood cooled.

"What made you scream like that? It sounded as if you were being attacked."

Embarrassing heat rose in her face. Screaming at the sight of a bug seemed childish. For some reason, she wanted him to think of her as a mature woman, not a silly schoolgirl. "It was nothing. A spider caught me off guard."

"A spider?"

She ignored his mocking tone and gave the gown a good shake, making certain the creature hadn't decided to take up residence in the folds. Only dust motes fluttered from the garment. She wouldn't require any more *saving*.

"The spider is gone now. You can put your pistol away."

He gave a throat-clearing cough and shoveled the gun into the holster belted to his waist. "Are you fully covered? Can I turn around?"

"Not yet, give me…" She slipped her arms into the gown and started working on the buttons. Fingers shriveled and soft from being immersed in water all day refused to cooperate. She fumbled and fidgeted. None of the loops would hook. *Rooster's teeth.* At this rate, she'd be here all night. The sooner Lieutenant Booth and his wit-robbing gaze departed, the better.

"Miss Talbot?"

"Just a minute…" She focused on the task and finally managed to get all the buttons hooked. "There. Done. You can turn around now."

He turned slowly, shucking off his hat as he moved. He glanced from her to the tub and back. Flames flickered in his eyes. Surely he wasn't imagining her sitting in the bathwater—naked. More heat climbed in her throat and burned in her ears.

He waved his hat in the direction of the tub. "I see you got the bathing tub."

"Um…yes, we did. And everything else on our list too. Thank you for having them sent so promptly."

"Only doing my duty. Is there anything else you need?"

She shook her head. "Nothing that I can think of at the moment."

As she stepped forward to collect the wet towel, her foot hit the puddle of spilled water and slipped out from under her. The floor came up to meet her backside. She sat there, blinking in surprise, water seeping into her gown and chilling her bottom.

Boot heels thumped across the floor. Before she could stop him, the lieutenant was there, leaning over her, his warmth enveloping her like a blanket. He was so close she could see the gold flecks speckling his eyes. The skin around his mouth and jaw glistened with silky smoothness. He'd shaven. The deliciously seductive scent of bay rum assailed her. Her head spun, and she couldn't stopper a moan.

His hand curled around her upper arm. "Are you all right? Did you hurt yourself?"

She would never be all right. Not while he was around to twist her wits. She shrugged out of his grasp. "It was just a little spill. I should have taken more care."

"Are you certain? It looked like a pretty hard fall to

me."

She was still falling. But he didn't need to know that. It would only embolden more fiery stares. She grabbed the edge of the tub and pulled herself upright. "There, you see. Fit as a fiddle. I could dance a jig if the yearning came over me."

"And do you…have a yearning?"

Not for dancing. She pushed out a laugh that sounded contrived even to her own ears. "I'm afraid I'd end up on the floor again. My stepmother said I have two left feet and both of them flat."

"Your feet look fine to me."

She tucked her bare toes under the bottom of her gown. She'd already exposed more of herself to him than she ever wanted.

"Yes, well…thank you again for all you've done for us, Lieutenant. I'll send for you if there's anything else we need." That would not be any time soon; she'd make sure of it.

Chapter Five

"He's right over there, Lieutenant. Fifth stall on the right."

The directions weren't necessary. The location of the disturbance was obvious. Screeching blasted from inside a horse stall where Indian Agent Samuel Finley stood in the opening, wagging a finger at whatever was causing the racket.

"Come out of there, you little whippersnapper," the agent scolded.

"No," came a shrieked reply. "You can't take her. I won't let you."

Preston angled for stall. He'd been delivering orders to the morning patrol when Private Womack arrived with news that he was needed in the stables to handle a problem with one of the Seaton House orphans. He'd sent Womack after Miss Talbot. Until she arrived, he would contain the situation as best he could. Considering the noise, he would have a wearying wait.

"What's going on here, Mr. Finley?"

The agent backed away from the opening, his face red and bloated as an overripe tomato. "Good, you're here, Lieutenant. I hope you brought a strap with you."

"What's the trouble?"

"This blasted child won't let me get to my horse."

Preston halted beside the agent. Inside the stall

stood a young boy shielding a horse five times the child's size. Tears streaked a dirty, disheveled face. Bits of chafe peppered curls so white they looked like cotton popping from a boll. Distinctive and quite memorable. As was his awkward and rather embarrassing encounter with the footstool in the Seaton House parlor—all due to this urchin and his penchant for rodents.

"Young man, come out of there before you get hurt."

A dirt smudged chin lifted. "Not until that man finds another horse to ride."

"Why does Mr. Finley need to find another horse to ride?"

"'Cause Honey is sick."

The mare stood solidly on all four legs, head up and ears pricked forward. She looked healthier than half of the mounts allocated to this godforsaken outpost. "The horse doesn't appear to be ill."

White curls whipped around the boy's head. "Well, she is."

Finley advanced a step, hand lifted as if to deliver a blow. "She's not sick. Now get out of there, boy. Before I give you a lesson in minding your elders."

The child yelped and backed against the horse. The mare shook her head and pranced in agitation. Preston's pulse crow-hopped. Finley was going to get the boy trampled. He couldn't let that happen on his watch. He would never forgive himself. Neither would Miss Talbot.

He stretched out an arm, stopping the agent. "Let me handle this, Finley. Chasing after the boy is only going to further rile him and the mare. One or both of them are likely to get hurt."

"Bah. I've already wasted enough time battling with this ragamuffin. I need to get to the reservation."

"I sent for the boy's guardian. She should be here soon."

"She'd better be."

"She will. Now back away."

Finley gave a piggish grunt and backed into the aisle. He stopped and hooked thumbs on the belt circling his ample girth. His beady gaze glowered into the stall. "What the boy needs is a good hide tanning."

The person needing the hide tanning was Miss Talbot. She'd definitely be getting an earful for letting yet another child escape her care.

The child returned Finley's glare. "You ain't gonna touch me or Honey, you mean ole hog."

"Here now, boy," Preston cautioned. "There's no need to be calling names."

"My name is Robbie, and he *is* mean. He beats Honey with a stick when she don't do like he wants. She has a hard enough time toting his fat behind around as it is."

Finley spluttered, his mouth yawing like a toad trapped under a gig pole. Preston stuffed down a laugh. Miss Talbot's flock certainly didn't mince words.

Finley muttered something under his breath as he fished a small red tin out of his breast pocket and unscrewed the lid. *Dr. Rumney's mentholyptus snuff.* Expensive stuff. And hard to come by. Odd that an Indian Agent could afford such a luxury. But then he didn't know a lot about Samuel Finley, other than what he'd observed at his previous post.

He and Finley had been stationed at Leavenworth at the same time. He'd run across the man during a visit to Madame Reynaud's. The doves were in a tizzy over Finley's refusal to pay for services rendered. Finley claimed the service was lacking in enthusiasm and talent. The women contested that he got what he deserved for selecting a young, untrained girl. The man was a cheat and a degenerate and some suspected him of preferring boys. Luckily, Finley seemed more inclined to take this youngster to the woodshed rather than a bedroom.

"Lieutenant Booth?" a familiar voice called from the stable entrance. "Where are you?"

It was about time. He leaned into the aisle. "Over here, Miss Talbot."

She dashed down the walkway with Private Womack trailing behind her. Worry lined her pretty face. "Where is Robbie? Is he all right?"

"He's fine. Or he will be once we get him to come out."

She sailed past him and into the stall. Her flowery scent kicked out at him. It was the same perfume that had attacked him the night before when he'd rushed into the jailhouse and found her half-dressed. It had taken all the will-power he possessed to keep from divesting her of the frilly undergarments that did little to conceal the curves beneath. She'd urged him to put his pistol away. If she'd known just how hard his *pistol* had gotten, she'd have screamed much louder and longer than she had at spotting a spider.

"Robert Wayne Edmunds." She hooked hands on her hips. "What in the world are you doing?"

Desire rifled through him fast and hard. He wanted to be cradling those slender hips, pulling her against him, feeling her flesh pressed against his. He growled under his breath and fisted his sword hilt. These carnal cravings needed taming. Perhaps a trip to the bawdy house in Mineral would put a bridle on them. Oddly, the thought of lying with anyone else made his stomach turn.

Miss Talbot wagged a finger at the boy. "I sent you to fetch water, young man. Yet here you are when I specifically told you the stables were off limits."

The boy's lower lip quivered. "I went to the well like you said. But there was too many people. I thought I'd visit the horses until the line got shorter."

"Well, you've had your visit." She held out a hand. "Come, let's go."

Robbie shook his head. "I can't. Honey needs me."

"Honey? Who is Honey?"

"It's what he calls Mr. Finley's horse." Preston nodded at the agent. "This is Samuel Finley, agent to the Creek Indians living on the nearby reservation. Finley, this is Miss Talbot, steward of the Seaton House orphanage."

Finley tipped his hat. "Miss Talbot."

"I'm sorry for all the trouble, Mr. Finley." She scowled at the boy. "Our children are usually better behaved than this."

Preston bit off a grunt. What world was she living in?

The boy crooked a finger, and she leaned over. Muslin stretched over rounded buttocks, treating him to a most pleasing sight. Too bad he didn't have time for a cooling dip in Dancer's Creek. His body would simmer for hours after such a taunting.

The boy whispered something, and she straightened. "He says the mare is sick."

"He already told us that. It's the reason he refuses to let Mr. Finley take the horse."

Finley's exasperated grunt rang out. "This is going nowhere. Have the boy come out of there this instant or I'll report this absurdity to Major Allen."

Great. Just what he needed…to have his commander involved. Any hint of ineptitude could hold up his request for transfer. "That won't be necessary, Mr. Finley. You'll have your horse shortly."

"No," the boy wailed. "He can't take her. Honey will die if he does. Please, Miss Talbot."

Miss Talbot cocked her head, her gaze fixed on him like a hawk sighting a rabbit. "Lieutenant Booth, is there anyone knowledgeable in the care of horses that can determine if the mare is indeed sick?"

"There is, but I don't see any reason to pull a trooper from his duties on the whim of a child."

She thrust up her chin, no less defiant than the boy. "This is not a whim. Robbie and I will remain right here until your man arrives."

His skull throbbed behind his eyes, crying for a respite. Unfortunately, there would be no relief until Miss Talbot and her flock vacated the fort *and* his life. He motioned to the soldier waiting in the aisle. "Private Womack, go to the parade ground and send Sergeant Reese here immediately."

"Yes, sir, Lieutenant." Womack swiveled in a squelch of boot leather and raced for the stable entrance. Quick and agreeable. Just like orders should be obeyed.

Finley paced the aisle, clucking in disapproval. "Such contrariness. Someone ought to take a strap to the *both* of them."

Miss Talbot pulled the boy against her legs. Protective. Like a mother bear with her cub. His gut clenched at the thought of anyone causing either of them pain.

"There'll be no flogging, Finley," he said.

"Humph." The agent halted his pacing and poked a beefy finger in the air. "Even the Indians know their place."

Miss Talbot speared the agent with a glare. "Like the ones burning down farms and killing people?"

Touché. She certainly had gumption; he'd give her that. His Irish grandmother would have cheered such boldness.

Footfalls echoed into the stable, and Sergeant Reese appeared, chest heaving from his hasty sprint. "You...sent for me, Lieutenant?"

"Have a look at Agent Finley's mare. See if the animal is healthy enough to ride."

Miss Talbot took the boy by the shoulders and herded him to the side of the stall. Reese walked around the horse, examining the mare from head to hoof. The trooper slid a hand over her chest, across her withers, and down her back. The mare didn't move. He checked her shoulders and barrel. Not a flinch. Yet when he pressed her lower flank, the mare flattened her ears and bobbed her head.

Reese looked up, his face penciled with concern. "There's some swelling in her belly, sir. She may have an intestinal cyst, possibly from worms. I wouldn't recommend riding her until she heals."

"Could she die?" Miss Talbot asked.

"If the cyst ruptures, she could." At Robbie's gasp, Sergeant Reese supplied the boy with a reassuring smile. "She'll be just fine, son. I promise. I'll mix up a tonic to give her. It might turn her droppings yellow, but she'll be back to normal in a week or so."

Damn. The horse *was* sick. If he were a betting man, he'd have lost the farm. "Looks like you'll need to find another mount, Mr. Finley. Sergeant Reese will help you select one from the remuda."

The agent's eyes took on a weaselly gleam. "Amazing. The mare seemed to be off her feed a bit. I thought it was just female contrariness. How did you know she was unwell, Robbie, is it?"

"He's just attuned to animals." Miss Talbot aimed the boy for the stall door. "Nothing out of the ordinary."

Finley rubbed his chin, eyebrows arching. "Quite out of the ordinary, I'd say."

Just dandy. The agent's attitude toward the boy had twisted from disgust to interest—and not in a good way. Preston stepped aside to let the pair pass. "Good day, Miss Talbot. I suggest you keep a tighter rein on your charges. We can't have them wandering unescorted all over the fort. It's too dangerous."

"I give you my word; it won't happen again."

Right. Like the sun promised not to shine. He'd best be on guard for the next transgression. Especially with reprobates like Finley just waiting to take advantage.

****

Water rushing downstream burbled a serene song. Even the breeze whistled merrily. Meredith sank to her knees on the creek bank and briefly closed her eyes. It was just the tranquility she needed. Her body quivered with tension. It bubbled and churned inside her like a geyser preparing to erupt.

After returning to the jailhouse, she'd blasted Robbie for disobeying her orders and directed him to gather the ashes from the potbelly stove as punishment. His woeful expression ate at her. He was just a child and adored his animal friends. Clearly, the stress of moving to the fort was turning her into someone she didn't know or particularly like—a shrew, as Lieutenant Booth had claimed.

With a heavy sigh, she dipped the metal pail into the rushing water and let it fill. The line at the community well had indeed been long just as Robbie had complained. When asked about another place to draw water, a soldier had pointed her to Dancer's Creek located just outside the rear pedestrian gate. While only six feet across, it ran swift and deep and flowed with clear, crystalline water. It probably originated in the Shoehorn Mountain that shadowed the valley and would taste much better than musty old well water.

She placed the bucket on the bank and sat back on her haunches. Birds calling to one another drifted across the grassy meadow that stretched beyond the creek. Trees had been cleared for a good distance around the fort. Where the wood line picked up again, splashes of white from the later flowering trees dotted the greenery. The soldier had warned her not to dally, but such serenity couldn't be rushed. Surely the renegades wouldn't venture this close to a garrison filled with armed men. She could spare a few more minutes to enjoy the lovely view.

As she bent to fill the second bucket, a breeze kicked up and white cotton puffs danced around her. The source was a tall cottonwood that stood sentinel a few yards from the creek. Thick, gnarled roots shoved up through the ground like the oak at Seaton House. She missed that old behemoth, even though it had caused her no end of grief.

She set the filled bucket beside the other and swiped at the perspiration trickling from her brow. The heat was oppressive today, and it wasn't even at the height of summer yet. She dreaded returning to the fort where the tall stockade walls cut off any chance of a breeze.

A few feet away, the shelter of the cottonwood's canopy beckoned. She could spare a few more minutes before leaving such a haven.

She rose and moved into the cooling shade. The trunk of the cottonwood was at least three feet in diameter and covered with rough, gray bark. While impressive, she made sure to stay well clear of it. She'd had enough of unreliable, disjointed visions.

Just up from the cottonwood, a tangle of honeysuckle embraced a cluster of decaying stumps. Pretty trumpet-like blooms dotted the lush vines. A sweet, nostalgic sadness spread through her.

She crossed to the vines and plucked a bloom. She pulled out the stem and placed it in her mouth. Sweet nectar bathed her tongue. She smiled. She and her stepbrother had often snuck off from their studies to enjoy the white honeysuckle growing along the pasture fence. They had called the collection of vines their candy store. It was one of the few enjoyable memories she had of Charles before…

No. She tossed the bloom to the ground. All that darkness was behind her. She wouldn't let the memories haunt her. Couldn't. The pain was too unbearable.

She spun to return to the creek. An ominous rattling rose from a tangle of tree roots. She froze. Mildred had warned her to keep a watch for the venomous rattlers that were as plentiful in the territories as bugs at a picnic. Her wool-gathering had placed her smack in the middle of danger.

"Don't move, Miss Talbot," a familiar deep voice warned.

She couldn't move even if she wanted to. Fear frosted her veins and petrified her muscles. The rattling increased until it reached a crescendo. The snake was about to strike.

A gunshot sliced the air.

She flinched and stumbled backward. Her hands met the cottonwood. Warmth shot through her palms. Her head spun, and darkness overran the sunshine. Red and yellow flames burst into her vision, darting and dancing in a macabre ballet. The image was much fuzzier than usual, less distinct. Probably because it came unbidden.

A door and a window shimmered through the fiery haze. *A building was on fire. Where?*

Firm hands coiled around her waist and tugged her away from the tree. The vision vanished in a flash of light. Buzzing filled her ears. Her stomach roiled. She gasped and slumped against the lieutenant's chest. The pungent aroma of horse and wood smoke filled her senses.

He gently laid her on the ground. "Are you all right? Did the snake strike you?"

She tried to answer, but the words wouldn't come. The aftereffects of the vision still had her in its clutches.

He shoveled her skirts to her knees and started probing her calves. His touch was warm and tender and most intoxicating. Venom from a rattler couldn't be any more lethal.

"I don't see any fang marks," he said.

His hands left her, taking their warmth with them. She swallowed and located her voice. "I-It didn't…strike me."

"Good." He pulled her skirts back over her legs. "A bite would have been disastrous."

For her or for him? She pushed up on her elbows. The earth spun like a toy top. Two heads swam in front of her. No three. She grimaced. Lordy, one of him was more than enough.

"Hold still. You're white as those cottonwood puffs."

She managed a slight shake of her head. "I'll…be fine."

"Can I get you something? Water? A wet cloth?"

"No. Just…give me a moment." *Or two or three.* She focused on the tree roots snaking through the grass. One of them wasn't a root at all. It was the rattler, now headless and unmoving. A shudder pulsed through her. If the lieutenant hadn't been there to save her, she could have been bitten. She might have died.

Her whirling head finally settled enough that she could look up without losing her lunch. The lieutenant had shucked off his hat. Dribbles of sunlight burnished his short-cropped brown hair. An angel's halo, Becky would have called it. He was her savior, yes. Angel, that was debatable.

"Thank you for rescuing me, Lieutenant. I should have been more cautious."

"Yes, you should have. But you shouldn't have been out here in the first place. What if renegades had attacked you instead of a snake?"

Overbearing man. She hefted her chin in a show of defiance. "I only intended a quick outing. We needed water, and the wait at the well was too long."

"If you were that determined to go outside the fort, you should have requested one of the soldiers accompany you. Or better yet, come and asked me."

Better yet? In her experience, tempting the devil never ended well. "I know how busy everyone is with the overcrowded conditions. I didn't want to take you or anyone else away from their duties."

"You are my duty, Miss Talbot."

Oddly, she wanted to be more to him than an obligation. "That must stick in your craw. It's evident how much you dislike having to deal with me and the children."

The firm lines around his mouth softened. He lifted a hand. "You have something…"

His fingers grazed her hair. Tingles shot across her scalp and ricocheted down her neck. She sucked in a breath. Being under the clutches of a vision wasn't nearly as mind-numbing.

He tugged and then held out a twig. "There. Got it."

She released the breath she'd held captive. How could such an innocent gesture feel so brazen, so seductive? Her scalp still prickled from his touch.

"As to your allegation…" His mesmerizing gaze slid down and locked with hers. "My duty assignment, while not my first choice, has its appealing aspects."

A nervous chuckle snuck past her lips.

"Appealing? What is so appealing about watching over noisy children and their steward?"

He leaned toward her. "You."

His mouth covered hers, gentle and soothing, like a soft caress. He pulled her bottom lip between his teeth, nibbling, tasting. Fire raced through her veins. A moan rose in the back of her throat. This could not be real. Maddie must have slipped a love potion into the lieutenant's drinking water.

He groaned and broke away. "Are you a witch, Miss Talbot?"

Her heart missed a beat. "Wh-what?"

"I usually have better control of myself than that. I believe you have bewitched me."

"I believe you are the one who was snake bit, Lieutenant."

He gathered himself, pulling away, retreating behind his stony barricade. "You are right. You were stunned by the near bite, and it was wrong of me to take advantage. It won't happen again. You have my word."

Part of her wanted the pleasurable experience to happen again—repeatedly. The sane part of her, the part that grasped the gravity of such closeness, shouted that she should run as fast and as far away from him as possible.

He collected his hat and pushed upright. "We should get back inside the fort before some other misfortune befalls you."

Too late. Misfortune had already latched onto her and wasn't letting go. She couldn't get that kiss out of her mind. She touched a finger to lips that continued to tingle and burn.

Burn. Fire. The vision. She stiffened. She'd left

Robbie cleaning the potbelly stove. Considering her luck lately, anything could have happened.

"Why did you seek me out, Lieutenant? Is it the jailhouse? Is it on fire?"

"Not that I'm aware of." Confusion stamped his face. "Why would you think the jailhouse was on fire?"

Because a silly old tree told me. "I suppose I'm just overly tired from the move and worrying about the children. My imagination goes places it shouldn't." She lifted a hand. "If you could just help me…"

His fingers closed around hers, sending quivers parading up her arm. She levered to her feet and pulled out of his grasp. If he noticed her response, it might encourage more touching, more kissing. She couldn't fall down that rabbit hole again. She might never climb out.

To her relief, he turned and retrieved the water buckets from the creek bank.

"Ready to go?" he asked.

More than ready. "Yes. And thank you for helping with those."

"I'm happy to be of service."

She batted aside the notion of exactly *what* service he was happy to perform. A white puff drifted between them. She gestured to the tree, seeking a more mundane topic. "I'm curious…why was this cottonwood left standing when all the other trees were cleared?"

"I asked the same question when I first arrived. One of my troopers said Major Allen ordered the tree to be left untouched. The commander likes to come down to the creek and sit in the shade to fish. I suspect to nap as well." His gaze shifted to the west. "I prefer a good swim. Just over that hillock, the creek widens and slows. It's the perfect place for a dip."

Images surfaced of his sleek body sluicing the water. She quickly washed the pictures from her head. The less she thought of him in such an intimate fashion, the easier it would be to keep her desires submerged.

She fell into step beside him. He had a long stride. She had to double-step to keep up. "You never answered my question, Lieutenant. Why did you come out here? Were you checking on me, or was there another reason?"

"Both, actually. Major Allen and his wife invited us to a supper party tonight."

"Us? You and me?"

"Yes. There will be other officers and their wives in attendance…as well as several prominent citizens from Mineral."

It sounded like a large gathering. After the day she'd had, she doubted she could string together two words, much less carry on a conversation. "I'm afraid that's not going to be possible. Please give your commander my regrets."

"It's not a request. Major Allen made it quite clear he and his wife expect both of us to attend. What Mrs. Allen wants; Mrs. Allen usually gets."

She kicked through the grass, searching for an excuse. Major Allen had been nothing but kind to her and the children. She didn't want to offend him or his wife. The dirt staining her hem prompted an idea. "As much as I'd like to go, I don't have anything suitable to wear thanks to those renegades."

"Mrs. Allen heard about your hardship. She and some of the other officers' wives organized a clothing collection. They sent a trunk of donated items over to the jailhouse. There should be something suitable for you to wear."

Rooster's teeth. It would be rude to refuse to dine with such kind-hearted women. "I suppose I will have to accept their invitation."

"Excellent. I'll call for you at seven."

Tightness coiled around her neck and shoulders. Any serenity she had gathered at the creek had perished—shot and beheaded like the rattler.

Chapter Six

"Where in Pennsylvania are you from, Miss Talbot?"

Meredith shifted in the over-stuffed chair. If only she could disappear into the hollow cratering the seat cushion. Interrogations always put her on edge, especially when the questions pried into her past. Earlier, when asked about her place of birth, she had given a vague answer. Luckily the supper chatter had moved on to other topics. Now that the ladies had adjourned to the parlor, the focus on her had returned and didn't appear to be budging.

She took a sip of tea, using the interval to gather her thoughts. She didn't want to reveal *everything* about her past—just enough to satisfy their curiosity. A few details should suffice.

She set her cup in the saucer balancing on her knee. "I'm from a township north of Philadelphia. My father owns and operates a large cattle farm there."

"Philadelphia." Edeline Wentworth, whose husband owned the Shoehorn Silver Mine, beamed like a child who knew the answer to a math puzzle. "Our daughter Alice lives there with Stanley's parents, Benjamin and Mary Wentworth. Do you know of them? They are prominent patrons of *The Franklin Institute.*"

Meredith shook her head. "I'm afraid I don't recognize those names. We didn't go into the city very often." Well, her father and stepmother had. She hadn't. Not once her *talent* had manifested.

"A cattle farm, you say?" Mrs. Troutman, wife of the town physician, leaned forward in her chair. Brown curls and ribbons dangled from her head like trimmings on a festive tree. "That must be quite the enterprise."

"It is. Before I left, the estate had swelled to over five thousand acres. Father was forever procuring more land. He boasted of eventually owning the largest cattle ranch east of the Mississippi." Mostly at his new wife's urging. Cordelia Wright Talbot seemed quite taken with wealth and status and pushed her husband into acquiring more and more. The woman had a powerful hold over her father—almost supernatural.

"And your mother?"

Meredith fingered the brooch pinned to her dress, an opal that rested in a gold filigree setting. Not a day went by that her mother hadn't worn the piece. It had belonged to her mother, Grandmother Agnes. And before her, Great-grandmother Margaret. It was one of the more harmless family heirlooms handed down from mother to daughter.

"My mother passed when I was a young girl."

"That must have been very difficult for you. I'm sorry for your loss." Mrs. Troutman's eyes glimmered with sympathy, the sort of kindness that didn't pose behind half-masted eyelids. "What made you decide to come out here to the territories?"

The answer to that question would send these fluffy women running for the door. A half-truth would have to suffice. "I came to assist my Aunt Mildred with the orphanage."

"How noble and self-sacrificing," their hostess said

from her perch beside the serving tray. Mrs. Allen wore a ruffled gown of black silk flecked with white and gray. Streaks of white striped her dark hair and even dotted her eyebrows. She looked like the speckled hen that nested in the cattle barns and chased after anyone who ventured near her territory.

"No more noble than your donation of clothing." Meredith raised her teacup in tribute. "Thank you again for your thoughtful generosity. All of you. It was much appreciated by everyone from Seaton House."

Mrs. Allen stirred sugar into her tea, her spoon tinkling against the porcelain. "We were just doing our Christian duty. Perhaps you could tell us about the orphans under your care."

"What is it you wish to know?"

"We've heard rumors that the children at Seaton House are…well, odd."

Hopefully the woman had heard nothing more than ignorant speculation. Meredith put on her most engaging smile—the one she used to calm frightened children and placate overbearing matrons. "They are no different than other youngsters. Little Becky is afraid of the dark. Anna is shy and avoids strangers. And the boys, well, they are just like any other young men. Rough-housing, teasing the girls, and collecting all sorts of insects and reptiles. Surely you know of what I speak."

"Indeed." Mrs. Cavendish, who operated the dry goods store with her husband, gave a shudder worthy of a theater performance. "My son Peter brought home a rat. A *rat*, for heaven's sake. Said it was his pet. I had James exterminate the thing immediately. Nasty, vile rodent."

The mayor's wife Alvena Wood wagged her head. "My Dilbert adopted a stray mongrel which he absolutely refused to give up. I made him keep the mangy creature in the barn with the other animals."

"What about you, Miss Talbot?" Mrs. Allen peered over the rim of her teacup. "Do you have any special pets? Any you converse with after a long, exhausting day?"

Meredith clenched the cup handle, mooring herself under Harriet Allen's pungent gaze. If the woman was looking to fuel her suspicions about Seaton House, she wouldn't provide her with any kindling. "I don't have any pets. Besides, with my Aunt Mildred away, I have more than enough on my hands caring for the children."

Mrs. Allen set her cup and saucer on the serving tray and laced her hands into a pious fold on her lap. "You seem to keep to yourselves out there in the backwoods with only your work staff venturing into town for supplies. We thought you would at least bring the children to Sunday services. In Romans 10, the Bible says, '…faith comes from hearing the message, and the message is heard through the word of Christ.' "

Meredith met Harriet's stare straight on. This fishing expedition had gone far enough. It was time to dock the boats. "Our handyman is a retired minister. Mr. Hoggard conducts Sunday services and instructs the children in Bible study every evening." There. That ought to appease the sanctimonious woman.

Instead of pacifying, the comment goaded Mrs. Allen into more histrionics. The woman took to the floor, hands waving and lips flapping as she expounded on the merits of a Christian upbringing, her own included. Meredith's temples thudded. Harriet Allen must certainly enjoy hearing herself talk. Shakespeare himself couldn't have delivered a more vigorous soliloquy.

A maid toting a tray of sweets pushed through the connecting door and allowed an unfettered view of the dining room. A low-hanging cloud of smoke swirled over the men gathered at the table. Lieutenant Booth sat to the right of Major Allen, sipping an after-dinner spirit. His mouth was tilted down as Anna would say. He didn't look any happier to be here than she did.

His gaze shifted and caught hers. Tingles skipped from the top of her head to the tips of her toes. Such a powerful attraction. It was almost magical. And most definitely dangerous.

She looked away and fussed with the folds of her skirts, a simple tea gown of russet brown she'd discovered in the trunk the ladies had sent over. It was pretty and showed little sign of wear. She felt almost acceptable in the gown. Almost.

"The men should be joining us soon," Mrs. Allen said from the piano bench where she'd finally roosted. "Do you sing, Miss Talbot?"

At last, the theatrics had ended. Her pounding head wouldn't last much longer without exploding. Meredith procured a wry smile. "I'm afraid that is one talent I never mastered." *Among others.*

"William says I make the cats howl. Naughty man." Mrs. Allen ran up the scale. "So I simply let the piano do the singing for me. Come everyone, join me."

Meredith rose with the others, but instead of joining them, she tucked behind a small table in the far corner of the room. Out of sight; out of mind.

A bust of President Washington sat on a pedestal

next to the table. She bent and read the inscription etched on the base. *Happiness and moral duty are inseparably connected.* Insightful. Just like Major Allen. The commander was nothing like she had imagined. He listened before speaking, and when he did talk, it was in a friendly and a non-judgmental manner. Too bad his wife didn't share his disposition.

Mrs. Allen was very forthright with her views, almost to the point of fanaticism. Odd that the major didn't take her in hand, considering his position as fort commander. Yet at the dinner table, he had allowed his wife to spout her opinions without comment. It was only after her dramatics rattled the dinnerware that he steered the conversation to a safer topic. Perhaps he'd learned early on when and where to wage his battles.

Meredith set her tea cup and saucer on the table beside a book resting spine up. She tilted her head to better read the title. *Witch Trials of Salem.* Of course. She should have recognized Mrs. Allen's line of questioning. It had been straight out of the Puritan journals of yesteryear. Would she next be inspected for blemishes or moles?

The dining room door swung open, and the menfolk filed into the parlor. Like a moth drawn to a flame, she sought Lieutenant Booth. He wasn't with them. Panic fluttered in her chest. Surely he hadn't left her alone in this den of lions.

"Mayor Wood," Mrs. Allen called out. "You have a marvelous singing voice. Come join us at the piano."

The room soon reverberated with the foot-tapping melody of *The Battle Hymn of the Republic.* The jovial music usually served to cheer her. Not now. Not after a tiring day of dodging snakes and evading wolves in ladies clothing.

A movement in the doorway caught her attention. Lieutenant Booth filled the opening. His gaze swept the room not stopping until he found her in the corner. His lips winnowed into a malnourished line. Was he upset with her? He always seemed to find her lacking.

He crossed to the middle of the room and leaned in to speak to his commander. The major's expression darkened, and bushy eyebrows bunched into a foreboding streak. His gaze fled to her hiding spot. Her stomach churned around what little supper she'd managed to choke down. Something was afoot—and that concerned look said it involved her.

She left her haven and joined the two men. "Lieutenant Booth. Major Allen. You look troubled. Is anything amiss?"

"I'm afraid there is, Miss Talbot," the major said. "Perhaps you should sit."

Her heart struck a bad chord. If he thought she should sit, then the matter was indeed dire. "Please tell me what is going on. Is it the children? Has something happened to them?"

"Not the children," the lieutenant said. "It's the orphanage. The evening patrol just rode in with news that renegades attacked and set fire to Seaton House."

Her knees went weak. She grabbed for the back of a nearby chair. Of course. The burning building from her vision had been the orphanage. If only she had seen more…perhaps she could have prevented it from happening.

"What of Mr. Hoggard? Did they find him? Is he…?" She couldn't put voice to the words. To say them aloud might make them come true.

"There were no signs of your handyman or anyone else," Lieutenant Booth answered.

She plucked up her skirts and raced for the door. "Then I have to go find him."

"Miss Talbot…wait."

The hallway runner bunched beneath her feet, but she didn't let the rug or the lieutenant's barked command slow her down. She tugged open the front door and bolted outside. In the distance, a faint red glow slashed the night sky. She pulled to a stop, her breaths coming in shallow draws. What had become of Joseph? Had he been hurt or worse? Her vision had been too brief and fuzzy to know for certain.

Footfalls thudded behind her. "Meredith, you cannot go to Seaton House. It's too dangerous."

Meredith. Any other time she would be thrilled to hear her name cross his lips. "I have to go. Joseph might need me."

Lieutenant Booth moved in front of her, blocking her path. "I told you the patrol didn't find anyone. And if Mr. Hoggard *was* inside any of the buildings…well, going there tonight won't help him."

"I want to see for myself."

"What possible good would that do?"

She stepped around him, hands fisted at her side. Anger was much less painful to hold onto than heartache. "If you won't help me, I'll find a way to get there myself."

"Fine." His fingers curled gently around her elbow. "I'll take you. But not until morning. I won't risk you or my men by going out there tonight."

He was right. She couldn't rush headlong into danger. Her run-in with the rattler had underscored that sharp-fanged point. The children needed her alive and healthy.

"Very well, but we leave at first light." She gave him a firm look. "Not a minute later."

****

Fingers of smoke curled up from the burnt remains that had once been home to laughter and the patter of little feet. There were no windows or doors. No walls or roof. The only thing left of Seaton House was the main chimney. It overlooked the destruction like a grieving mourner, its bricks dark and weeping with smut.

Meredith drew in a ragged breath, the charred air scraping her throat. What would they do now? Where would they live? Rebuilding would require time and money—neither of which they had to spare.

Something metallic glinted amidst the ashes. She bent and rescued the object. It was one of Gabe's jacks, blackened and twisted from the intense heat. Had she not agreed to move the children to the fort...

No. She briefly closed her eyes, watering now from the smoke and the strangling feeling of powerlessness. She wouldn't think that way. Couldn't. Her heart was already heavy enough without the added burden.

Something brushed her arm, and she turned. Lieutenant Booth's gaze met hers, strong and steady, an anchor in a storm. She latched onto it.

"How are you doing?" he asked. "This is a lot to take in."

She shoved her hand into her pocket and held it there, fisted around the jack rock. The little piece of metal would be a reminder that although warped, it had survived. They would all survive.

"I'll manage. The worst part of all this is Joseph.

Have you found any clues as to what happened to him?"

"I wish I had better news. We searched through the rubble here and at the barn. We also made a sweep of the surrounding woods. There's no sign of him."

"Where could he be? Do you think the Indians took him?" Lord help him if they had. The newspapers back east had been full of horrific accounts of the tortures the merciless Indians inflicted on their captives. A gentle soul like Mr. Hoggard stood little chance of surviving such savagery.

He shook his head. "I won't sugar coat the situation. This particular band of renegades isn't known for taking prisoners."

He didn't say what the renegades usually did with their victims. But he didn't have to. Her throat closed around a sob. She should have tried harder to convince Joseph to join them at the fort instead of staying at the orphanage where he would be alone and vulnerable. Now he might be gone from them forever.

Lieutenant Booth's arms went around her, gentle, as if cradling a fragile flower. It had been a long time since she'd been held in such a tender embrace. After her mother died, her father had retreated into his shell and stayed there until the evil siren Cordelia lured him out. Even then he ignored his only child. Was it because she reminded him of the wife he'd lost? Or had her affliction so revolted him he couldn't bear to look at her? The sob she'd held at bay bubbled to the surface.

"Everything's going to be all right," he whispered into her hair. "We'll find Mr. Hoggard. I'll make sure of it."

The arms around her tightened. She should pull

away, should rebuff the inappropriate gesture, kind though it was. But she couldn't. His strength grounded her—stopped her world from spinning out of control. She rested her head on his chest and let the steady beat of his heart soothe her rawness.

After a few minutes, he loosened his hold and leaned back. "Better now?"

Better? Not even close. But she would pull herself together and march on—for Joseph's sake. She managed a nod.

He skimmed a hand along her arm in a comforting caress. "It's possible Hoggard escaped into the woods. We'll keep looking for him. My men are very diligent. They won't leave any stone unturned."

"I appreciate all your efforts. Joseph means the world to us. I don't know what we would do without him. He's like a father, brother, and uncle all rolled into one. The children adore him…we all do. Even the livestock flock to him."

"I'm more than happy to help in any way I can." He dropped his hand to his side. "Speaking of livestock, I forgot to mention we came across your milk cow during our search."

"Bessy? Is she all right?"

"She appears to be unharmed. Your neighbor's one-eyed mutt was with her. Most likely protecting her from predators. I had her secured to the wagon. We'll take her back to the fort with us where you can look after her."

Robbie would be relieved. He'd worried day and night about how the animals were faring. "What of the chickens? Did you see any of them?"

The flock normally roosted in the barn, but that too

had been gutted by the fire. Miraculously, two adjacent walls had remained upright—charred and listing, but still standing. It was probably the reason Bessy had managed to escape. The good Lord willing, Joseph had done the same.

"Unfortunately, the chickens have scattered throughout the woods," he answered. "We just don't have the time to round them up right now."

"I suppose they will have to manage as best they can." Just as they all would.

Voices drew closer. She stepped away and pretended an interest in the burnt remnants of the porch steps. She didn't need people speculating about a blossoming relationship between her and the lieutenant. For that matter, she didn't need to be speculating on such a thing either.

"Do you recognize this?" He held out a hand. "It was found in the front driveway. There's mud on one side as if it was recently dropped. Is it one of the children's?"

A small wooden dowel that looked similar to a clothes pin rested in his palm. The children had few toys, and she could easily eliminate it. "No. I've never seen it before. Did one of the attackers drop it?"

"I can't say for sure. It doesn't look like anything an Indian would own. It's too smooth and polished as if factory made. I'll just hold onto it for now." He stuffed the pin into his jacket pocket. "Is there anything you want to take back with you? Not much of value left. The fire unfortunately torched everything it touched."

Jack rock points bit into her palm. "No. As you said, there's nothing left worth salvaging."

"Very well. We'll start preparing to leave soon.

The renegades have probably moved on, but just in case, we should get everyone back to the safety of the fort."

"What about Mr. Hoggard? We can't just abandon him."

"We won't do that. I'm leaving half the patrol behind to continue searching. If he's out there, my men will find him."

From his lips to God's ears. "Thank you. You've been very kind and helpful through all this…" Her throat closed around the rest of her words. Fresh tears surfaced hot and heavy in her eyes.

His hand closed around her elbow in a gentle squeeze. "I'm sorry this happened, Meredith. I know it's going to make things harder for you and the children. If there's anything I can do, all you have to do is ask."

He didn't know the half of how hard it would be. Would probably never know. A ragged "thank you" was all she could manage.

He looked as though he wanted to say more but turned and strode away. He wasn't the same cold-hearted, inflexible man she'd collided with when they first met. He'd changed—had let her see beneath his armor. And she quite liked what she saw.

She drifted toward the old oak. Heat from the fire had seared the bark to a blackish brown. Many of the leaves were scorched and curled in on themselves. She couldn't imagine the pain it must have endured.

She lifted a hand to touch the trunk, but drew back. There were too many people roaming about to risk being observed using her talent. Besides, all of her recent visions had been full of bad tidings. As much as she wanted to know about Mr. Hoggard, she just couldn't bear any more heartache.

A raised voice drifted across the short distance. "What in God's name is that thing, Lieutenant?"

"It's a dog, Agent Finley. He might look like a brute, but he's tame enough. Buster watched over Miss Talbot's cow after it escaped into the woods."

She couldn't help but stare in awe as Preston knelt and gave the dog a friendly pat. *Preston*. After being in his arms, after being treated to his gentleness and his compassion, she felt comfortable thinking of him that way.

"It's detestable what those renegades did to these poor folks. You need to find those Indians and hang them from the nearest tree."

Mr. Finley's anger and frustration mirrored her own. The Indian Agent had happened upon them as they were leaving the fort and insisted on accompanying them to help in any way he could. It was kind of him to offer, though from the look of things, there wasn't much he, or anyone, could do.

"We will find and punish the guilty parties; make no mistake about that." Preston rose and motioned for her. "We're ready to go when you are, Miss Talbot."

Miss Talbot. Back to formalities—as it should be. She waggled a discreet wave to the scorched tree. *Get well, old friend. I will be back soon. I promise.* One way or another, she would return. This was her home now. The place she felt safe and protected. No fire, no matter how destructive, could torch that feeling.

****

With no clouds to check its potency, the midday sun assaulted the earth. The roadway shimmered with dancing waves of heat. The nearby trees sagged, their leaves wilted and lifeless. Even the birds had gone silent, most likely sheltering in the dense canopies. The only sound came from the driver seated beside her on the wagon as he hummed a solemn tune.

Meredith fished a handkerchief from her sleeve cuff and swiped perspiration from her brow. She might be baking on the outside, but ice coated her insides. The only thing salvageable from the fire-ravaged orphanage had been Bessy. Secured to the back of the wagon, the cow walked quietly as if content to leave behind the chaos of the night before. Bessy could be the last living soul to have seen Mr. Hoggard alive. Did she know what happened to him? Where he had gone? When they got back to the fort, she would have Robbie speak with the animal and find out. The tricky part would be relating any information they learned to Preston.

He rode twenty yards ahead of the wagon, turning his head from side to side, ever watchful. He was her guardian. Her savior. A good friend who wouldn't let anything happen to her. Her body heated with the memory of his arms wrapped around her, comforting her. Yet friend was all he could be. To consider more would put her and everyone at Seaton House at risk of being exposed.

Private Greene broke off his humming. "There's a canteen of water under the seat if you're needing a drink, Miss Talbot."

She tucked the handkerchief back under her sleeve. It would take more than a canteen to drown her sorrows. "I'm fine for now. Thank you for offering."

He must have heard the ache in her voice. His tone softened. "I'm sorry 'bout what happened to your orphanage. It was a horrible thing to do. Those savages deserve to swing from a rope."

The word savages conjured images of painted, hide-wearing Indians she'd seen depicted in the newspapers. While only drawings, they still gave her the shudders. "It's quite upsetting to think there are people in this world capable of such evil."

"Unfortunately, there are far too many of them. And not just Injuns." He slapped leather to a flagging mule. "Hup there, Mack. I hope they find your handyman alive and well. I'll be sure to keep him in my prayers."

She also prayed for his safe return. Yet considering the viciousness of the attack and the passage of time, the hope of finding Joseph alive hung by a thin thread. She tugged at bonnet laces that had tightened snugger than a noose.

"I reckon the fire is gonna make things even harder for the children," the trooper added. "I know some of them weren't too keen on moving to the fort to begin with. Now they won't have a home to return to."

"It is going to make things more difficult, that's for certain."

"I'm a fair hand at carpentry if you need help with rebuilding."

He had big hands, paws almost. Her maid back at Hickory Hills said big hands on a man meant a big heart. He must have one the size of a watermelon. "I appreciate the offer. We will need all the help we can get."

"I know there'll be others willing to help. Before the war, Private Brown was involved with the renovations at the Willard Hotel in Washington City.

He has a good head for construction and such. I'm sure he'll volunteer his services…once we get those renegades caught and jailed, that is."

"I hope that happens soon…for all of us."

"Me, too. All this burning and killing needs to stop. Been going on way too long."

The wagon rolled past a deep gouge in the roadway. It was the spot where their first attempt to make it to Fort Dent had resulted in a broken axle…and where Private Greene had been tossed to the ground. Only a small strip of white bandage peeking from beneath the trooper's hat brim indicated he'd suffered an injury. On the ride to the orphanage, she'd been too consumed with thoughts of Joseph to consider the driver's welfare. No time like the present.

"How is your head, Private Greene? You don't appear to be suffering from your fall."

"Doc Troutman says the gash is healing just fine, thanks to the excellent care I got when it happened. I'm grateful to you and Mrs. Clement."

And Maddie, but he didn't need to know about the special potion that had aided his healing. In her experience, kindness didn't mean acceptance, especially when it came to the unexplainable.

"We were only too happy to help." She inclined her head to the ditch, cleared now of wood shards and shredded clothing. "I see the soldiers retrieved the wagon and our trunks."

"Yes'm. Though most of the wood ended up on the kindling pile."

The army wagon and trunks might be gone, but the stark memory of finding their severed clothing remained. Shirts, pants, and dresses ripped to shreds.

Not by one slice, but many. Over and over. The viciousness of the deed had left her feeling exposed and violated...as did the attack on the orphanage. She slipped a hand into her pocket and fisted the jack rock.

A flash of color flickered in the nearby woods. She squinted against the sunlight. Blue shimmered among the greens and browns. Something or someone was in there. Her heart leapt. *Please let it be Joseph.*

"Stop the wagon, Private Greene. I think there's someone in the woods."

He pulled back on the reins. "Whoa, mules. Where? What did you see?"

She pointed to the area where she'd seen the movement. "Over by that thick stand of pines. Something blue flashed in the greenery."

He rose and let out a whistle. Preston turned, and Private Greene motioned to the spot she'd indicated. Preston unholstered his pistol and nudged his horse over the ditch and into the woods. He quickly disappeared into the heavy brush.

Minutes passed. Or was it hours? Voices floated from the thicket. There was a shout. And then silence returned.

A few minutes later, his horse trailing behind him, Preston emerged on foot with his arm slung around a man wearing mud-splattered coveralls and a tattered blue shirt. *Joseph.* He was alive.

She scrambled from the wagon and raced toward them. Dried blood caked a gash on the handyman's forehead. His eyes were bloodshot and rimmed with dirt. One foot dragged the ground. He was alive, but not unscathed.

She shouldered under his other arm. "There, now,

Mr. Hoggard. We have you."

"Run, Miss Talbot," he muttered. "Demons. Fire."

Preston shook his head. "He's keeps rambling on like that. Must have hit his head pretty hard."

Not a good sign. "It's all right, Joseph," she crooned. "The Indians are long gone."

"White demons."

"White men?" Preston asked. "You must have been confused, sir. We found Creek arrows in the rubble at the orphanage."

"Not Creek. Branded horses."

Agent Finley rushed over to them. "Poor man. He's clearly out of his head. Doesn't know what he's saying."

Joseph wagged his head. "Saw them…they—"

His voice and knees buckled, and he started sinking to the ground. Meredith struggled to keep him upright.

Mr. Finley sidled beside her. "Let me help get him to the wagon for you, Miss Talbot."

She stepped aside and let the agent and Preston handle Joseph. She trailed behind them as they carried the handyman the rest of the way to the wagon. Joseph slumped in their grasp, his chin bouncing against his chest. She prayed he had only succumbed to unconsciousness and not to death's call.

The two men lifted Joseph onto the wagon bed, and with Preston's help, she climbed in beside him. His eyes were closed, yet his chest rose and fell evenly. He lived. Thank you, Lord. She dabbed a corner of her skirt at the crusted gash. At least the bleeding had stopped, though considering his ramblings; the worst of the damage was most likely hidden underneath and would require a doctor's attention.

"Quickly now, Private Greene," she urged the driver. "He needs medical care as soon as possible."

The trooper whipped up the mules, and the wagon lurched forward. She pulled Joseph's head onto her lap to cushion him against the jolting. He didn't need to further aggravate an already severe injury.

Preston trotted his horse beside the wagon. He unhooked a canteen from his saddle and tossed it beside her on the wagon bed. "There's some water if he needs it. I'm going to ride back to the orphanage and let the search party know your man has been found."

A judder jostled the wagon, and Joseph's eyes flickered open. He blinked, and blinked again. Muddy blue eyes focused on her. "Miss Talbot?"

"Yes, it's me. We're on our way to Fort Dent. You hit your head. It bled some, but has stopped now."

"Running. Fell…"

She uncapped the canteen and held it to his lips. "Drink some water. Slowly now."

He took a sip and then collapsed back to her lap. His fingers clamped around her wrist, cold and quivering. "Seaton House. Couldn't stop them. Too many…"

She patted his hand. "You're safe. That's all that matters."

"Fire. Burning…nothing I could do."

"It's all right. We'll rebuild once the renegade Indians are captured."

"Not Indians… White."

He really was befuddled. "Shhh. You just close your eyes and rest. Once we're back at the fort and you're feeling better, you can tell Lieutenant Booth all about what happened."

Chapter Seven

Preston batted aside the canvas flap and ducked out of the tent. He swiped sweat from his brow before tucking on his hat. After a night of stifling mugginess and little sleep, a dip in Dancer's Creek sounded quite appealing. Not that he'd had much luck cooling himself at that particular waterway. Kissing Meredith had heated his blood to near boiling, and it hadn't abated a degree since. Her lips had been soft and pliable and tasted of honeysuckle. He couldn't get the sweetness out of his mind. Even now, he hungered for another taste.

On the other side of the field, the jailhouse shimmered in the morning sunlight. Smoke poured from the chimney, and the window glowed with welcoming lamplight. The occupants were awake. Perfect. He had questions that needed answers. His desires would have to be grated and banked.

The door swung open, and a short squat cockroach of a man stepped onto the stoop. A bit early for Finley to be making social calls. Whatever the agent was up to, it wasn't good.

Preston made a beeline for the jailhouse. As he drew closer, Meredith filled the doorway. His pulse bolted as it always did at the sight of her—much to his annoyance. He usually had better control over himself. Around her, he acted like a pimple-faced private fresh off a long patrol.

"Just let me know if you or the children need anything, Miss Talbot." The agent's tone dripped with sugary mash. "I'll be more than happy to acquire it for you."

"Thank you, Mr. Finley. It is kind of you to offer."

The agent looked like a dog's dinner his Irish grandmother would have said, with his bright blue jacket, white waistcoat, royal blue ascot, and gray-striped trousers. A colorful getup for a morning visit. Was the man aiming to court Meredith? Not that he had any say in the matter. He didn't have any hold on her. But her safety was his responsibility, and there was something about the Indian Agent he didn't trust. Any man who would strip the last coin from a drunkard with twelve mouths to feed didn't merit well in his book, even if it was at the poker table.

"Agent Finley." Preston rested a foot on the stoop. "What brings you out for a visit? Shouldn't you be preparing for our excursion?"

The agent looked down his patrician nose like the emperor Caligula dismissing a plebeian. "I made time to come by and check on Mr. Hoggard. After seeing his precarious state yesterday, I was quite concerned about the man."

Right. Finley only cared about anything or anyone that could further his ambitions or line his pockets. A poor handyman was neither of those.

Preston shifted his attention to Meredith. Perspiration dotted the skin at her neckline. Odd how sweat looked like a string of pearls on her. "I assume if you are allowing visitors, Mr. Hoggard is doing better this morning?"

Her dazzling smile rivaled the sun. "He is greatly improved; I'm pleased to say. His head is much clearer."

"Yes, much clearer," Finley shoved in. "Thanks to the wonderful care he is receiving."

Preston stuffed down a gag. Hopefully Meredith could see through the man's snake-oil slickness. "I'd like to speak with him if I may. Get his account of what happened at the orphanage."

"Certainly, Lieutenant." Meredith stepped back from the doorway. "As long as you keep your visit short."

Short he could handle, provided it netted him the information he needed. He tugged off his hat, yet before moving onto the stoop, he speared the agent with a hard glare. "I'll see you back at the stables, Mr. Finley. Noon. No later." If the pompous jackass delayed their mission, there'd be hell to pay. He wasn't going to get his ass chewed out because of Finley's tardiness.

He followed Meredith into the jailhouse. The last time he'd been inside, he hadn't taken much notice of anything except the nymph tempting him with her wet flesh and barely concealed curves. Even now he had trouble putting one foot in front of the other without tripping over the memory.

The main chamber had been transformed into a crude parlor with curtains at the windows and a rug in front of the pot belly stove. The floors and walls gleamed, and a flowery aroma rode the air. It was a nice change from the stench and filth of a few days ago. Amazing what women could do with a little soap and water.

In the far corner of the room, several of the

children sat around a table. Some read from books, others marked on slates. The two boys sat on the floor, playing with a set of small wooden pins. His neck hairs prickled. What the hell? He stalked across the room and snatched up a pin. It matched the one he'd found at the orphanage the day after the fire.

He wagged the pin in the air. "I thought you said you didn't recognize this toy, Miss Talbot."

Her pretty chin lifted. "I didn't at the time. That pin is part of a game called *Nine Pins*. Mr. Brown at the Sutler's store recently purchased a whole crate of them. Since many of the local children have a set, he thought the orphans might enjoy playing with one. So he sent a set over yesterday evening. I even saw a group of soldiers playing with them at the mess hall last night."

Any number of people, including his troopers, could have dropped the pin at the orphanage. Damn. That shot his potential lead all to hell. He'd have to find another clue to the identity of the raiders.

"If you're finished interrupting the boys' game, you can follow me."

Prickly as a porcupine. He couldn't blame her, though. He'd all but accused her of lying. Yet, he couldn't help himself. Dishonesty riled his gut worse than boiled boot leather.

He returned the pin to the boys and trailed her to the archway leading into what used to be the jailing section. Curtains draped the iron-barred doors in an attempt at privacy. Cots and pallets filled each cell. They couldn't be comfortable living in such cramped conditions. Unfortunately, with the orphanage now a pile of ashes, they could only look forward to more discomfort.

"How are the children taking the news of the fire?"

"As well as can be expected. They're worried about what will happen to them once the renegades are caught."

"I'm sure the townsfolk will pull together and help you rebuild."

She didn't comment, merely stopped in front of the last cell on the left. "You have another visitor, Mr. Hoggard. It's Lieutenant Booth. Go on in, Lieutenant."

Preston stepped past her and entered the cell. Hoggard reclined on a cot, his head swathed in a thick, white bandage. His skin was still pasty, but his eyes were clear and focused. Good. The first rule of warfare—identify the enemy. As the only living witness to the attackers, the handyman could very well provide the evidence he needed.

"Are you feeling well enough for some questions, Mr. Hoggard?"

"My head feels like Lucifer stabbed it with his pitchfork, but I'll manage." Hoggard motioned to a chair in the corner. "Please, come in and have a seat."

Meredith brushed past him. "I'll just change that bandage while you talk. That way when you're done, Mr. Hoggard can rest. Is that all right with you, Lieutenant?"

Hardness crusted her sweet tone. After his earlier blunder, he'd best agree else he'd find himself tossed out on his ear. He gave her a brief nod and took up a position at the foot of the cot. He wanted a clear field of vision for this interrogation.

Meredith moved to Hoggard's head and began unwinding the bandage. He imagined those slender fingers touching *him*—combing through *his* hair, sliding over *his* flesh, enticing *him* with their siren song.

"Lieutenant?" Hoggard prodded. "You have some questions?"

Horse crap. Caught gathering wool. He cleared his throat of fluff and forced his focus onto the task at hand. "Now that you're more lucid, I'd like to hear your account of what took place at the orphanage. Tell me everything you can remember about the attackers. Clothing, horses, conversations. Anything."

"My memory is still a bit muddled."

"But you remember some of it. Yesterday, you were adamant the attackers were white. You called them demons."

Hoggard's face wilted. "I'm afraid all the panic and confusion made me a bit rattled. The wallop I took when I fell didn't help matters any."

The man went quiet as Meredith removed the last of the bandaging. She dipped a clean cloth in a basin of water and leaned over to dab the crusted wound. More images roused—of her warm breath fanning his face, her breasts grazing his shoulder. He shifted his weight, seeking a more comfortable position against the stirring in his loins. She was definitely a witch. Nothing he did seemed to break her spell over him.

"You said they were riding branded horses," he continued. "Were you able to see the brands?"

Hoggard dropped his hands to his lap and picked at a fingernail. "I remember it being dark as pitch that night. I had gone to the barn to settle Bessy when I heard riders approaching. Figured with all the attacks lately, there might be trouble. So, I doused the lantern and watched through the cracks in the wall slats. The renegades were riding around like devil hounds, yipping and hollering and setting fire to the orphanage. With all the commotion, I just can't be certain what I saw."

"You call them renegades. Were they Indians then?"

"They were wearing face paint and animal hide clothing, I recall that much." Hoggard licked his lips. "Miss Talbot said you found Creek arrows in the rubble."

Hoggard's memory *was* scrambled. He had mentioned yesterday they found some arrows. "That's right. We discovered a number of arrows with Creek markings at the orphanage."

"Well, there you go."

On the contrary, this interrogation was going nowhere. "Did you get a good look at them? Could you identify anyone?"

"I didn't linger long enough for that. Once I realized there were too many of them to stop on my own, I released Bessy from her stall and with a prayer in my heart, fled into the woods."

Hoggard's account sounded reasonable. Yet something didn't ring solid. He couldn't put his finger on what it was, but it was there. Like an odd smell—not unpleasant, but not agreeable either.

Meredith wrapped a clean bandage around the wound and tucked in the tail end. "There. All done. I think that's enough questions for today, Lieutenant. Mr. Hoggard needs his rest."

He doubted he'd get anything more useful from the befuddled man anyway. "I have all the information I need for now. Good day, Mr. Hoggard. Thank you for your time."

He followed Meredith back through the jailhouse and out onto the porch. Heat engulfed him. It was going to be a long, miserable day. Not that he expected anything less. These days, ill-weather and ill-luck seemed to be hot on his trail.

Dainty frown lines creased her brow. "You urged Mr. Finley not to be late for your excursion. Are the two of you going somewhere?"

"Major Allen ordered me to go with Mr. Finley to the reservation. He wants us to apply pressure on the Indians to provide more information about the renegades. We're leaving at midday."

"Won't that be dangerous? Going into the lion's den, so to speak?"

Was she concerned for his sake or for Agent Finley's? His stomach turned at the thought of her developing feelings for the smarmy agent. "It will be worth the risk if we can uncover the identity of the renegades. From what we can gather, it's just a small group that has splintered off from the tribe. The sooner we catch them, the better."

"I will pray for your success then."

He'd need all the prayers he could get. He stepped off the stoop and turned to look up at her. Sunlight played over her pretty face. He memorized the sight to savor later if things with the Indians did indeed turn ugly.

"I don't know how long I'll be gone. We'll most likely set up camp outside the reservation and return after our meeting. Could be one maybe two days."

Her lips tipped into a gentle smile. "We should be able to manage for a few days without you."

Would she miss him? He would definitely miss that lovely smile. It made the loneliness of living in the backwoods more bearable.

"If you need anything while I'm gone, send for Private Womack. He'll relay your needs to Major Allen, or if Mr. Hoggard needs medical attention, he can send for the doctor."

"Thank you, Lieutenant. Hopefully there will be no need for the doctor. Mr. Hoggard appears to be on the mend."

Speaking of Hoggard… "A bit strange that his account of the attack changed so abruptly from yesterday."

She shrugged. "Head injuries are known to upset the memory."

"I suppose that is true." He tucked on his hat and headed back to his tent. He'd come to get answers, now all he had were more questions.

****

The children walked behind her, orderly and quiet, like dutiful little ducklings. The previous excursions to the fort's dining hall had proceeded uneventfully. With any luck, this one would turn out the same. Every venture outside the jailhouse tempted trouble.

A patrol of troopers rode by, their uniforms and mounts gray with dust. Begrimed faces sagged with weariness. The sight triggered thoughts of Preston. He'd only been gone for a couple of hours, yet she missed him. Missed the tenderness that crept into his eyes when he let his guard down. Missed his strength and confidence in the face of adversity. Missed how his touch warmed her body and her soul. Despite her efforts, she had developed feelings for him—feelings that refused to be corralled. And that frightened her. In her experience, caring for someone usually led to anguish and heartache. She didn't think her heart could take any more pummeling.

Gabriel hefted his nose in the air, sniffing. "Mmm. Something smells scrummy."

"I hope they have boiled carrots like yesterday," Robbie peeped.

The army cook had added sugar to the carrots, making them taste like a sweet dessert. She'd have to remember that trick to encourage the finicky ones to eat their vegetables. A few loved greens and carrots and would even eat them raw. Others would turn up their noses. In her younger years, when her father's favorite mashed turnips were on the menu, she would feign a sour stomach. She couldn't, in all fairness, be critical of the children's pickiness.

She stopped at the bottom of a short stoop leading into a long rectangular building which the soldiers referred to as the *mess hall*. Odd that they called it that. The dining chamber was always neat and spotless. Not a *mess* in sight.

"All right children, get your supper and sit at the same table as yesterday. And remember, mind your manners."

"We will, Miss Talbot," Robbie and Gabe said as they bounded onto the stoop.

The girls trailed behind the boys, faces aglow and eyes sparkling...all except for Lily. The older girl wore a guarded expression. It would be a long while before she trusted people enough to relax around large crowds.

As the last duckling entered the hall, a tall, slender woman approached. She looked to be about Meredith's age, yet carried an old look in her eyes—as if she'd seen more of the world than she cared to. Blonde braids wrapped her head in a pretty arrangement. Her gingham dress, while thin and faded, was clean and pressed.

"Pardon me, this is vhere supper is served, yah?"

The Dutch community in Philadelphia had spoken with a similar accent. Because of their speech and unfamiliar customs, they were shunned by the local citizenry. This unfriendly treatment caused the immigrants to avoid contact with others…something she understood quite well.

Meredith nodded. "This is the dining hall, or *mess hall,* as the soldiers call it."

"Tank you. I am new to the fort. So many buildings and such strange names. Vera confusing."

"Yes, it can be quite the labyrinth." Others might be unkind to the unusual sounding immigrants, but she wouldn't. She gave the woman a welcoming smile. "I'm Meredith Talbot. I oversee the orphans from Seaton House."

"I am Mrs. Valder. Jana Valder. From Pennsylvania. I moved into the Mineral town last month."

Footsteps clicked on the stoop, and a small hand closed around hers. "Are you coming, Miss Talbot?"

"Yes, Anna. I'm coming." She dipped a nod at the woman. "Excuse me, I should go inside. The children are waiting for me. It was a pleasure to meet you, Mrs. Valder."

"Yah. It vas pleasure to meet you."

A riot of sound and people met her inside. Dozens of civilians sat at crudely-made plank tables. Others waited in line to be served. There wasn't enough room for everyone at the fort to dine at the same time, so the commander had ordered all meals to be taken in shifts. The townsfolk ate first and then the soldiers. So far, the arrangement worked very smoothly and efficiently—quite an accomplishment considering the overcrowded conditions.

Meredith joined the queue waiting to be served. The line moved along quickly, and she soon had a steaming bowl of soup in hand. She carried her supper to the table where the children were busy devouring their meal. Only a few slices of bread remained in the baskets dotting the tabletop. Hungry, indeed.

She sat next to Anna, gave a quick prayer of thanks, and dove into her meal. Her taste buds sighed at the delicious fare. Chunks of venison and summer vegetables floated in a tasty broth. What a blessing to have such a competent cook—one less hardship for the soldiers to bear in the remote outpost.

The clink of silverware and muted chatter filled the room. Most of the civilians appeared to be focused on eating—all but one. Jana Valder stood near the soup kettle, looking around the room, her face cratered with uncertainty. Poor woman. There was little space left at any of the tables, and no one seemed inclined to make room for her. What was wrong with these knot-headed people?

Meredith rose and waved her hand, catching the woman's attention. She motioned for Mrs. Valder to join them. A smile blossomed on the woman's face, and she headed for their table.

"Scoot over, Robbie," Meredith said. "Give our guest some room."

The boy did as asked, and Mrs. Valder settled

beside him on the bench. "Tank you, Miss Talbot. I vasn't sure vhere to sit."

"You are always welcome to join us, Mrs. Valder."

"Please, call me Jana."

"Of course. And you must call me Meredith." She resumed her seat and picked up a basket. "Would you like some bread? There are a few pieces left."

"Yah. It looks vera tasty."

Jana plucked a slice for herself and also gave one to the eager-eyed boy beside her. Thoughtful and kind. A woman she could easily call friend.

"You mentioned you were from Pennsylvania," she said as she set the basket back on the table. "I used to live outside of Philadelphia in Montgomery County."

"Vee lived in Allentown...until Mr. Valder decided vee should go vest. To California. To the land of opportunity, says he." Sadness crept into Jana's face and into her voice. "My husband passed to God three months ago. He did not get to see his opportunity."

"I'm sorry for your loss. I know that had to be hard on you. If there is anything I can do, please let me know."

"Tank you. You are vera kind."

Meredith lapsed into silence. As much as she hungered for conversation with another woman her age, she should let the poor soul eat in peace. She didn't have enough fingers and toes to count the number of times she'd ended up with dyspepsia after balancing eating and answering the children's questions.

"Vhere are you staying, Miss Talbot? I haven't been out much since moving into the fort."

Apparently Jana didn't require quiet to eat. Maybe she had a good constitution. Or perhaps she too craved friendly conversation.

Meredith dabbed her mouth with her napkin. "The army quartered us in the jailhouse on the east side. It's set off from the main part of the fort."

"In the jailhouse?"

Meredith chuckled at the woman's astonished tone. "It's not the finest of accommodations, but at least we are all together. It took a lot of hard work, but we made the place livable. You should come by and visit some time."

Mrs. Valder wagged her head, amusement crinkling the corners of her eyes. "I vill certainly have to do that. I vould like to see vhat you have done with this jailhouse."

A shadow fell over the table. "You shouldn't be consorting with the likes of her, Miss Talbot."

The familiar condescending voice set her neck hairs on edge. Meredith swiveled on the bench seat to confront the intruder. "The likes of whom, Mrs. Allen?"

Harriet Allen pointed a bony finger at Jana. "That one. She's the scourge of good people."

Meredith shot to her feet, anger fisting her hands and heating her blood. "Because she talks and dresses differently? What nonsense. The woman just lost her husband. You should show more compassion."

"I have no compassion for a woman who sins."

Sins? What was the harpy rattling on about now? The woman spewed her pious poison like pus oozing from a boil.

Mrs. Allen's cronies gathered behind their general, clucking like agitated peahens. "We have no room here for the likes of you," Alvena Wood huffed. "We want you to leave. Go back to your house of depravity."

Jana rose from the bench, the color fleeing from her face. "I should not haf come."

"No, you should not have darkened this fort or our town with your filth." Mrs. Allen pointed to the door. "Go back to that rock you crawled from under."

Not while she drew breath. No one, no matter who they were or what their circumstances, deserved to be mistreated. Meredith moved to Jana's side and rested a hand on the woman's quivering arm. "Don't you go anywhere, Jana."

Mrs. Allen bristled. "Are you condoning what this woman does? At least the floozies in the saloon halls know better than to flaunt their wares around the good people of Mineral."

Jana was a prostitute then. Not that it mattered. "How can you be so narrow-minded? With no husband to support her, Mrs. Valder is doing what she has to in order to survive. Surely you *good* people can understand that."

"What we understand is she's rubbish. You will regret aligning with her. Most assuredly."

Mrs. Allen punctuated her words with a poke to Meredith's shoulder. Meredith stumbled back and nearly fell into the diners seated behind them. As she righted herself, Nel rose from the bench, hands fisted at her sides.

"Dorothea is disappointed in you, Mrs. Allen," the girl scolded. "She says you should remember Reverend Bosch's teachings and how you felt when the other children excluded you from their games because of your stuttering."

Harriet Allen's mouth yawed like a catfish tossed out of the water. Beady eyes narrowed, and Mrs. Allen leaned toward Nel, her brow knitted into a formidable line. "How do you know such things, young lady? My mother is deceased, and I have never spoken of my stammering, which I might add, I outgrew."

Nel shrank back, color draining from her face as she realized her mistake in revealing conversations heard from beyond the grave.

Meredith moved to shield Nel from Mrs. Allen's vicious talons. "She must have overheard you talking at some point. You do like to go on about yourself."

"Humph. She's a witch, I say. A devil-consorting witch who should be burned at the stake."

"Yes, burned," Alvena and Edeline repeated.

The oil lantern sitting on the table began to shake, the glass globe rattling. The flame sputtered and sparked. Black smoke began pouring from chimney. A second later, the lantern tipped over and fell to the floor amid a shatter of glass.

People shouted and leapt to their feet. One man threw his coat over the spreading puddle of flaming oil. The three peahens backed away, screeching about fires and witches.

Fear glazed Meredith's insides. Her worst nightmare had come to pass. She plucked Anna from the bench and urged the other children to follow her.

As they rushed for the door, Harriet Allen called after them, "Go, you heathen witches. Leave this fort, or we'll run you out."

Chapter Eight

Burning logs sizzled and popped. Smoke tails billowed upward and caught on the wind. The flaming fire pit called to mind the torched orphanage and Meredith tucked in his arms. His body had clamored for more than a comforting cuddle. During the ride to the reservation, he'd come to one undeniable conclusion. He couldn't fight his attraction any longer. He wanted her. And not just for one night. He wanted her every night—in his bed and in his life.

Once he returned to the fort, he would start the courting process. It was the logical thing to do. He would eventually need a wife, and she was a good fit. When she talked of the children, of keeping them safe, he thought of his troopers. It was a connection that would only grow and strengthen. She might refuse his suit. But if the way those sparkling eyes lit up and her pretty mouth parted when she saw him was any indication, he needn't worry about a refusal. Those sweet lips would soon be his for the tasting any time he pleased.

A noise kicked into his daydreaming. On the other side of the rock-rimmed pit, dark-skinned faces watched him with wariness. He gave himself a mental thump. Best quit his woolgathering and focus on the task at hand before he needed an undertaker instead of a minister.

He set his face into a steady, non-provoking response. He wasn't going to give the Creeks any reason to get riled. He would smoke their peace pipe and garner their respect and with any luck, their cooperation. Though many of his fellow officers would have resorted to swords and bullets to get results, he preferred to loosen lips with honey—in the form of the finest tobacco the Sutler's store had to offer.

Bathed in late afternoon sunshine, the pipe holder stood in front of the gathering, holding the bowl in his left hand and the stem in his right. He pointed the pipe to the east and chanted in his native tongue. He then sprinkled some tobacco onto the ground and loaded a pinch into the bowl. The Indian did this at each of the compass directions, filling the pipe and chanting.

Once again facing east, he touched the stem to the ground and then lifted the pipe above his head, angled toward the sun. After a few minutes, he lowered the pipe and lit the bowl. The pipe was passed around to each of the gathered guests. Some whispered a blessing before smoking, others remained silent. Some did not smoke at all, just held the pipe before passing it on.

Preston accepted the pipe from the Indian seated next to him. A bluestone bowl sat at the end of a long hollow reed. It reminded him of the carved wooden pipe the army had given his father when he retired from service. From that day on, the man lived with that pipe, either clenched between his teeth or clamped in his hand, emphasizing his gestures. Maybe one day he would be presented with such a fine retirement gift. He first had to come out of this parlay with his scalp intact.

He drew in a mouthful of smoke and puffed it out. Smooth and woodsy with just a little burn to the tongue and throat. Well worth the expense.

He did this three times as the others had done and handed the pipe to Agent Finley seated next to him. Once the pipe had completed its journey, the pipe holder smoked the last of the tobacco, cleaned out the ashes, and tossed them onto the ground. He then separated the stem from the pipe and placed both in a pouch. The ceremony was over. Now the tournament could begin.

His head adorned with a large bonnet of eagle feathers, Chief Red Wing sat cross-legged in the forefront of the gathered warriors. The leader of the Red Ground tribe of Creek Indians wore a blue-and-white striped jacket belted at the waist and animal hide leggings—quite the eclectic mix. Yet it was his eyes that caught and held one's attention. They were black as pitch and piercing, like the bird of prey he was named for. He would make a most intimidating opponent. Luckily, they sat across from one another in peace.

Red Wing lifted a hand. "The sacred pipe has been smoked. Let us speak with truthful words, truthful hearts, and a truthful spirit."

The truth. Good. That's what he was after. It certainly helped that the chief had a fair grasp of English. Many words got lost in translation. "Thank you for agreeing to speak with us, Chief Red Wing. We appreciate your cooperation in this urgent matter."

The chieftain nodded. "We help any way we can."

"As you have no doubt heard, there is a rogue faction of Creek warriors attacking and killing homesteaders."

Lines cratered the chief's leathery face. "How you know Creek warriors have done this?"

"We know because arrows with your tribe's markings were discovered scattered in and around the destroyed homesteads."

"Anyone could make such arrows and use them to accuse us."

An astute observation, one he'd considered until Hoggard had corroborated the evidence. "What you say is true. However, there was a survivor who reported he saw Creek warriors attacking his homestead. We have no reason to distrust this man. We need to know who these renegades are and where they are hiding."

"As I said to Agent Finley, we know nothing about these attackers. They are not of our people."

Finley snorted. "There. I told you this would be a waste of time."

Preston shot a glare at the agent. "And I told you to hold your tongue and let me handle this discussion."

The agent ignored his warning and continued spouting. "I've been trying to negotiate with this stubborn mule for months on behalf of the Southern Railroad. He won't budge. Says he won't surrender what little land was given to them as part of the treaty agreement."

"That's his prerogative, Finley."

"Bunkum. I've tried to explain the benefits, but he refuses to even consider it. Many of his warriors have been openly hostile toward me. I wouldn't be surprised if they are indeed the renegades and Red Wing is at the helm."

The crowd behind the chief stirred, their voices rising like bees in a disturbed hive. Preston's gut tightened. He had to calm the waters, fast. Before things escalated and someone did something that couldn't be undone.

He caught and held Red Wing's gaze. "The army is not accusing you or any of your peaceable tribe members of anything. We just want to put an end to the violence."

The chieftain barked in his native tongue, and the group quieted. Red Wing nodded. "We also want to stop these attacks. They bring much disharmony between our people."

"Whitewash," Finley muttered. "We should just move them onto the more secure reservation with the Choctaw and be done with them. That will put a stop to all this nonsense."

The crowd erupted, some jumping to their feet and jabbing fists in the air, others waving their weapons. To put the Creek and their long-time rivals together would be like tossing gunpowder onto a fire. Instant explosion. Preston cursed inwardly. Finley's flap-happy tongue was going to get them killed. He needed to diffuse the situation. But how? Meredith had calmed her agitated flock with sweet words and a calm demeanor. He couldn't manage sweet, but he could do calm.

He pushed to his feet, hands raised. "If you'll just settle down for one moment," he said in a loud but composed tone.

Wary eyes lit on him. He held their gazes, hoping they would respect his boldness, if nothing else. "I understand your anger. But believe me; we have no intention of moving any of you to another reservation. All we want is to find the men responsible for the attacks. Please, let us honor the peace promised with the smoking of the pipe."

The din slowly subsided. Those standing settled

back to the ground. Preston let go the breath he'd seized and lowered his hands. One issue dealt with…now for the other.

He leaned over Agent Finley and adopted a forceful tone that usually had his troopers quaking in their boots. "If you open your mouth one more time during this discourse, Finley, I will stuff it with one those burning logs. Two if need be."

Finley's eyes went wide as wagon wheels. His mouth sagged as if he wanted to respond, but he snapped his lips shut with a click of teeth. Smart man—for once.

Preston sank back the ground and returned his focus to Chief Red Wing. An appreciative glint lit the Indian's eyes. He hadn't put Finley in his place to garner approval, but if it encouraged the chieftain to cooperate, all the better.

"As I said, Chief Red Wing, we have no intention of moving your tribe. All we ask is a little cooperation. You are a wise and perceptive leader. Have you heard or seen anything that might help us locate these renegades? They have been uncommonly elusive."

Eagle feathers swayed. "I have heard nothing. My son took a scouting party to look for these *chitto*. We wait for his return."

"That was a risky thing to do. Your son and his men could be mistaken for the renegades." The Creek were not allowed to leave the reservation without Major Allen's permission. Could Finley's allegations have merit? His gut said no. Something in the chieftain's eyes and tone of voice resonated with honesty. If anyone was going to be deceitful, his bet would be on Finley.

"Black Hawk will use caution. I will send word to you when he has returned."

"Thank you, Chief Red Wing. I will let my commander know of your assistance. He will be very grateful for any information you can provide us."

Red Wing crossed arms over his chest. "Ask this commander about our provisions and cattle. None have been sent since last winter. These things were promised by the paper I marked with your man from Washington."

What the hell? Preston turned to Finley. As their assigned agent, the Indians were his responsibility. "Why haven't the allotments been sent to them?"

Finley puffed up like a perturbed hedgehog. "I appropriated for the provisions as required by the treaty. You'll have to ask the senators in Washington why they are not getting sent."

"That's your job, Finley. Not mine."

"I cannot be held responsible for greedy government contractors who only want to line their pockets."

Preston itched to knock the teeth out of Finley's belligerent attitude. The Red Ground tribe may not be part of the current attacks, but if the agent continued on his current path of negligence and intolerance, that peacefulness could turn deadly.

"Make no mistake, Agent Finley…you *will* be held responsible. As soon as we return to Fort Dent, you will follow up on those allotments, even if it means making a trip to Washington." He punched steel to his tone. "Or you'll answer to me."

The skin around Finley's jaw twitched as if considering his options. Preston grunted inwardly. Not much to consider. The man either complied, or he'd be eating gruel for the rest of his life.

The agent gave a resigned grunt and shifted his attention to the other side of the fire pit. He lifted a hand, palm outward. "You have my word, Chief Red Wing. I will look into the delay of your provisions."

Finley's *word* was worth about as much as a bucket of tobacco spit. But a boot to the backside would ensure the man followed through on his promise. Preston met the chieftain's gaze. "I know words will not fill your people's bellies, but I assure you this oversight will be rectified. Soon."

Red Wing nodded and rose in a smooth, effortless movement. The meeting was over. There would be no more discussion. Pledges had been made. It was up to each of them to honor those vows or suffer the consequences.

****

Firefly sparks flashed in the encroaching darkness. Clicks and whirrs rode the air. The insects were tuning up for their evening performance. Normally she would stop and listen, absorb the tranquility. Not tonight. Tonight she had a mission, and nothing could distract her, not even her own misgivings.

A tall shadow basted the softly-lit canvas wall. Meredith tightened her grip on the soup bowl. After hours of continuously checking through the jailhouse window, she'd seen Preston arrive at his tent. While she cheered his safe return, seeing him, being near him, turned her into someone she didn't recognize. She couldn't think around him, could hardly draw breath. All she wanted was more of what his heated gaze promised. Her reactions were senseless and quite unnerving. There could be nothing between them. He was a man of strictness and practicality. He would never accept her for who she was and what she could do.

Yet she had to meet with him. He needed to hear about the incident at the mess hall from her...not from spiteful gossipmongers who might twist the truth into something ugly and heinous.

She stopped outside the tent and gathered herself with a deep breath. She would tell him about the latest developments and leave. Friendly and business-like, nothing more.

"Lieutenant Booth? Do you have a moment?"

Shuffling sounded from inside, and then the tent flap swept open. Preston ducked through the opening, wearing a partially buttoned white shirt tucked into clean trousers. Suspenders dangled at his sides. He must have just finished bathing. His hair was still damp from a recent washing. One lock dangled rakishly over his forehead. She wanted to smooth it back. She lifted the bowl instead.

"I saw you had returned, so I brought you some supper. It's well past mealtime. I thought you might be hungry."

His fingers grazed hers as he took the bowl. Quivers danced up her arms, and she braced herself against the onslaught. *Friendly and business-like. Friendly and business-like.* The mantra did little to quell the rebellion building inside her.

"You shouldn't have troubled yourself with bringing me anything." He lifted the bowl to his nose. "Smells wonderful, though."

"It was no trouble at all, and the stew *is* wonderful.

Mrs. Clement made it from a rabbit Gabe and Private Womack trapped in the woods outside the fort."

His brow mashed into a frown. "Did the mess hall run out of fare? Or is army food so bad that you resorted to cooking your own?"

"Neither. There's another reason we are cooking for ourselves. It's why I sought you out."

The only movement breaking the gloom came from the darting bats seeking their dinner. She and Preston were alone. But that may not last for long. Not if the past few days were any indication.

She inclined her head to the tent. What she needed to tell him required privacy. "May I come inside for a moment?"

Hesitation jack-rabbited across his face. He glanced from her to the jailhouse and back. He clearly wanted no part of being alone with her. Somehow that only added to her unease.

"Please. It's important."

His balking expression surrendered, and he stepped back from the opening. "As you wish."

Heart thumping, she stooped and entered the tent. A narrow cot covered with a wool blanket sat against the far wall. Precisely folded uniforms filled an open trunk at the foot. A chair rested next to small table that held a book and a softly-glowing oil lamp. The living space was neat and orderly—unlike hers. She moved through life like a whirlwind. She and Preston were as different as night and day. She would do well to remember that.

He moved into the tent and motioned to the ladder-back chair. "Please have a seat."

She settled on the chair and fussed with her skirts,

unable to meet his gaze. Her nerves were in tatters. One tender look from him would be her unraveling.

"How was your expedition with Agent Finley?" She fluffed out a rather unruly crinkle. "Productive, I hope."

"Not as productive as I'd hoped, but we may know more in a few days."

"That's good."

The soup bowl thumping on the table startled her. She looked up and into a scowling stare. Her gown became suddenly too tight, too hot. She wriggled beneath his glare.

"What's wrong, Meredith? You're squirming worse than a worm on hot sand."

Meredith. She would never tire of hearing her name cross his lips. "I'm afraid there was some trouble while you were gone."

"What kind of trouble?"

The worst sort. "Some of the townsfolk are not happy with me or the children. They want us to leave the fort."

"Why would they want you to leave? What happened?"

She wished he would sit down. His hovering set her pulse to galloping, and she wasn't ready or equipped for a ride.

She pushed back against the chair and concentrated on not squirming like a worm. "There was a disagreement a few days ago at the supper meal. The local ladies were unhappy with my decision to associate with someone they felt was beneath me. You many know of her. She's a German immigrant. Mrs. Valder. Jana Valder. She moved into town last month. Her husband passed away during their trip west, so she had to resort to…um, coarse means in order to survive."

"Yes, I am aware of who Mrs. Valder is and what she does."

His mouth tightened, and he scrubbed a hand through his hair. Had he visited with the widow? The thought of him being with another woman sent an arrow zinging into her chest.

She clasped her hands into a tight ball in her lap, holding onto a courage that was fading fast. "There was little eating space available in the mess hall, so I invited Mrs. Valder to join our table. Mrs. Allen and her lady friends were very vocal in their disapproval. Very vocal. I stood up against them and their vicious attack."

"Was that wise? You had to know doing so would only provoke them."

"I wasn't going to let them assail Mrs. Valder. No one deserves to be ill-treated, no matter what they do for a living." If he didn't understand or approve of that, how would he ever accept an outlier like her? Her decision to keep him at arm's length was the right one.

"While your intentions were honorable, they won't endear you to the good ladies of Mineral. Is this the trouble you wanted to tell me about?"

"That's part of it." Best to tread softly. Preston Booth had a knack for reading between the lines, even if they were blurred. "During the dispute, one of the children cited some personal details about the commander's wife, details Mrs. Allen claimed no one else knew about."

"How did the child know these things?"

Homing in on the key aspects—just as he always did. She wouldn't want to be his adversary on a battlefield. "Nel must have overheard Mrs. Allen mention them at some point. The major's wife is quite garrulous and enjoys speaking about herself to anyone and everyone."

She hated lying to him, but she didn't have a choice. As much as she wanted to divulge the truth of Nel's knowledge, she had no idea how he would react to the notion of speaking with the dead.

"During the disagreement," she continued, "someone jostled the table. The lantern tipped over and smashed to the floor. That misfortune, combined with Nel's remarks, had Mrs. Allen and her lady friends screaming of witchcraft and ordering us to leave the fort."

His disparaging snort ripped the air. "Witchcraft? What nonsense. Officers' wives are expected to behave with decorum and discretion. They are supposed to be role models. While I respect Major Allen, he allows his wife too much freedom. She needs to be taken in hand. No wife of mine would bring such taint to me or my career."

A warning well received. "I'm afraid the confrontation didn't stop at accusations. Since that night, we have had numerous threats. Rocks thrown at the windows. Intimidating notes tacked to the door. Someone even left a dead rat on the stoop."

"Did you inform Private Womack of these incidents?"

She shook her head. "Not at first. I thought if we ignored them, the bullies would grow weary and cease their activities."

"But they haven't."

"They've gotten worse. This morning, a group of

children attacked Robbie and Gabe at the community well. The boys suffered cuts and bruises. It would have been much worse if a stray dog hadn't jumped in to protect them." He didn't need to know that Robbie had summoned the dog for help.

"I hope you went to Private Womack after that."

"I did. He escorted me to the fort headquarters, so I could inform Major Allen of the deeds. But the major was in ill health and couldn't meet with me. When I saw you had returned, I figured I had best come and relay what had transpired before you heard about it from someone else."

His fierce expression lightened. "I'm glad you did. Rest assured; I will speak with Major Allen about this tomorrow when I deliver my report. I'm sure he will put a stop to all the nonsense."

A weight lifted from her shoulders. Preston would see the matter righted. He was a man of honor and principle. It was one of things she admired most about him. It was also the thing that kept them apart.

She rose from the chair. "Thank you. The hostility is frightening the children. They can barely sleep."

He moved closer, his fresh, soapy scent washing over her like an incoming wave. "What about you? Are you sleeping?"

She wasn't. Not just because of the spiteful harassment. But because of him. Because of her longing to have what she denied herself—the love of a decent, caring man.

His hand drifted up and cradled her cheek. Warmth from his touch trickled down her neck and spread like an umbrella under her ribs. Breathing became a struggle—speaking near impossible. It took every ounce of control to keep her knees from buckling.

"I missed you, Meredith. Missed your sunny smile. The way your eyes dance when you're agitated. The way they go soft when you're kissed."

"Preston. I'm not…that is, we shouldn't…"

"Say it again."

"S-say what?"

"My name. It's the first I've heard it cross your lips. I like the sound. You should say it more often."

She swallowed her last bit of moisture. He sounded so tender, so loving. Yet that tenderness would surely turn to disgust once he learned the truth about her. He had already declared an officer's wife should behave with decorum and discretion. He would most definitely consider her affliction a taint to his reputation.

Gray-brown eyes drank in her face. His lips parted and with a ravenous growl, he lowered his head. His kiss was gentle at first, and then more demanding when she didn't resist. She couldn't resist. Her bones had turned to mush.

He trapped the back of her head with his palm and proceeded to devour her with little nibbles and flicks of his tongue. He teased her lips apart and slipped inside. A groan erupted in her throat. This was the toe-curling, mind-numbing kiss her maid had gone on about. Her head spun, and all thoughts evaporated like raindrops on parched earth.

Deft fingers worked at the buttons on her blouse. Before she knew it, cool air bathed her exposed skin. Her nipples grew taut with want. Preston obliged. He slid a hand under her blouse and fingered a needy peak. Heat swept through her and pooled between her legs. She moaned again and arched against him.

His mouth left hers and travelled down her neck. His warm breath whispered over her flesh, leaving a fiery trail in its wake.

"You want me." He pulled her against him. "As I want you. I've fought my hunger for as long as I can. But it's a battle I cannot win."

His male hardness pressed into her belly, and cold reality flooded her brain. Being with him this way was wrong. So very wrong. And dangerous.

She pulled away. "Preston…w-we can't."

"Why can't we?" He planted kisses along the hollow at the base of her neck. "We're two consenting, unattached adults."

Tingles budded around his touch. "It's not proper. W-we hardly know each other."

"We get on well enough. Besides, I know all I need to know about you. You're smart and loyal and captivatingly spirited. We could have a wonderful future together."

He said nothing of his feelings for her—nothing of love. A bucket of cold water couldn't have cooled her faster. She pushed out of his arms and backed away, fastening buttons as she moved. "I c-can't do this."

"Meredith—"

"Goodnight, Lieutenant Booth." She batted aside the canvas and fled into the night, chased by the strident bugle notes of *Taps*.

Chapter Nine

Meredith plucked a carrot from the basket and sliced it into strips. Cooking them wouldn't take long. The vegetables were already limp from the incredible heat. So was she. She swiped perspiration from her forehead with her apron. Preston must be suffering, too. Those wool uniforms trapped warmth like a lid on a pot. Though in all reality, she had probably inflicted a lot more discomfort than the heat.

As much as she hated causing him pain, she couldn't allow herself to be drawn into such a dangerous whirlpool. Getting involved with him, getting close to him, made the likelihood of her secret being uncovered ever greater. Even if she did tell him, he would cast her off just as her family had. Her battered heart couldn't bear his rejection.

She chopped with more force than needed. The knife tip grazed her finger. Red bubbled up from the gash. She gasped and lifted the stinging finger to her mouth. Of all the dumb things. She shouldn't let herself be distracted by her own troubles. She needed to focus on the children and what they were going to do once the renegades were captured.

She retrieved a strip of bandaging from the medical basket and wrapped it around her finger. The bleeding stemmed, she returned to her task and to more productive thoughts. Preston had suggested approaching the townsfolk for assistance with finding a place to stay until the orphanage could be re-built. She'd have better luck trying to convince the sun not to rise. After the mess hall debacle, they were more likely to be chased out of town with nothing but the clothes on their backs.

Everything is going to be all right, Miss Talbot.

The child's voice echoed inside her head. Meredith spun on her heels. All the children sat quietly on the other side of the room, working on afternoon lessons. None were paying her any mind. Several were just about to nod off, heads bowed and eyelids drooping. Even the ever-studious Maddie was using her lesson book as a pillow.

"Which one of you said that?"

Sluggish gazes rounded on her. Robbie stretched his arms out and yawned. Maddie lifted her head, blinking sleep from eyes.

"Said what, Miss Talbot?" Lily asked.

"I heard someone whispering to me in my head. Which one of you did that?" None of them, to her knowledge, had mastered such a feat.

Gabe plopped his slate on the table with a grunt. "Wasn't me. But I wished it was. I woulda told you it's too dang hot in here for lessons."

Robbie nodded. "Can we go outside and play? Please, Miss Talbot? We ain't been outside in three days."

"We haven't. And I'm sorry, but we can't go outside. Remember what happened when you and Gabe went to the well? We want the townsfolk to forget we are here. Then maybe they'll leave us alone."

Hopeful faces plummeted. Her heart fell with them.

She didn't want to be so merciless, but she had to—for their safety.

The front door squealed open, and she turned to see who had arrived. The doorway was empty. So was the yard beyond it. Nothing stirred, not even the curtains at the window. A breeze hadn't blown open the door…

Meredith leveled a glare at the culprit. "Gabe, close that door."

His brow puckered. "Aw, Miss Talbot. If we can't go outside, can't we at least let a little air in here? It's so hot, I can hardly breathe."

"We can't give those mean-hearted people such easy access to us. Not until Major Allen puts a stop to all the harassment. Now, close the door." When it didn't budge, she put more steam into her tone. "Gabriel Hunt."

"Fine." The door slammed shut, making the window curtains billow inward. She couldn't blame him for the display. She was just as frustrated by the situation, but she couldn't let anger drive her to be reckless. It would only make matters worse.

"All right, now back to your studies."

Groans met her decree. Someone grumbled about turning into a roasted hunk of meat. Another claimed to be a puddle of melted butter.

Lily closed her history book. "I agree with the others. It's too hot to concentrate. I keep reading the same passage over and over, and I still don't know what it said. Perhaps we could practice our *other* lessons for a while. Clear our heads."

Eager eyes plowed into her, pleading for her agreement. It was hard to say no to such sweet-faced cherubs. She scooped the carrots into a pan of sugared water and set it on the stove to boil. "Very well. But restrict your practicing to small tasks and most importantly keep your voices down. We don't want anyone coming to investigate strange noises."

Yips and the scraping of chair legs greeted her announcement. Meredith walked to the window and tugged the makeshift curtain closed. Even though it cut off any chance of a stray breeze, she couldn't risk prying eyes observing the abnormal activities.

She crossed to where Robbie and Becky sat on the floor. The pair had coaxed a chipmunk through a hole in the mud chinking and were busy conversing with the inquisitive creature. On the other side of the twins, Gabe had his jacks spread out in front of him. One at a time, the metal spikes rose, floated for a second, and then clattered back to the floor.

"Try making a pattern suspended in the air," she urged.

"Like what?"

"Form them into the outline of a star."

Half a dozen jacks lifted, began to spread, and then clanked to the floor. Gabe's expression curdled. "I can't do it. Not all at one time."

"Yes, you can. Concentrate. See the pattern in your head. Move each jack until they line up as you want them." Mildred had used the same positive encouragement when teaching her to control her gift. She could only hope it worked better on Gabe.

The jacks rose again. This time, the cluster unfurled slowly, and the outline of a star began to form. All of the jacks remained airborne until they molded into a perfect pattern.

Gabe's frown blossomed into a satisfied grin. "I

did it. I made a star."

She gave a soft grunt. Maybe she was better at mentoring than she thought. "So you did. Keep practicing. Try more difficult patterns."

Sitting beside him on the floor, Sally tapped his arm and pointed to the flower design on her dress.

"You want me to make a flower?" Gabe asked.

Sally nodded. Gabe's sister hadn't yet shown any signs of a *talent*. She didn't even speak. The doctors couldn't find anything physically wrong with her. They attributed her muteness to the tragedy of losing her parents at a young age and insisted she would talk when ready. Meredith's heart went out to the girl. She supposed something that heartbreaking would cause any child to crawl into a cave of silence.

As Gabe worked on creating a flower pattern, Meredith moved to the table where Lily and Maddie sat huddled over a dealing of tarot cards.

"What is it, Lily?" Maddie asked. "What do you see for my future?"

Ten-year-old Madalene Fontaine and her devoted nanny had fled New Orleans when her guardians attempted to use her special skills for nefarious purposes. They found refuge with a tribe of Choctaw Indians and lived there until the aging nanny succumbed to an illness. Not long after, Mildred had discovered the girl and convinced her to come to Seaton House. No doubt the girl's future would hold just as much drama and intrigue.

Lily tapped the first card. "This is the Chariot. It tells me that you will be the commander of your destiny. That no matter what the odds you will be successful."

"I like that card. Tell me more."

"It also warns that your determination to succeed may lead to a desire to win at all costs. Winning isn't everything, Maddie. It's the start of things."

"Pooh. What does that other card say? Will I find a nice, handsome husband? Preferably one that doesn't drink or swear or use his fists." Maddie's mouth pinched into a frown. "Uncle Abelard was like that. He was meaner than a copperhead."

Lily moved to the next card. "This is Justice. The man in your life will need to find balance before you can discover each other. He has lived too long in one world. To balance the scales, he will need to be level-headed and not be tricked by emotions or passion."

"Humph, I'll just mix up a potion. Then he'll fall in love with me, and we can marry."

Meredith sank onto a chair. "Is that what you want, Maddie? For a man to love you because a potion made him? Don't you want him to love you for yourself? For who you are?"

Maddie cocked her head and studied her with keen eyes. "Is that why you won't set your cap for Lieutenant Booth? Are you afraid he won't love you for who you are?"

Leave it to Maddie to call a spade a spade. "We're not talking about me right now."

"But we should." Maddie scooped up the cards and handed them to Lily. "Let's do a reading for Miss Talbot."

"Not today, girls. Maybe another time." Why be reminded of a future that held no chance at happiness with a man, and most certainly not with Lieutenant Booth?

Lily shuffled the cards. "Give it a try, Miss Talbot. Maybe the cards will help you see things differently."

And maybe they wouldn't. "I appreciate the offer, but I believe I will decline."

Undeterred, Lily shoved the cards toward her. "What's the harm? You can take the message to heart or not. Just cut the deck with your left hand, and I'll do the rest."

"Why my left hand?"

"Because it's closer to your heart and will show what's inside it."

The only thing the cards would show of her heart was a raw, weeping wound. Two expectant faces peered up at her. Very well. She would play along. As Lily said, what could it harm?

She cut the deck, and Lily placed the bottom half on top and peeled off a card. The girl's forehead bunched. "The High Priestess. She shines a light on what you might not otherwise see. But you will need some time alone, some quiet time to reflect on your feelings."

Meredith nodded. "Good advice."

"It also shows that secret paths and hidden dangers will be revealed, either passed on by someone else or coming by way of visions."

Great. Just what she needed more visions. She'd be sure to stay away from any deep-rooted trees.

"Now for the lieutenant's card." Lily turned over a second card. A smile blossomed on her face. "Lovers. He is powerfully drawn to someone or something. But he has a choice to make."

Of course he did…her or his career. Misery toppled her stack of cards. There was no doubt in her mind which he would choose.

****

"My door is open if your mind is changed, Meredith."

All her mind seemed to do lately was change. From wanting Preston, to knowing she shouldn't. He had mentioned having a future together. Part of her wanted the normalcy of a husband and a family. The sane part of her shouted her life would never be normal.

"Thank you for the offer, Jana. But I think we will just stay at the jailhouse for now. The harassment seems to have died down. We should be safe."

"I'm glad to hear it. I vas vorried I might have caused more problems than you needed."

"We will be fine."

"Vera well. Good day to you, and tank you again for all your kindness." Jana waved to the children playing on the back stoop and headed for the roadway.

A cloud rolled across the sun, plunging Jana into gloom. Meredith's arms prickled with gooseflesh. She prayed it wasn't an ill omen. Jana had decided to move back into her home, confident the Indians would prove less dangerous than the unfriendly townsfolk. She had even offered to let Meredith and the children stay with her. It was a kind offer, one that required thoughtful consideration. Poking a hornet's nest would be most unwise *and* unhealthy.

Meredith stopped beneath the thin rope stretching from the jailhouse to a tall pole planted in the ground. During the free time from his duties, Private Greene had erected a makeshift clothes line for them. They were lucky to have such a kind and generous man as a friend. Too bad there weren't more like him. It would make life at the fort so much more tolerable.

She plopped the basket of laundry onto the ground, sending long-legged grasshoppers scattering in all directions. The insects seemed to have multiplied overnight. Yesterday, only a handful had plagued her chores. Today, there were dozens more. She would have to remember to shake out the clothes before bringing them inside, else they risked having unwanted guests.

As the sun broke free of the clouds, she plucked a shirt from the basket and pinned it to the line. Next came a pair of pants, one knee sporting a silver dollar-sized hole. The boys went through clothes like mice through burlap. She envisioned a young Preston being just as rough on clothing—running through the woods, climbing trees, and crawling over rocks while chasing imaginary foes. Little would stop the hard-charging youngster who had become a harder-charging man.

Brisk bugle notes blasted the air. She stilled and listened. *Morning Assembly*. Private Greene had taught her what the various bugle sounds meant. This one called the soldiers to formation for their morning drills. There was also *Mess Call*, which even the children recognized and without being told, lined up for the trek to the dining hall. *Tattoo* was the last call of the day. Private Greene had told her that before the influx of civilians, the entire command would parade around the central field in the evening for an inspection of equipment and discipline. Major Allen had curtailed that practice due to the overcrowding. That was unfortunate. The children would have enjoyed such a grand spectacle.

She bent and retrieved another pair of pants.

Preston had probably learned all the various bugle calls at an early age, considering his father had been in the military. A classmate from her primary school had complained about never being able to stay in one place for long because of her father's frequent reassignments. Perhaps that was why Preston only gave a vague reference to a possible future for them. He was incapable of putting down roots.

A shadow darkened the ground, and the man plaguing her thoughts materialized. Her pulse set to hammering, just as it always did around him.

"Was that Mrs. Valder who just left?" he asked.

"It was." She draped the pants over the rope. "Why do you ask?"

"I have some news, and part of it involves her."

"Oh? What is that?"

"Not yet. First…" Preston captured her hand and caressed the tops of her fingers with his thumb. "You left last night before we could finish our…conversation."

She wanted to pull away, should pull away. Letting him hold her in such an intimate fashion would only encourage him to think she had reconsidered. But his tender touch held her mesmerized.

She averted her gaze. One look from those smoldering eyes and she would buckle. "There's nothing more to discuss."

"I disagree. You ran out of my tent as if being chased by the hounds of hell. What are you afraid of, Meredith? You know I would never hurt you."

Of course he wouldn't. Not intentionally. What hurt was the ache to be with him, yet knowing that would never be possible. She tugged out of his grasp and busied herself with hanging the laundry. She didn't want him to see the pain that had to be clearly visible on her face. Her eyes burned with it.

"I realize I carried things too far last night." His tone rang with sincerity and regret. "I apologize for that. It was ungentlemanly of me. I promise to restrain myself in the future. I'd like to court you if you'll allow it. So we can get to know one another properly."

He wanted to court her, to build a relationship—one that could possibly end with a proposal of marriage. Her insides twisted. Instead of the laundry, she jabbed her finger with the clothes pin. She jerked away with a yelp.

"What have you done?" He moved to her side and reached for her hand. "Let me see."

She avoided him with a retreating step and rubbed her smarting finger. "There's no need. It's fine. I'm just a little clumsy this morning. I didn't sleep well."

"Because of me? Again, I apologize for upsetting you. It wasn't my intention. I want to make things right between us…" His lips puckered. "Although I don't know how much time we'll have together before I have to leave."

Her heart shriveled. "Leave? Where are you going?"

"A few months ago, I requested a transfer to another post. That reassignment could be granted any day now. So what do you say? Will you let me call on you in the short time we have left?"

Everything inside her screamed yes, but her answer had to be no. Her gift would be a huge obstacle, not only to his career, but for her as well. He would want children, and she couldn't take the chance of passing the family curse to a daughter. It would be a chasm neither of them could span.

He stood there, waiting for her answer, his expression expectant like a child eyeing a festively wrapped gift sitting under a Christmas tree. The last thing she wanted was to crush his spirit. She would just have to let him down with softly couched words.

"I don't think that is a good idea, Preston. There are just too many uncertainties right now with the burning of the orphanage and worry over the renegades."

He shook his head. "You may not have to worry about the renegades any longer. A patrol arrived earlier this morning. They captured a band of Indians believed to be responsible for the recent raids."

"The renegades have been captured? Why, that's wonderful news."

"Wonderful only if they are proven to be the culprits." Skepticism spiked his tone.

"What makes you doubt they are the ones?"

"They were apprehended without a fight a few miles from the burning Bowen homestead last night. Why would they give up so easily if they were guilty?"

"Perhaps they realized fighting would be futile."

His shoulders went up in a shrug. "Perhaps. But Chief Red Wing assured me this scouting party was only searching for the real renegades."

"People are known to twist the truth when it suits their needs." Disgust churned inside her. She was no better. She'd been doing the exact same thing with her secrets.

She snatched up a piece of laundry to hang on the line. It was a pair of her bloomers—the frilly ones

Preston had inadvertently seen her wearing days ago when he burst into the jailhouse. Heat climbed in her neck and burned in her ears at the reminder of that encounter. She dropped bloomers back into the basket as if they were on fire.

"Um…so how does Jana figure in all this?"

"I'm getting to that. First, with the capture of the renegades, we'll need the jailhouse back. You and children will have to move out."

With all the recent turmoil, she hadn't had a chance to search for another place to stay. Her shoulders sagged under the weight of her burden. "This is all so sudden. Where will we go?"

"No need to worry. I've spoken with several respectable families. Each of them has agreed to take in one or two of the children until you can find other accommodations."

No. No. No. She would not allow the children to be divvied up like leftovers. "I won't separate the children. They've been through so much already."

"There's no other choice, Meredith."

There were always other choices…some not as agreeable as others, but they had to be considered. A grasshopper vaulted onto her arm. She brushed it off with a flick of her hand. If only she could sweep away her problems as effortlessly.

"Jana offered to let us stay at her place. We can move in with her."

"That brings up what I wanted to tell you about her. Major Allen spoke with his wife and her lady friends. He convinced them to end their hostilities against you and the children. They agreed but insisted you must cease any association with Mrs. Valder."

She fisted her hand around the clothes pin. "So you want me to ignore my convictions and surrender to their narrow-minded demands."

"If you want the persecutions to stop, then yes. You will have to abide by their demands. It's for the best, Meredith. As you said, the children have suffered enough. Don't let the stress of being homeless be compounded by tension with the townsfolk."

The air went out of her. He was right. Staying with Jana would only make matters worse. She was no Socrates, but it didn't take a brilliant mind to grasp that she needed to make wise decisions concerning the children's welfare.

She dropped the clothes pin into the pail. "Tell me the names of these people and what you know about them. I want to learn everything before I place any of the children in their care."

Chapter Ten

Preston loaded the last of the luggage onto the wagon—two trunks, four satchels, and a small crate of toys. The Seaton House evacuees had amassed quite a collection during their stay at the fort. Folks had been generous…well, up until the incident at the mess hall. Thanks to Major Allen, all that ugliness about witches and burnings at the stake was water under the bridge, and with proper diligence, would never surface again.

The children watched from the jailhouse steps. Living in less than optimal conditions didn't appear to have caused them too much hardship. Although subdued, they looked healthy and well fed. They could handle being separated from each other for a few months. They were a lot stronger than Meredith gave them credit for.

Despite being forced into their unfamiliar world, he was glad for the experience. Children weren't so bad. They were just miniature recruits, requiring patience and guidance—more of the former than the later. Their unfiltered outlook on life made him look forward to having his own children. He might not be the best father in the world, but with Meredith by his side, he would damn sure try.

Meredith would be a perfect mother. What he once considered willfulness, he now knew to be uncompromising protectiveness. After the dust settled, he would try again to convince her to let him call on her. That night in his tent, he'd let lust overpower his good sense. He would take things slower, court her as she deserved, and when the time was right, ask her to be his wife. He wasn't going to let her slip away. Not while he had a chance at something wonderful.

She walked toward the wagon, herding the children ahead of her. Her eyes were sad and needful, a wounded bird seeking shelter. He would be her refuge.

"Ready to go?" he asked.

She sighed and nodded. "I suppose so."

"Everything will work out just fine. Have a little faith."

Her lips turned up in a weak attempt at a smile. "You sound like Aunt Mildred."

He wanted to kiss away her bleakness. With the orphans looking on, he cupped her elbow instead. "She would want you to be strong. For the children...and for yourself."

"You're right; she would want that." She motioned to the wagon. "Go on, children, get in. We don't want to hold up Lieutenant Booth any longer than necessary."

As the children lined up to board the wagon, she glanced at the jailhouse. Her pretty mouth dipped into a frown. "Where is Robbie? I sent him to get Bessy. He should have returned by now."

Why wasn't he surprised? "I'll go get the boy," he said.

For all Meredith's loving goodness, she just didn't have the firm hand needed to guide young boys into manhood. He'd do his best to fill that void during the time he had left at Fort Dent, though as an only child and tutored at home, he didn't have any real experience to draw on. He'd just have to rely on the leadership training drilled into him at West Point. It had served him well thus far.

Twenty yards beyond the jailhouse, the boy stood beside the grazing cow, hands waving and head bobbing. He appeared to be having a one-sided conversation with the animal. Some might call him odd. Some had labeled him a witch. Anger stomped inside him. How could anyone hurt such an innocent? There was nothing wrong with play-acting. Hell, he'd done the same thing as a youngster, using sticks for guns and trees for bank robbers—on the rare occasions his father allowed him time away from his studies.

"You there, Robbie," he called out.

The boy turned. "Yes, Lieutenant Booth?"

"You were supposed to bring that cow to the wagon ten minutes ago. Everyone is ready to leave."

"Sorry, sir. Bessy wanted a bite to eat before we left."

"Tell her she can eat her fill at her new home in the town stable." Claude Gunderson had agreed to house the animal at his livery until a new orphanage could be built. He had a passel of youngsters and could use the milk.

Robbie peered up at him, his expression puzzled. "You know I can talk to animals?"

"You have a way with them, there's no denying that."

"Do you talk to them?"

He leaned over and lowered his voice. "Don't tell anyone, but I have been known to discuss thorny issues with my horse. It helps me sort things out in my head."

"Does he answer you?"

"Not in so many words. But he has grunted an answer a time or two."

Amusement danced in the boy's eyes. "I like you, Lieutenant. I don't care what the others say." He tugged the cow's lead rope. "C'mon, Bessy. It's time to go."

An odd feeling settled over him, like the warmth of a wool blanket on a cold winter's night. His father was wrong. Children could be seen *and* heard. All you had to do was open up to them, see things from their perspective. The result was quite rewarding.

He trailed behind the boy to make sure no other distraction delayed their departure. He wanted to be well on the way before the captured Indians arrived. He didn't want the sight of them upsetting the little ones or Meredith.

Robbie twisted his head around. "You're sweet on Miss Talbot, ain't you?"

Was the boy a mind-reader? "She's a special lady."

"Lily says she's your soul mate. Whatever that means."

Indeed. "You just focus on leading that cow to the wagon. We're already late leaving as it is."

As they rounded the jailhouse, an approaching parade caught his eye. Five Indians, hands bound and feet hobbled, were being escorted by a four-man detail. Damn. He was too late.

"Are those the renegades?" the boy asked.

"It appears so."

The sullen captives trudged past, heads held high, gazes focused on the jailhouse...their home for the foreseeable future.

Robbie frowned and looked up at him. "Bessy says

they aren't the ones, Lieutenant."

"Aren't the ones what?"

"The ones that attacked Seaton House. Bessy got a good look at them before she ran off into the woods. Those aren't the Indians she saw."

The boy sure did have some imagination. Perhaps one day, he'd be a writer of fantasy stories. He'd be good at it.

Meredith and the other children sat quietly in the back of the wagon, eyeing the renegades. They didn't appear to be distressed by the sight...more curious than anything. One of the younger girls was up on her knees and waving to them. The boy Gabe leaned over the side, trying to get a better view. Any farther, and he'd topple onto his head.

Adding his own brand of absurdity to the spectacle, Agent Finley rode up and dismounted. He strode to the wagon and doffed his hat. "Good-day, Miss Talbot. I didn't expect to see you here. I thought you and the children would be gone by now."

Preston grunted under his breath. So did he.

"Good-day to you, Mr. Finley," Meredith replied. "I'm afraid we took longer than anticipated with our packing and delayed Lieutenant Booth. We were just about to leave."

"I hope the sight of these heathens doesn't upset you or the children. Such nasty, violent creatures."

Finley's oily tone and crass words left him feeling the need for a bath. Preston fixed the agent with a glare. For all the good that did. The man only sidled closer to the back of the wagon and to Meredith.

"They don't appear to be very menacing," Meredith said. "All shackled and guarded by armed soldiers. One has a horrible scar on his cheek. If anything, I feel sorry for them."

Finley clucked. "You shouldn't feel the least bit sorry for them. They are vicious barbarians. If they weren't shackled, they could easily break free and cause all sorts of mayhem."

Now wasn't that a pretty picture. Finley sure knew how to put women and children at ease. "Step aside, Mr. Finley," he barked. "We need to be on our way."

The agent ignored him and remained rooted like a bad mushroom. "I'm sorry you had to be ousted from the jailhouse, Miss Talbot. Have you found homes for the children? I'd be happy to watch over one or two if need be."

Like hell he would. "The children have all been placed." Preston held out a hand. "Give me that lead, Robbie. I'll take care of securing Bessy. You hop in with the others."

The boy handed him the rope and climbed into the wagon. Preston tugged the cow closer. Finley had to scuttle sideways to avoid being trampled. It would serve the intrusive bugger right if he got a few crushed toes. Shouldn't be sticking his feet or his nose where they didn't belong.

Robbie settled beside Meredith and leaned over to whisper in her ear. A frown creased her pretty face. Whatever the boy said, it didn't sit well.

Finley edged closer. "What's that, young man? What did you say that cow told you?"

Robbie ducked his head. "Nuthing."

"Can you talk to other animals, too? What about birds? I had a cousin who could recall everything he'd ever read. Word for word. Said it stayed in his memory like a photograph."

Meredith's mouth sagged, and her eyes widened to the size of a robin's egg. Finley's comments were even less appetizing than the boy's. Damn the man. A rock had more common sense.

Preston secured a taut knot in the rope. Too bad he couldn't wrap the thing around Finley's neck. "The boy is just repeating what he overheard Mr. Hoggard say during his delirious ramblings. Nothing more."

"Is that so?" The agent reached over the side, his hand settling like a talon on Robbie's shoulder. "I'm afraid your cow has it all wrong, young man. Those *are* the renegades that attacked Seaton House, aren't they Mr. Hoggard?"

The color retreated from Hoggard's face. He glanced at the Indians, and then back to Finley. His Adam's apple bobbed with a hard swallow. "That's right. Those are the renegades."

Warning bells clanged in Preston's head. There was something going on between Finley and Hoggard—something that smelled like a fly-blown carcass.

****

The wagon rattled through town, the bed emptier than it had been an hour ago. Her stomach churned around breakfast. She had promised to look after the children—to keep them safe. Yet here she was delivering each of them right into the snapping jaws of danger.

Before leaving the fort, she'd given each of them a trinket from her treasure box, items from her past that held loving memories. Like the wooden pony Charles had carved for her. And the tortoise shell comb her father had presented her on her sixth birthday. She cherished those little baubles. She could only hope they gave the children some measure of solace during this difficult separation.

Lily and Maddie had been dropped off at Major Allen's quarters. Preston's commander had insisted on housing two of the older children, and since he had been instrumental in quelling the hostilities, she couldn't very well refuse his offer. Mrs. Allen had been uncharacteristically quiet and non-confrontational during the exchange. Meredith's only consolation was knowing the girls would be able to lean on one another if their stay became strained.

Next had been Bessy at the stable. Poor Robbie had been so distraught. He started sobbing from the moment they arrived. Preston had to pry the boy's arms from the animal's neck. He wasn't harsh with Robbie, just matter of fact. Told him he could visit Bessy whenever he wanted, and that they'd all be back together soon. If only she had his confidence. Perhaps she wouldn't be leaving a piece of her heart behind with each delivery.

Nel had been left with the banker and his wife. The older and wiser girl had faced plenty of strife over the years and had emerged stronger for it. She should be able to deal with any difficulties.

Gabe and Sally were dropped at the mayor's residence. The Woods were pleasant enough, but something didn't feel right about the pair. She couldn't put her finger on what made her uneasy. Maybe it was the odd gleam in Alvena's eyes, or the quirk to her mouth as if she'd eaten something distasteful when told Sally didn't talk. Gabe would look after his sister, but who would look after Gabe? He had a knack for finding trouble. She'd visit as often as she could and hopefully keep him on the straight and narrow.

The elderly couple who ran the feed store had invited Mr. Hoggard to stay with them. Meredith envisioned cozy nights of checkers, chatting about days gone by, and warming old bones by the fire. Joseph would recover nicely in such a setting. It was the only delivery that soothed her sorrow instead of making it worse.

That left Robbie and Becky. They were to stay with Dr. Troutman and his wife, an older couple whose children had left the nest years ago. Having the twins living with a physician ought to ease her mind. Not to mention Suzanna Troutman had been quite welcoming at Major Allen's dinner party. But those positives did little to lessen her worry. The twins were so young and vulnerable. They didn't understand why their lives had to be plagued with such upheaval and misery. She could barely fathom it herself.

"Here we are." Preston reined the mules to a stop in front of a building midway down the street. The place looked well kempt, the wall boards painted and gleaming; the door decorated with a ribbon-festooned wreath. Bright yellow curtains adorned the front window, and the glass shimmered from a fresh polishing. Surely anyone who took such loving care of their home would be just as attentive of their guests.

A soft sob carried from the back of the wagon. She turned and her heart sank further. Little Becky's bottom lip quivered, and her eyes glistened with tears. So miserable and forlorn. She hated what this separation was doing to them.

"Can't we stay with you, Miss Talbot? Please?"

Anguish made her head spin. She gripped the edge of the wagon seat for support and swallowed back a sob. "I wish you could, Becky. But, there's only room for me and Anna and Mrs. Clement at the church rectory. You'll be just fine with Doctor and Mrs. Troutman."

"But I don't want to stay with anyone else. I want to live with you."

Seated beside her, Preston held his mouth in a firm line. She would take a page from his book and be strong but positive. "I would love nothing better than to have all of you stay with me. But it's just not possible. Not right now. You're a brave young lady, Becky. I know you can do this."

Preston gave an approving node. It wasn't easy, but she was trying. He climbed down and reached up to help her out. Any other time, she would revel at his touch. Now all she felt was numbness.

She rounded the back of the wagon and held out her hands for Becky. The child melted into her arms and snuggled against her. Meredith held tight. She would not let this train leave the station without Becky knowing she was loved and wanted.

Preston helped Robbie to the ground. He stood beside the boy, his hand resting lightly on Robbie's shoulder. Her heart went out to him for that small gesture of comfort. Such things didn't come easy to a man accustomed to holding his emotions in check.

The door swung open, and Doctor Troutman and his wife walked out onto the boardwalk. Becky sucked in a sharp breath and stiffened.

"Everything's going to be just fine, sweetling," she whispered into the girl's hair. "You'll adjust to this just as you always have."

"What if they won't let me leave a candle burning at night?"

Becky's quivering voice sliced into her. Meredith called on her last reserve of strength, which at this point wasn't much. "I'm sure if you ask nicely, the Troutmans will allow you to have a nighttime candle. Besides, Robbie will be there with you. He'll keep you safe."

"I will…miss you," Becky said around a sniffle.

"And I will miss you. So very, very much. I'll come to visit as often as I can. You be strong now, all right?" At Becky's nod, she unwound the girl's arms from her neck and set her down.

Robbie moved beside his sister and slipped his hand into Becky's. The pair stood shoulder to shoulder, eyeing their new caretakers. Her heart nearly split in two at the sight.

She assumed a smile, though there was little to be cheerful about. "Good morning, Doctor. Mrs. Troutman. These are the children who will be staying with you."

Suzanna Troutman's round face beamed like an All Hallows Eve jack-o-lantern. "We're so happy to have you."

Robbie shucked off his hat. "I'm Robert Edmunds, but you can call me Robbie. And this is my sister Becky. Thank you for letting us stay with you, ma'am. We appreciate your kindness."

Polite and mannerly—just as she'd coached him. She couldn't have been prouder. He was growing into a fine young man.

"It's our pleasure, Master Robbie." Dr. Troutman

motioned to the open doorway. "Miss Talbot, Lieutenant Booth, won't you come inside? Have some tea before you go?"

It would be better for the twins if she made a clean, quick break, like yanking a bandage off a crusted wound—painful, but only for a short while. "Thank you for the invitation, but we must be off to our last stop at the church."

"Very well. Come back after you're settled, Miss Talbot. You are welcome here any time."

"Thank you. I will do that." She squatted so she was eye level with the two youngsters. "Take care of each other. Remember, this is only temporary. We'll all be back together soon. I promise."

Though Becky's lip quivered, she managed a nod. Robbie secured a thin smile and tugged his sister toward the door.

Meredith wobbled upright. If not for Preston's hand on her arm, she would have collapsed right there on the boardwalk. He helped her back to the wagon and onto the seat. She stared straight ahead, unable to look back. If she did, she might splinter into a thousand shards.

Preston joined her on the seat. His hand closed over hers, warm and comforting. Tears she'd held in check slid free. One day, she'd have all of the children back under one roof, and she'd never let them be taken from her again. Never.

****

Meredith propped the broom against the pew and sank onto the bench seat with a sigh. She had offered to clean the church in preparation for Sunday service. The smell of freshly polished wood usually calmed her, and the physical toil would sweep aside her worries. But neither activity served her today. Her heart still dragged like a battle-scarred soldier.

The past few days felt like months. She had visited Robbie and Becky the day before. The twins appeared to be well cared for...with clean clothes and clean hands and faces. But their eyes and tone of voice told another story. Both were dull. Sluggish. As if they were slowly dying inside—just like her.

She missed the children. Missed Aunt Mildred and the security of Seaton House. Most of all, she missed Preston. She found strength in his unshakable optimism. If she was honest with herself, she missed the comfort of his embrace. He had come by earlier to tell her he was going out on patrol and wouldn't be back for a few days. He must have seen the anguish in her eyes. Once they were alone, he pulled her into his arms and just held her. She loved him. Didn't know when or where it happened, but it had. The crack in her wall had widened until he flooded inside, swamping her with a need for his love.

Little good it would do.

He wouldn't return those feelings. The army held his heart. Always would. There was no use wishing for something she would never have.

She grunted to her feet and snatched up the broom. A little hard work would douse all those gloomy thoughts. She moved to the altar and attacked the dirt with renewed vigor. Footprints stamped the dust on the short stairs, made earlier when Reverend Scott came by to rehearse his sermon. He'd recited the story of the mustard seed and how even a small amount of faith can move mountains. He'd talked about forgiveness and of turning the other cheek. She would do her best to follow that advice, to have faith—to be a better Christian.

A soft murmuring broke into her thoughts. She whirled around. No one was there. Odd. She would have sworn someone called her name.

She resumed her assault on the floorboards. Dust motes rose up and drifted around her. A fly circled her head, buzzing noisily near her ear. She brushed it away with a flick of her hand. Pesky insect.

The murmuring came again, louder and more distinct this time. *We're coming, Miss Talbot.* It was a mental message, just like the one she'd heard in the jailhouse.

She halted her sweeping and focused on sending a reply. *Who is this? Where are you?*

The only sound came from the bothersome fly. She hurried to the window. Nothing moved in the street or in the short expanse of yard. She heaved a sigh. Clearly, the strain of separation had her all out of sorts.

She moved away from the window and traded the broom for a polishing cloth. She picked up one of the candlesticks flanking the altar. Tarnish stained the silver. Just like her and the children, the shine was hidden. But with a little hard work, it would soon be restored.

A scuffling noise sounded. She turned to find Gabriel and Sally standing in the rear doorway. Her dreariness lifted. She plunked down the candlestick and rushed down the aisle. A beam of sunlight pouring through the open doorway painted Gabe's face. A dark circle with faint, fingerlike extensions branded his cheek. Anger iced her veins. He'd been struck. Hard.

She halted in front of him and gently cupped his chin. "Who did this to you, Gabe?"

He twisted out of her grip. "No one. I fell."

"No fall could cause a bruise that looks like a handprint. Did Mr. Wood hit you?"

"Not him."

Mrs. Wood, then. The evil woman. "Let's go outside so I get a better look at your face." She nudged him through the doorway and into the full sunlight. The whites of his eyes were clear, his nose and mouth unblemished. The damage appeared to be limited to his cheek. A relief. But it didn't lessen the fact that he'd been mistreated.

"This is totally unacceptable."

Gabe shoved back his shoulders and hefted his chin. "I didn't use my gift or cause any trouble, if that's what you mean."

"I didn't mean you. I meant Mrs. Wood hitting you. When did this happen, and why would she do such a thing?"

"It was just after the noon meal. Mrs. Wood started hollering at Sally for not answering her. I told her Sally couldn't talk, but she wouldn't listen. She just kept shaking Sally's arm, trying to make her speak. So, I stepped in to stop her. That's when she hit me. Called us witch's spawns."

The only spawn was Alvena Wood—a daughter of Satan himself. "You did the right thing by protecting your sister. Did she hit you anywhere else?"

"Just my cheek. I turned the other one, just like Mr. Hoggard says we should."

Good for him. But the woman shouldn't have hit him to begin with. She turned to Sally who had followed them out the door. The girl clutched Charles' carved pony against her chest.

"What about you, Sally? Did the woman hurt you?"

Sally wagged her head. Her eyes held a haunted, wary look, and her face had no coloring. The child may not have been physically hurt, but she had been mentally traumatized. Meredith stuffed down her outrage. She would save her anger for the person who deserved it. God would have to wait a little longer for her to be a good Christian.

"Was it you who talked in my head, Sally? Here and before at the jailhouse?"

The girl averted her gaze and fiddled with the pony. Her bottom lip quivered ever so slightly.

Meredith smoothed down a rebellious curl. "It's all right. I'm not upset. I just want to know for certain who sent me those messages. Nod if it was you."

Moss-colored eyes lifted and poured over her. After a few seconds, the girl dipped her head.

"I thought it might be."

Sally held the trinket out to her. Meredith pushed her hand away. "You don't have to give the pony back. It was a gift from me to you."

Sally wagged her head. She pointed from the toy to her head and then to Meredith.

Realization dawned. "You used my pony to talk with me."

Another nod. Meredith sighed. The odds were highly in favor of Sally having a gift. She just didn't expect it to be mental conversing—though it made sense. Her brother could move objects with his mind. Why shouldn't his sister be able to use personal items to send mental messages to others?

"Ain't that something? I knew you was special, Sally. Just didn't know how much." Gabe puffed up his chest. "Course since you're *my* sister, you have to be gifted with something impressive."

Sally smiled up at him, the wariness fading from her eyes. She poked his ribs with a finger. He yelped and leapt away, holding onto his side in a dramatic show. Meredith smiled for the first time in days. It was good to see them being playful after what they had suffered.

"I'm glad you finally feel comfortable using your gift, Sally. We'll talk about it later, all right?" At the girl's nod, she motioned to the footpath. "For now, let's go to the rectory where we can decide what to do with the two of you."

Gabe's sunny expression retreated. "You're not going to send us back to those people, are you? Mrs. Wood ain't right in the head. I saw her smearing horse dung on her face one night when Mr. Wood was away. It smelled awful. She preened in front of her mirror, like she was a queen or something."

Something hideous, that was for certain. "You will absolutely not be sent back to that woman."

"So we can stay with you then."

The rectory alcove wasn't large enough to hold any more occupants. Something else had to be done. Something Mrs. Allen and the rest of the townsfolk weren't going to like.

They would just have to turn the other cheek.

Chapter Eleven

The acrid scent of burnt wood rode the air. A few yards away, two of his troopers strained to lift a thick beam from the blackened mound. There wasn't much left of the Bowen homestead. The house and barn resembled the remnants of Seaton House—nothing but charred wood and smoldering ashes. Thankfully, this time, no one had been harmed during the attack. Zeke had the good fortune to be visiting his wife and children who were staying at the fort and consequently avoided the raid on his farm.

Preston tossed the last of the chimney stones onto a pile and brushed soot from his gloves. Although stained, the stones could be reused. Zeke vowed he would rebuild. Said he wasn't going to let a few bad Indians scare him off. As word spread about the capture of the renegades, more people would be adopting that attitude and returning to their farms. Hopefully none would regret that decision.

He crossed to his horse and untied the reins. He'd purposely taken his patrol by the Bowen homestead. Not to assist with the clean-up…well, he would have done that any way…but he wanted the chance to look for clues. Things just weren't adding up. The captured Indians were adamant about their innocence. Claimed they had only been riding toward the fire to uncover the real criminals. His gut told him Red Wing's son was telling the truth. If Black Hawk and his band *had* set the fire, it only made sense that they would have fled or fought with the arriving patrol. They would not have surrendered without incident as they had done. Their arrest deserved more than just a sweep under the rug.

He mounted and reined his horse to the west where Bowen had cleared land for planting and pasture. Dust and ash billowed around his horse's hooves. With little rain and plenty of comings and goings, any clues left by the raiders had been obliterated. He'd have to look in a less sullied spot for evidence.

In addition to torching the buildings, the attackers had run off the livestock. A few of the beef cows had returned and now gathered in the far corner of the pasture. One big heifer with a calf nosed under her belly lifted her head, took his measure, and then resumed grazing. Although the cows seemed to be unaffected by the raid, the crops weren't as lucky. Broken stalks of summer wheat littered the adjacent field. Many shoots were already turning brown and shriveling. It looked like a battlefield after a bombardment of cannon fire. Finding anything useful in this mess was going to be harder than tracking a blood trail in the rain.

He reined his horse back toward the east. Woods formed a semi-circle around the site where the house once stood. Just to the northeast, a stand of trees clustered together in a thick grove. It would be an ideal spot for remaining concealed, if nefarious business was on the agenda.

He dismounted at the edge of the tree line and secured his horse to a stout sapling. The grove wasn't very large, an acre at the most. It consisted mostly of pines, a few scrub oaks, and a lot of undergrowth. He stepped over a vine-snarled bush that looked more like a green hairball than a plant.

On the other side of the bushy hedge, a dense cluster of trees offered the perfect barricade for watching and waiting. He angled for the spot, his footfalls quieted by a thick layer of pine needles. The forest floor seemed more packed than normal as if recently tread upon, yet there were no discernable footprints.

He slowed and shoveled the toe of his boot under the needles. Only dead branches and pinecones rolled up to the surface. Nothing of note there.

He expanded his search, shuffling through the trees in an ever widening arc. Sunlight dribbled through the overhead canopy and sparkled on something shiny and red. He squatted and exhumed the object. It was a small tin—*Dr. Rumney's mentholyptus snuff*, the same brand Agent Finley preferred. Quite an interesting find.

There was no rust on the container, no dents. He opened the lid. It was half full and the tobacco still damp. The tin had been recently dropped. He replaced the lid and shoved the evidence into his pocket. It might prove to be nothing at all, but its presence near the torched homestead definitely warranted looking into.

Moving outward, he continued his hunt. At one shaggy pine, he stooped to duck under a low-hanging branch. Manure droppings littered the ground on the other side. Most intriguing was the shod hoof print stamped in the middle. He toed the mound. The droppings were dry, but not hard, maybe a day old at most. And colored yellow.

That day in the stables, Sergeant Reese had told

little Robbie he'd give Finley's sick mare a tonic—one that would turn the horse's manure yellow. Instinct screamed that the snuff tin and the yellow droppings were not coincidental, and that Finley was somehow involved in this attack. However much joy it would give him to pin the raid on the obnoxious Indian Agent, it would be best to question Zeke Bowen before jumping to conclusions. The last time he thought he had evidence pointing to the identity of the raiders, it turned out to be a bust.

He left the thicket and led his horse to the clearing. He stopped beside Zeke, who was busy hitching a pair of mules to a farm wagon. Most folks didn't waste time or money putting shoes on draft animals. Zeke was no exception.

"Fine looking mules, Mr. Bowen. You own any more we need to search for? What about horses?"

Zeke shook his head. "Wish I did. Had to sell off my mare last winter to pay for dry goods and feed. These two plow mules are all the animals I got left. Lucky for me I had them with me in town when the Injuns came 'round."

Times were harsh out in the territories, especially for farmers trying to eke a living out of the inhospitable land. "You have any visitors lately?"

Bowen set the pull chains. "None that I can recollect. Been busy with the stock. Some of the cows came down with swollen udders. Another one got the bloat."

"I can send Sergeant Reese out to have a look at them if you want. He's quite learned when it comes to doctoring animals."

"Thanks for the offer, but I got things under control

for now. My main focus will be on rebuilding, which will be a sight easier now that you've captured those damn heathens."

Maybe. "Before the raid, do you recall seeing anything out of the ordinary?"

"Such as?"

"Cattle acting spooked. Things missing or misplaced. Anything unusual."

Bowen shook his head. "No. Why do you ask?"

"Just checking. I found day-old manure and a shod hoof print over in that grove to the northeast. And this…" He fished the snuff tin out of his pocket. "Is it yours?"

Zeke snorted. "Too expensive for my wallet. Most I can manage is a bag of pipe tobacco on occasion."

"Anyone come by that this might have belonged to?"

"Nope. No one has called on us since folks moved into the fort for protection. You think it might be tied to the raid?"

"I don't know. But I aim to look into it. Let me know if you remember anything that might help. Anything at all."

He had a promising lead, but he wasn't going to get his hopes up. Charging a man with criminal wrong-doing required a thorough investigation, especially with someone as slippery as Samuel Finley. He wanted any charges brought against the man to stick like pine tar on a boot heel.

****

Compared to a few days ago, Fort Dent looked like an empty shell. No long lines choked the community well. No crowds gathered outside the mess hall or swarmed around the officers' barracks. The only activity came from small pockets of soldiers going about their duties. One stopped his raking and tipped his hat to her and Nel as they walked past. Meredith nodded in response. The soldiers must be relieved to have their garrison back to normal. She was about to do the same with her household. Well not quite normal, more like tolerable. And this was the last stage of her operation.

Her target sat just ahead...a single-story cottage situated at the end of a row of similar buildings. Fresh whitewashing coated the clapboard planks. Sunlight glistened on spotless window panes. Even the door had been wiped free of grime. Mrs. Allen appeared to work diligently to keep her residence presentable, not an easy undertaking on a garrison where boots and hooves kicked up copious amounts of dust and mud.

Meredith stepped onto the spotless veranda and rapped on the door. Hopefully Mrs. Allen was home and not out on one of her gossiping sprees. This mission needed to be over and done with as soon as possible.

The faint thud of footfalls sounded on the other side. The door clicked open, and Lily appeared in the opening. Surprise and then delight swept across the younger girl's face.

"Miss Talbot." She rushed into Meredith's arms. "It's so good to see you."

Meredith squeezed Lily against her. Tears brimmed in her eyes. She needed this reunion almost as much as Lily did.

The smell of beeswax polish and lye soap surrounded the girl. Meredith gently pushed Lily away and slid her hands down until they were clasping each other. Lily's fingers were rough and dry, and grime streaked the apron covering her dress. She looked more like a washer-woman than a young lady.

"How have you been, Lily? Are the Allens treating you well?"

Before Lily could answer, a squeal resounded in the hallway and a second later, a brown-headed whirlwind plowed into her. Maddie wrapped Meredith's legs in a ferocious bear hug. Meredith smiled and cupped the girl's head. This enthusiastic welcome confirmed what her heart already knew. She was doing the right thing.

Maddie tilted her head back. Dark circles ringed her eyes. "Did you come for a visit, Miss Talbot? How are the others? Anna? Sally? There's Nel. It's so good to see you. I miss everyone so much."

"Everyone is fine." She brushed a hand over soft curls. "And this is not just a visit."

Brusque footfalls snapped on the floorboards. "If this is not a visit, then what is it? You are taking the girls from their chores."

Harriet Allen's harsh tone reverberated against the walls. Maddie's grip tightened. Lily stiffened and sucked in a breath. Clearly the girls were uncomfortable around the gruff woman. *Not for long.*

Meredith disentangled herself from Maddie's embrace and gave the girl a nudge. "Both of you go and pack your things."

Maddie's eyes brightened. "Why? Where we going?"

"I'll explain later. Go get your things."

As the girls rushed from the foyer, Meredith

squared herself. Harriet Allen could bluster and froth all she wanted. She wouldn't be intimidated. This was a battle the tyrant would not win.

"Thank you for taking Lily and Maddie into your home, Mrs. Allen, but your hospitality is no longer required. I have found other accommodations for the children."

"What other accommodations?"

"A place where we can all be together under one roof."

Harriet's gaze narrowed. "And just where is this place you have *found*?"

"All you need to know is that the children will be well cared for."

"You could not have located suitable accommodations in just three days. There are only a handful of places in Mineral that could house all of you together. Unless…" Mrs. Allen puffed up like a chicken who'd been bothered by a rooster. "I will not allow you to take those children to a bawdy house."

"You have no say in the matter."

"It's my God-given right to ensure those children are not mistreated or led down the path to sin."

Wasn't that the pot calling the kettle black? "You should turn that righteous indignation on yourself. I see what you have done with Lily and Maddie…working their fingers to the bone. They've never looked so ragged."

"A little hard work never hurt a child."

"Lily and Maddie were not placed with you to be slave laborers. Even if I hadn't found other accommodations, I would remove them from your care."

Arms folded across a broad chest. "William will hear about this. Make no mistake."

"Do what you must. I'm taking the girls with me."

Mrs. Allen eyed her like a she-cat sizing up an opponent. Her breaths were coming in noisy exhales; her upper lip curled back in a snarl. At any moment, claws would unsheathe.

Lily and Maddie skipped into the foyer, satchels in hand. Perfect timing. Any longer and she might burst into flames from Mrs. Allen's evil glare.

"Girls, thank Mrs. Allen for her *generosity*, and we'll be on our way."

The pair murmured their thanks and rushed through the open doorway. As much as she wanted to bolt with them, Meredith held her ground and mustered as much politeness as she could, which wasn't much. She was near the bottom of her barrel of civility. "You have a wonderful day, Mrs. Allen."

Indignant huffs followed her out the door. Meredith marched off the veranda and into the street. She wouldn't let Mrs. Allen's displeasure ruin her joy. She had her children back, and no one was ever going to take them from her again.

"Where are we going?" Lily asked. "I heard you tell Mrs. Allen you found another place where we can all be together."

"She called it a bawdy house," Maddie added.

"Mrs. Valder's is not a bawdy house." At least not while the children stayed there. Jana had agreed to cease her business until they found another place to live. Meredith sensed Jana was relieved to suspend her trade and decided to help the woman find other means of employment once things settled down. But that was a conversation for a later date.

She motioned the girls forward. "Come. Mrs. Clement and the others are already there waiting for us."

"What about Mr. Hoggard?"

"There's not enough room for him at Mrs. Valder's. He's going to remain at the feed store for now." Which was a good thing. She didn't want to put the retired preacher in an awkward position of living in a house of ill repute. While he wasn't happy with her decision to move the children into such a place, he agreed it was for the best.

Lily skipped into step beside her. "Your aura is glowing a soft blue color, Miss Talbot. You're quite pleased with everything in your life."

Most everything. Preston would have to be dealt with, but she would cross that bridge when the waters calmed. "I have all of you back together with me and under one roof. That makes me very happy."

"What made you change your mind?"

"An unexpected turn of events. I'll tell you about it when we get to Mrs. Valder's."

Maddie tucked in on her other side and snuggled her hand in Meredith's. "My charm worked then."

"Your charm?" Her pulse hopscotched. "Oh, Maddie. Don't tell me you practiced your talent."

"It was just a simple potion. No one saw me. I buried it the other night beneath a big cottonwood tree near the creek outside the fort."

Dread coiled in her stomach. She knew that exact spot. It was where a deadly rattlesnake had almost bit her. Where there was one snake, there was most likely more.

She tightened her grip on Maddie's hand. "You shouldn't have done that, Maddie. You could have been hurt or worse."

"Lily came with me. We weren't out for very long. A half hour at most."

A half hour too long. "What if someone saw you and informed Mrs. Allen? I can assure you, she hasn't forgotten about that evening in the mess hall. One whiff of anything abnormal, and she'll be back on her witch hunt faster than a hound after a rabbit."

Maddie squeezed her hand. "We were careful, Miss Talbot. We waited for clouds to cover the moon before going out. The darkness covered us."

"Even so, it was a dangerous thing to do. Promise you won't do anything like that again."

"I promise. No more charms or nightly adventures." A frown puckered Maddie's brow. "Although Major Allen could use a charm."

"Why do you say that?"

"He's been suffering with a sour stomach for days. Lily says she saw his aura turn blackish green when he drank his morning coffee. She says that meant he'd been touched by something evil."

"Something evil…like poison?" At Lily's nod, Meredith picked up her pace. The sooner she got the girls away from the fort and Mrs. Allen, the better.

As they neared the garrison gate, a pack of soldiers surged past them, rifles at the ready, their expressions grim. The squad surrounded a group of mounted Indians assembled outside the stockade walls. Within seconds, a crowd collected, trapping her and the girls in place.

One of the soldiers leveled his gun at an Indian

wearing a bonnet of eagle feathers. "You shouldn't be here, Chief Red Wing. Go back to the reservation before you find yourself joining your son in the jailhouse."

The Indians gathered around the chieftain stirred, their rumbles rising like the drone of disturbed bees. Meredith stiffened. She had to get the girls to safety before hostility overrode good sense.

"Let's go back inside the fort, girls."

Lily and Maddie turned with her, but Nel didn't budge. The girl stood transfixed, her gaze focused skyward, mouth agape.

"What are you doing, Nel? We need to go."

"It's amazing," the girl whispered. "Do you see it?"

All she saw was a throng of dark-skinned men with tense faces and tenser hands gripping their weapons. Even their horses were agitated. Some snorted at the gathering. Others pranced in place. Both riders and mounts were powder kegs waiting to go off.

"We need to go, Nel. Now."

"I've never seen such a thing before," Nel said, her voice dripping with awe. "The Indians have a rippling cloud of white hovering over them…the spirits of their ancestors."

Wonderful. Now the spirit world had joined the fray.

The one called Red Wing held up a hand, and the Indians surrounding him quieted. The chieftain nudged his horse forward. He wore an odd combination of trappings, a blue-and-white striped shirt and animal hide leggings. She prayed the cultivated side would win out over his savagery.

"We want no trouble," the chief stated. "Release my son and his warriors, and we will leave."

The soldier wagged his head. "I can't do that, Red Wing. Your warriors are being held for attacking innocent people and setting fire to their homesteads."

"These things they did not do."

"That is for Major Allen to decide."

The chief crossed his arms over his chest, and his face took on a mulish bent. "Then bring this Major Allen here so we may talk."

"Major Allen is busy."

"We will stay until he is not busy."

"I can't let you do that. Turn around and go back to the reservation, or…" He signaled to his soldiers who took a step forward, closing in on the Indians like a noose. "We will use any means to force you back."

Meredith's veins turned to ice. They were going to get caught in the middle of a gun battle. Stupid, stupid men.

She snagged Nel's hand and tugged. "Come. We must go back inside the fort where it's safe."

The girl dug in her heels. "We can't leave. The Indians need our help."

"There's nothing we can do, Nel."

"We can stand with them. Show our support."

A man standing nearby gave Nel a piercing look. Meredith's stomach fell. Moving in with Jana was going to cause enough friction with the townsfolk. Defending the Indians would only add fuel to that fire.

****

Preston leaned forward as his mount topped the low rise. In the shallow valley below sat the mining town of Mineral. The northern end contained the false-fronted business district with the saloons relegated to the outskirts. Boarding houses and residential homes occupied the southern end, built away from the more congested commercial section, mostly due to the dust in the summer and mud in the spring—and because the good ladies refused to live cheek-to-cheek with the prostitutes, gamblers, and drunks.

The place was growing fast. Talk of a railroad spur coming through had drawn people like ants to a picnic. Since his arrival twelve months ago, they had constructed a theater and a new school for the children. A decent-sized hotel was going up, the spines already reaching skyward. Not that he would be around to see its completion. Once his transfer came through, Mineral would be a page in his memoirs.

A wide thoroughfare flowed through the center of the town, stretching all the way to the entrance of Fort Dent where—he fisted the reins. *Oh, hell no.* Soldiers ringed a small band of Indians collected at the gate while a large group of civilians looked on. Even from a distance, tension slugged the air like a boiling thundercloud.

He prodded his horse into a gallop. He had to hurry before someone did something stupid. If the soldiers opened fire, innocent people, both white and red-skinned could be hurt or killed.

After skirting the log jam of people, Preston reined up near the stockade wall. Infantrymen of the Sixth had their weapons trained on the Indians. Civilians crowded behind the soldiers—some curious, most wagging fisted hands and shouting angrily. A familiar face caught his eye, and his stomach bucked. *Meredith.* What was she doing out here? He had to diffuse the situation, fast...before he lost something he'd only just discovered.

He dismounted and headed for Sergeant Wilson, the ranking soldier of the squad. Thankfully, the Creeks didn't appear too agitated. The Indians sat their mounts quietly, hands cupping rifles resting on their laps, not aggressively, but at the ready should the need arise. He hoped to hell it didn't.

"Stand down, Sergeant." While not directly under his command, Wilson would still have to respect and obey his rank.

The soldier turned to face him. "Lieutenant Booth, Chief Red Wing refuses to return to the reservation. He insists we release the incarcerated renegades."

"I said stand down, Sergeant. Now." He spiked his tone with steel. "Before I have you arrested for disobeying orders and tossed in jail *with* those renegades."

Wilson's frown deepened. After a few seconds of jaw-twitching reflection, he lowered his rifle. "Stand down, men."

Weapons slowly sank but were held in readiness. Distrust choked the air, stagnant and potent as a fetid marsh. Preston crossed to the eagle-eyed chief, one he was quite familiar with. Their previous encounter had ended on good terms. Hopefully this one would too.

"Chief Red Wing, I understand why you have come, but I urge you to go back to the reservation. Your presence will only make things worse." If the situation couldn't be contained, a whole lot worse.

"We will stay until I have spoken to your Major Allen about his jailing of my son and his scouting party."

"There's no need for that. Black Hawk and the others are being treated with great care. I give you my word."

Red Wing shook his head. "They should not have been arrested. They did nothing wrong."

"They killed innocent people," someone in the crowd shouted. "I say hang 'em all. Starting with this mangy bunch."

Though his eyes narrowed, Red Wing's bearing remained steady and collected, presumably to avoid inciting the warriors gathered behind him. A sound strategy.

Preston turned to the crowd, hands raised and expression calm, even though his insides churned like waves in a nor'easter. He focused on the stocky, livid-faced man at the forefront of the group. If he could get the ringleader to stand down, the others would follow.

"I realize many of you have lost homes, livestock, and loved ones. But now is not the time for vigilante justice."

"All we want is for them savages to get what's comin' to 'em," the man said.

Preston nodded. "We *all* want justice for the atrocities that were committed. Rest assured, Major Allen will make sure that justice prevails—in a fair and just manner. There's no need to incite more trouble. I urge you to go back about your business. Let the army deal with the Indians."

The ringleader sized him up and then gave a nod. While the crowd around him didn't disperse, they did grow quiet, the fire in their bellies banked—for now. Preston let his hands relax to his sides. It was a start. Now all he had to do was remove the kindling.

He turned back to the Indians. "Chief Red Wing, as I said, justice will prevail in an equitable manner. Your son and his warriors will be given a fair trial. If they are found innocent, they will be released."

"Why should we trust this?"

"You, like I, are practiced in measuring a man's integrity. I know my commander. Major Allen is a rational man. He will listen to all sides before passing judgment. Whatever his decision, it will be obeyed."

Black eyes pierced into him, assessing his claim. Preston stood his ground. To show uncertainty would doom their discussion.

"You have faith in this Major Allen."

"I have every faith in him. He is sensible and honorable. He will do the right thing."

Red Wing's shoulders went down a fraction. All the chieftain needed was a little push to get him off the fence. Preston lowered his voice and leaned in. What he had to say was for the chief's ears only.

"I have uncovered something that I believe will shed new light on *exactly* who is behind the attacks."

"What is this you have found?"

"I can't divulge that information until I have spoken with Major Allen. But if this turns out to be what I think it is, I assure you, all wrongs will be righted. Give me a week to sort things out."

Red Wing didn't look convinced. Preston held up his hand, palm outward. "I swear on the sacred pipe we shared that I will not stop until I have looked under every rock. If my investigation proves your son and his warriors are innocent, and I believe it will, I will make sure they are set free."

The chief considered this for a moment and then

nodded. "I will hold you to your word, Lieutenant Booth. You have one week." Red Wing barked a command, and he and his braves reined their horses to the west.

"Let them pass," Preston called to the soldiers.

The infantrymen parted, and Preston watched until the Indians were safely on their way before he wheeled around. Now to make good on his word.

"Sergeant Wilson, send someone to find Agent Finley and bring him to headquarters, post haste."

Wilson tendered a brisk salute and rushed to carry out his orders. As soldiers and civilians began dispersing, Preston threaded through the throng, angling for one civilian in particular. Her pretty face beamed like a beacon in the sea of agitation.

He caught hold of her arm. "What are you doing out here, Meredith? I thought you were staying at the church in town?"

Violet eyes flashed with a mixture of relief and defiance. "I was collecting Lily and Maddie from Mrs. Allen. When we arrived at the gate, we were caught up in this...whatever it was."

Dangerous is what it was. He wanted to pull her into his arms, stroke her hair, her face. Assure himself she was safe. But this wasn't the place or the time. Later, when they had more privacy...

"The altercation is thankfully over. You can take the girls and go now." He softened his tone and his stance. As much as her presence at the standoff alarmed him, he didn't want there to be any tension between them. "I'll come by the church after I give my report to Major Allen. We can talk then."

Color fled from her face. "I won't be at the

church."

"Why not? Where will you be?"

Her gaze shifted from him to the dwindling crowd and back. She fidgeted with the broach pinned to her blouse—a nervous twitch if he ever saw one. Something was up, and whatever it was, his gut told him he wasn't going to like it.

He guided her to a more secluded spot beside the stockade wall and turned her to face him. "What is going on, Meredith? Why won't you be at the church?"

She shrugged out of his grasp. "Because I'm staying somewhere else."

"Where?"

"At Jana Valder's. I gathered all the children, and we're living with her now."

"What? Why would you do that? I thought we had already discussed Mrs. Valder."

She shoved up her chin, no less strong-willed than Chief Red Wing. "Things have changed. I discovered some of the children were being mistreated, so I decided it was best to collect all of them and move in with Jana. She has agreed to suspend her...er...business until we leave."

She would do anything to keep her flock safe— even if it put her own life in jeopardy. He wanted to be angry at her. Living in a whorehouse would only make things more complicated, even if Mrs. Valder had suspended her trade. But all he could think about was planting kisses along that slender, arching neck.

"You are one determined lady, Meredith Talbot."

"When it comes to the children, yes, I am."

"Go on then. We'll talk later." *Among other things.*

"Bye, Lieutenant," one of the girls cooed. "Thank

you for defending those Indians. You were magnificent."

Her name was…Nel. A pretty girl just blossoming into womanhood. She was already catching the eye of his younger troopers. Yet another complication he didn't need.

Chapter Twelve

Meredith snipped the trailing thread and set the scissors and the repaired sock on the end table. Darning wasn't her favorite chore. It required patience and dexterity, not her strong suits. But it had to be done. The second-hand clothes while helpful didn't hold up long under youthful vigor. With any luck, Aunt Mildred would return soon with a satchel full of donated funds. Then they would be able to suitably house and clothe the children. For now, they would have to make do with the castoffs.

Robbie squirmed on the floor at her feet. He was supposed to be studying his primer. Little Petunia was doing more of the reading as the mouse darted across the pages. Meredith merely smiled. She didn't have the heart to chastise him—or any of the children, for that matter. After days of being apart, they were finally back together. She didn't want anything to spoil their happiness.

Sunlight poured through the large bay window and filled the parlor with brightness and warmth. Frilly white curtains replaced the heavy velvet ones that had concealed the previous guests from view. Cheerful paintings decorated the walls. A vase of lavender stalks sat on the sideboard and added a fresh perfume of innocence to the air. The transformation was almost complete. Soon, no one would recognize the house's former occupation.

The other night, after the children had gone to bed, Jana had broached the subject of making a change in her life. When she had first arrived in Mineral, an opportunity presented itself where she was able to trade her mules, wagon, and Mr. Valder's tools for a house on the outskirts of town. Unfortunately, the exchange left her with few resources. So she had done the only thing she could to get by—sell herself. Now she wanted to change that. Said with the coming of the railroad, she would like to turn her home into a boarding house. Meredith and Mrs. Clement had both cheered the idea and offered to help. It was the perfect solution for everyone.

Meredith's optimism dimmed. Not everyone would be as accepting. It had only been twenty-four hours since she had collected the children, and while all had remained quiet, there were sure to be repercussions. The question was when they would happen and how violent. She would just have to be extra vigilant and keep the children close.

As she reached for another sock, a muffled shout rang out. She stilled and listened. The noise sounded as if it had come from outside the house. It couldn't be Mrs. Clement returning from the general store. The housekeeper hadn't been gone very long, and she had a substantial list of goods to purchase.

Something thumped against the window. The pane shattered, sending glass shards and a large rock spilling onto the floorboards. Anna screeched and scrambled behind Meredith's chair. Little Robbie started, spilling book and mouse to the floor.

Heart racing, Meredith shot to her feet. "All of you

come over here and get behind my chair. Quickly now."

Gabe ignored her and ran to the window. "It's Pete Cavendish and his gang. I ought to send that rock back out there and hit each of them upside the head."

He would do it too. Meredith hurried to the boy's side and placed a restraining hand on his arm. "No, Gabe. That will only make things worse. Please come away from the window."

"Don't matter no how. They're running away." He shook a fist and shouted, "Cowards," through the opening.

Cowards, indeed. Pete Cavendish and his cohorts were the same bullies who had jumped Gabe and Robbie at the fort's community well…though she couldn't put all the blame on the young thugs. They were only mimicking their parents' intolerance and cruelty.

Jana raced into the room, her face pleated with concern. "I heard glass shatter. Is everyone all right?"

"Everyone is fine." Meredith pointed to the fracture glass. "Some boys tossed a rock through the window, but they've run off now."

"Evil mongrels. It is good thing they ran off. A sound switching is vat they need." Jana spun around with a grunt. "I vill get a broom. Clean up this mess before someone gets cut."

Wise suggestions. Both of them. The switching she couldn't do much about, but the other she could. "Come away from the window, Gabe, so we can clean up the glass."

The boy only leaned closer. "Look-it. Here comes Mrs. Allen with a herd of her lady friends and some soldiers. You think they're coming to make sure we're all right?"

Only if cows grew wings and flew. "I don't know. Just to be certain, I want all of you to go up to your rooms. Wait for me to call you down."

Anna scurried to her side and clung to her skirt. "I'm scared. I want to stay here with you."

Meredith gently extracted the girl and prodded her toward the door. "Everything's going to be all right. Go upstairs with Lily. I'm sure if you ask nicely, she'll recite your favorite story."

"The one about the angels?"

"Yes, the one about the angels." If Harriet Allen was here for the reason she suspected, they would need all the heavenly help they could get. "Now all of you go upstairs to your rooms. Be mindful of the glass as you leave."

Once the children were safely out of the parlor, she made her way into the hallway and to the front door. She grasped the handle. Now to navigate a bigger pile of trouble, one that had much sharper edges.

Her stomach roiling, she pulled open the door. Mrs. Allen led the pack, followed by Alvena Wood, Edeline Wentworth, and Suzanna Troutman—the four ladies of the apocalypse. The four soldiers trailing behind them were their multi-colored steeds. There was no telling what plague they intended to spread.

Meredith walked out onto the porch and pasted on her most welcoming smile. "Good afternoon, ladies. What brings you out on such a lovely day? Taking a stroll?"

Mrs. Allen stopped at the bottom of the stairs with her posse closing in behind her. "You know why we're here. Have the children gather their things and come outside."

"The children are staying right where they are."

Alvena Wood shoveled forward. "We won't allow them to live in a bawdy house. You bring them out here so they can be placed in decent homes, free of filth."

"Free of filth, you say?" Meredith pointed to the street. "I believe there's a pile of manure in the roadway, Alvena. Freshly dropped this morning. It would be the perfect face pack. That is what you do, isn't it? Smear yourself with excrement in hopes of enhancing your looks? Wherever did you learn about such a wonder treatment?"

Mrs. Wood's bottom jaw sagged. Her color faded to the hue of dried dung. Meredith smiled inwardly. Revenge served cold tasted ever so sweet.

Mrs. Allen shoved the witless woman behind her. "What Alvena does in the privacy of her home is none of our concern."

"The same could be said of Mrs. Valder's home," Meredith countered.

"The two are not the same and you know it. This is a house of sin. God's children should not be touched by such wickedness."

Jana stepped onto the porch, broom in hand. "I haf decided to turn my home into a respectable boarding house, so you need not take the children away."

"Respectable? Bah, you will always be tainted no matter what trade you employ."

Meredith glared at the woman. "And you call yourself a Christian? Mrs. Valder is trying to better herself. You should be supporting her, not casting stones."

Red climbed in Mrs. Allen's face. If she were a

volcano, lava would be spewing from her ears. "If you won't call the children to come out, we will go in and get them."

"By whose authority?"

"By my husband's. As post commander, he has jurisdiction over the fort *and* the town and has ordered the children to be collected so they can be placed in proper homes." Mrs. Allen motioned to the soldiers. "Sergeant Wilson, have your men round up the children. There are eight of them. Six girls and two boys."

Her insides turned to stone. Sergeant Wilson. The same soldier who had almost instigated a clash with the Indians at the entrance to the fort. Not a good sign. Not good at all.

Wilson turned to his men. "Jones and Abbott, secure the back entrance. Private Bolton, come with me."

As the sergeant and his lackey moved toward the porch, Jana stepped forward and blocked them with broom and body. "You vill haf to go through me first."

Meredith shouldered next to her friend. "Me too."

The two men slowed their advance, their expressions clouded with uncertainty. Mrs. Allen chopped the air with her hand. "Both of you harlots move out of the way. This instant. Or you will regret your interference."

Meredith stood her ground. She wasn't about to back down. "Threaten all you want. I won't let you take my children."

"Fine. Sergeant Wilson, use whatever force is necessary to obtain those children. Anything at all…on the order of your commander."

The two soldiers squared themselves and clattered up the steps. Private Bolton grasped her by the elbow. Meredith tried to wrench free, but to no avail. The soldier held fast.

She dug in her heels and glared up at him. "Let go of me, this instant."

His grip tightened. "I'm sorry, ma'am. But I must insist you move out of the way and let us do our duty."

Before she could tender a stinging retort, Jana swung her broom at the two men. Private Bolton ducked. Sergeant Wilson wasn't quite so nimble. He took a face full of straw. He stumbled back a step and then regained his balance. He grabbed for handle, and he and Jana struggled for control. No match for the burly soldier, Jana lost her purchase on the handle. She careened backward and collided against the wall with a pained yelp.

Meredith twisted against the soldier's grip. "Let me go. I need to see to my friend. She's been hurt."

Bolton released her, and she raced to Jana's side. She squatted beside the grimacing woman. "Are you all right? Where does it hurt?"

"Go. Save the children." At Meredith's hesitancy, Jana flicked her hand. "Go. I vill be fine."

Reassured by the color returning to Jana's face, Meredith pushed to her feet and turned, only to find the soldiers had already breached the door. She hiked up her skirts and rushed after them. They would not take her children. Not while she drew breath.

Sergeant Wilson and his men swarmed like cockroaches through the house, ignoring her appeals to stop. Not finding their quarry downstairs, they climbed the steps to the second floor. A door slammed shut.

Someone shouted. A thud rang out and then came the splintering of wood.

Meredith raced up the stairs, her footfalls matching the thump of her heart. "Stop," she cried out. "Leave the children be."

"You cannot stop them," Mrs. Allen shouted from the bottom of the staircase. "And if you encourage the children to use *other means* to resist…they will be dealt with as our Salem forefathers handled such miscreants."

Fear stomped her insides. If the children were observed using their gifts, they might be tortured or worse. She couldn't allow that to happen.

She stopped on the second-floor landing and gathered herself with several deep breaths. She needed to show calm and reassurance, else the children would not listen. "It's all right, children. You can come out, now."

"We can stop them," Gabe yelled from a nearby room.

The shriek of scrapping wood echoed into the hall. Sergeant Wilson grunted out a colorful exclamation, and then came the ominous click of a cocked weapon.

Meredith fled into the bedroom. An armoire barreled across the floor, heading toward the gun-wielding sergeant. Her heart skipped a beat. Gabe was using his gift, and it might very well get him killed.

"Gabe, stop. That's enough."

The scrapping halted. A head peeped around the side of the armoire. A smaller head of white curls appeared below it. The boys weren't using their gifts, just brains and brawn—the former of which Sergeant Wilson was lacking.

Meredith wagged a finger at the soldier. "Put that

pistol away, Sergeant. There's no need for weapons. They're just little boys, for heaven's sake."

The sergeant looked at the armoire and back at her. Indecision caked his face.

"The children will cooperate, I give you my word."

He hesitated, and then with an irritated grumble, holstered his weapon. The first intelligent thing he'd done since arriving.

"Come boys." She motioned for them to join her. "Let's go out into the hallway."

She called the rest of the children to her. As they gathered around, she put on her most encouraging expression, though her insides churned with hopelessness. "I know this is difficult and quite upsetting after we only just got back together. But I want you to go with Mrs. Allen. It won't be for long. I promise."

"What are you going to do?" Lily asked.

"I'm going to see someone who can put a stop to all of this."

****

Major Allen glared over his spectacles, his brow forming one bushy stripe of skepticism. The commander could be quite intimidating when the situation called for it. And this one screamed for a browbeating.

"Agent Finley. You claim this is *not* your snuff tin that Lieutenant Booth found at the Bowen homestead."

Finley crossed arms over his paunch. "That is what I said."

"Yet you freely admit this is the brand you favor and have purchased on many occasions. How do you refute the obvious connection?"

Preston leaned forward. He wanted to hear the man's explanation, too. See if the weasel could wiggle out of this one.

Finley met Major Allen's scowl head-on, nose cocked in the air. "Perhaps there is someone else who enjoys the same brand. I have never visited the Bowen homestead. Haven't even passed within a mile of the place. Therefore, I could not have dropped a snuff tin in the woods."

"*Dr. Rumney's* is an expensive brand that can only be imported from England. Not many folks in these parts can afford such a luxury."

Major Allen hovered over the seated agent, a tactic the commander used quite often and quite successfully to bring insubordinates in line. Yet Finley didn't cower. Hardly even batted an eyelash. Ballsy for a Nancy.

"You have no proof that tin is mine or that I was even at the Bowen place." The agent jabbed a finger in Preston's direction. "Besides, how do we know the lieutenant didn't plant it there and concoct this absurd tale to shift the blame to someone else? He has a soft spot for the Indians. I observed his kowtowing during our talk with Chief Red Wing."

Preston fisted his hat brim. He'd like nothing better than to wipe the smug lines off Finley's face. But now was not the time to give rein to his anger. "Are you calling me a liar, Finley?"

"If the shoe fits…"

The man's haughtiness grated like sand trapped inside his boots. It took all his willpower to keep his feet firmly planted to the floor. He forced restraint into his tone. "I'm glad you mentioned shoes… I also found a shod hoof print stamped in yellow-tinted horse manure near where that tin was dropped. If I recall, the stable master administered a tonic to your ailing mare that turns manure yellow. What are the odds those droppings and that shoe print came from your horse?"

Finley's left eye twitched slightly. Not enough to condemn the man, but enough to indicate he'd struck a nerve.

"You cannot find me guilty based on a hoof print or yellow horse droppings."

"Men have been hanged for less…much less." Despite his efforts, venom spewed up and spiked his voice.

Major Allen gave him a cautionary look—one he'd best not ignore. Not if he didn't want to be directing latrine duties for the next month.

Preston snapped his mouth shut and stood down. Finley should be grateful he was being judged by a level-headed man like Major Allen. If it were up to him, the cretin would be swinging from a noose.

An outsized map of the territories hung on the far wall. He picked out several ideal spots for abandoning Finley. Inhospitable and barren. Let the snake see how he would fare with just arrogance and sarcasm for sustenance.

Major Allen strode to the desk and tossed the tin next to a stack of papers. "You are correct, Mr. Finley. We cannot find you guilty on such tenuous evidence."

"Good." Daylight shined between the chair seat and Finley's ass. "Then I'll just be going—"

"Sit down," the major thundered.

When Finley failed to comply, Preston hooked a hand on his saber grip and took a step forward. The agent looked from him to Major Allen and back. The commander remained pointedly mute. Finley plopped back to the chair with a disgruntled huff.

"As I was saying," Major Allen continued in a more level tone. "It is my opinion that this situation requires a thorough investigation."

"There's nothing to investigate. I am innocent."

"I'll be the judge of that." Major Allen turned to the door and called for his adjutant.

A split second later, Simpson appeared in the doorway as if awaiting his commander's call. Eager and intuitive. Good qualities to have in an aide. Major Allen could read men like books and stacked the good ones around him. Finley didn't stand a chance against the adroit commander.

"Escort Mr. Finley to the jailhouse, Sergeant Simpson," the major said. "Have the guards lock him in a cell until further notice."

Preston smiled inwardly. Preferably in the same jail cell with Black Hawk. He'd pay for prime seating to watch that clash.

Finley squirmed on the chair, his face seething. "You cannot do this, Major. I'm a civilian. I have rights."

"Not on my post you don't. You will be detained while we look into your activities of the past few months. If nothing untoward is found, you will be released."

"But—"

"No buts." Preston couldn't hold back any longer. Finley's insolence had drained his last ounce of self-restraint. He leaned toward the agent, using height to push home his point. "You're going exactly where you belong, Finley…behind bars."

Finley shoved up his chin. "I have friends in Washington. I'll have you court martialed for this. Both of you."

Major Allen's mouth twisted into a smile that was miles from reaching his eyes. "We'll see just how loyal those *friends* of yours are. A telegram has been sent to Washington to determine if the treaty provisions were requisitioned for the Red Ground tribe and if so, why they were not sent. You are at the very least culpable of dereliction of duty."

"You can't do that."

"I can and I did." Major Allen flicked a hand. "Take him away, Sergeant."

Simpson snagged Finley by the collar and dragged him out of the chair. The agent's face went from blotchy red to gray to white. He looked as if he might spew. Preston moved back a step. The varmint could rot in his own soilings for all he cared.

The adjutant hauled Finley out of the door, and seconds later, blessed silence returned. Preston eased his shoulders down. That took care of the flea, now to soothe the bitten dog.

"Word will get out about Finley's arrest, sir. What should we do about the Creek scouting party? Chief Red Wing won't sit idle for much longer. He'll want them released."

"We'll continue to hold them for now. Make certain of their innocence before letting them go. Red Wing will just have to be patient." The major moved behind the desk and settled in his chair. "How confident are you of Finley's culpability?"

"Not as certain as I am that Black Hawk and his warriors are innocent, but pretty damn close."

"Good enough." Major Allen adjusted his spectacles and sifted through a stack of documents. "Since you already have a head start on the investigation, I'm putting you in charge. Find out what Finley would gain by attacking the Bowen homestead."

He would leave no stone unturned. He snapped a brisk salute. "Very well, sir. If you'll excuse me, I will begin making inquiries."

"Just a minute, Lieutenant. I have some news for you." The major slid a piece of paper from the pile and held it out to him. "You will have to be quick with your investigation. Your request for transfer was approved. You're expected at Fort Sill by the end of the month."

A combination of relief and dread trotted through him. This definitely put a ticking clock on his plans. He'd need an answer from Meredith and soon.

"I'll be sorry to see you go, Preston," the major said with uncharacteristic familiarity. "You're a fine officer and a great asset to my staff. The troopers under your command have turned into exemplary fighting men. But I understand your desire to move forward with your career. If you ever want to come back, the gate to Fort Dent will always be open."

High praise from a man he admired and respected. "Thank you, sir. I appreciate your understanding."

A door screeched open in the ante-chamber. Footfalls clapped on the floorboards and then Meredith filled the doorway, her chest heaving as if she'd run a footrace. Her gaze tripped over him.

"You cannot do this," she said. "I won't allow it."

Chapter Thirteen

There were no mirrors draped in black or a casket with a groomed body to mourn. Yet the house was funeral parlor quiet. There should be laughter and brotherly squabbling, the shush of little feet and the clap of excited hands. Instead, there was only darkness and silence. Silence so deafening, her ears rang with the clamor.

Meredith clawed at the laces clutching her chin. She needed air. Now. She ripped the bonnet from her head and drew in several deep breaths. If a person could suffocate from sorrow, she should be purple and bloated.

Footfalls clicked in the hallway. She briefly closed her eyes and drew on the last bit of strength left in her bones. She wouldn't let this setback defeat her. She would be strong. For the children. For her sanity.

Golden lamplight flooded the parlor, and Jana appeared in the doorway. "I thought I heard the door open. Vere you able to speak with anyone about getting the children back?"

Meredith crumpled the bonnet in her fisted hand. "I spoke with Major Allen, but no decision has been made yet. The children are still being held by Harriet Allen and her cronies, although the major did agree to allow Mrs. Clement to remain with them. At least the children have her for comfort."

"I am so sorry, Meredith." Jana hung her head. "My past choices haf hurt everyone."

"You mustn't blame yourself, Jana. You did what you had to do. It's those evil women who can't see past their righteous noses who are at fault."

"I vish there was something I could do."

So did she. But there was nothing either of them could do. The fate of the orphans rested in the hands of Major Allen, a man who had never been blessed with children of his own. How could he possibly understand the trauma a child endured when being removed from those they loved and trusted and forced to live with strangers?

Preston appeared in the hallway behind Jana. Strength and understanding shimmered in his eyes. She ached to anchor herself on his solid shores. He was just what she needed, yet nothing she could have.

Jana stepped to one side. "Good evening, Lieutenant Booth. Please…come in."

Preston swept off his hat and moved into the parlor. His towering presence chased the shadows from the darkened corners and eased her anguish enough that she could breathe without struggle.

"Vould either of you care for something to eat? I stewed a chicken for supper. There is plenty left."

The way her stomach churned, she doubted anything would stay down. "I'm not hungry. Thank you, Jana."

Preston shook his head. "None for me either, Mrs. Valder. Thank you for asking."

"Vera well." Jana set the lamp on a side table. "I vill take to my bed then. It has been a long day. Call out if you need anything."

As Jana left the room, the morbid silence returned. Meredith crossed to a chair and braced her hands on the back. The glass had been swept from the floor, and the shattered window covered with a board. Yet the malicious deed still hovered in the air, cold and cloying as the perfume of death lilies.

Footsteps thudded into the room, and then Preston was there, his essence wrapping around her like a blanket. She rested in the folds.

"Are you all right, Meredith? You didn't say two words between here and the fort."

If she let out a single word, agony would gush from her like a spring thaw. It thrashed just below the surface, roaring to be released. She took a step back, and her foot struck something. It was Robbie's primer, laying spine up on the floor. He'd dropped it when those ruffians had broken the window. She retrieved the book and clutched it to her chest. There was no give to the hard covering. No soft breaths. No squirming. No clean, soapy scent.

"I miss them so much," she whispered on a ragged breath.

"I know you do. But it won't last for long. Major Allen is a reasonable man. He seemed taken aback by his wife's fanatical behavior and with your revelation that the girls suspect she might be putting something in his coffee to make him ill. I'm certain he will see through his wife's rantings and order the children returned to you."

Her throat grappled with a sob. "What if he doesn't?"

"No one is more devoted to those children than you are. You treat them like they are your own. It's hard not to see that."

"In my heart, they *are* my own."

Anna's doll peeked from behind the chair. The strength went out of her knees. She sank to the floor and gathered the dolly, squeezing it and the book to her as if they might turn to smoke and vanish. Tears burned in her eyes. She couldn't hold back a moan. It scrapped up her throat and spilled over her lips.

"I let them down, Preston. I failed them."

He knelt and pulled her into his arms. She didn't resist. Couldn't. There was no more fight left in her.

"You have not failed them, Meredith."

"But I have. Many times. I'm not fit to be their guardian."

His lips brushed the top of her head, a gentle kiss that spoke volumes. "You are more fit than any woman I know. You have courage and conviction. Love and patience. Don't give up on the children *or* on yourself."

He was so positive, so grounded. He tethered her to the earth when she just wanted to float away. She tipped her head back and met his steady gaze. "Thank you, Preston. Your confidence means more than you know."

"It's only the truth."

"I'm blessed to have a friend like you. Someone I can lean on during the dark times."

"You don't need me or anyone else. You're a strong woman, Meredith. You would have survived this misfortune just fine without me."

Something darted across his face—guilt, sadness? Her pulse fluttered. "What is it, Preston? Is there something about the children you're not telling me?"

He shook his head. "Not the children. It's me."

"You? What about you?"

His gaze travelled over her, slowly, reverently, as if stamping her image in his mind to save for later. "I'm leaving soon."

The finality in his tone made her heart sink. "Leaving? Are you going out on a patrol?" Please let that be all he meant.

"Not on a patrol. My request for transfer came in. I've been reassigned to Fort Sill. I'm due there at the end of the month."

He was leaving her. She would never again be comforted by his tender embrace. Never be encouraged by his steady, confident voice. It was too much. The book and doll clattered to the floor. Everything was lost.

The arms holding her fell away, and he started to rise. Panic squeezed her chest. She grabbed for him. "No, don't go."

He stilled. "I'm not leaving…at least not right now. I was going to look for some spirits, a nightcap to take the edge off an exhausting day. I could use one. I'm sure you could too."

It would take an entire barrel of spirits to dull her pain. She pried reluctant fingers from his arm. "There's whiskey in the kitchen pie safe. Jana kept a bottle on hand for her…er, guests. Glasses are on the cupboard."

As he left the parlor, she gathered the doll and book and pushed to her feet. She set the items on the table beside the chair and grazed a finger across the hard cover and over braided yarn locks. Robbie and Anna would return. All the children would. She had to think positively. If she didn't, she'd sink into a black pit and might never climb out.

Preston returned with two glasses half-filled with amber liquid and handed her one. "Mrs. Valder has good taste in whiskey. It's Old Crow, a smooth Kentucky bourbon."

She accepted the glass and took a sip. Fire coated her tongue and scorched her throat. She drew in a raspy breath. "Smooth, you say?"

A smile stretched into his eyes. "It *is* an acquired taste."

She managed a smile of her own. "I prefer something a bit milder. Back home in Pennsylvania, our cook would make a crock of cherry shrub every summer. Juice from fresh Morello cherries sweetened with sugar and spirited with a gill of brandy. On especially hot days, we'd mix it with cool spring water. Quite invigorating."

Talk of the happier times at Hickory Hills blunted the sharpness of her pain. As did the whiskey. Subsequent sips took much smoother journeys down her throat. Her body and mind softened. She sank onto the chair with a moan.

Preston settled on the settee across from her. "You don't speak much about your life before coming to the territories. Tell me more about your home in Pennsylvania."

Oddly, she wanted to share every little detail, wanted him to know all there was to know about her…well, not everything, not yet. There wasn't enough liquid courage in her glass for that. The more mundane aspects would have to do for now.

"I grew up on a cattle farm just north of Philadelphia. *Hickory Hills*, my father called the estate, for the vast number of hickory trees growing on the property. We would gather the nuts every fall. Some were used for cattle feed, others for ourselves. Although, I don't miss the shelling part. Once you finally managed to break through the rock-hard hull, you have to pry the meat out with a small pick."

"Doesn't sound like it'd be worth the trouble."

"Oh, it was. Cook would toast the shelled meat and mix it in with a sweet batter. I had a hickory nut cake for every birthday that I can remember. Anna will be turning six soon. I just know she would enjoy a delicious cake with mounds of icing and..." Sorrow returned, snapping at her with sharp-edged teeth.

"Everything's going to be all right, Meredith. You'll be back with them before you know it, celebrating birthdays and all the other special events in their lives."

She blinked back a fresh round of tears. Any more leakage and her insides would turn into a desert. "I want to believe that; I really do. But I just can't stop the dark thoughts from creeping in. Everything I have ever touched has turned to ash. Why should this be any different?"

Preston set his empty glass on the side table and leaned forward, taking her hand in his. "It's going to be different because I say it will. Whatever it takes, I'll make sure you and the children are brought back together."

An eternity ago, he hadn't given two hoots about separating her and the children. Now, he vowed to do whatever it took to reunite them. This was the man who made her feel alive for the first time in years, the man she admired and respected, the man who had stolen her heart.

"Thank you, Preston. You don't know what that means to me."

He sandwiched her hand between his. She briefly closed her eyes and savored the comforting sense of being protected, of being cherished. It may be a long time, if ever, before she felt this way again.

His hands slid away. "You're exhausted. I should go. Let you get some rest."

Her veins turned to ice. If he left, the darkness would return, smothering her with its black void. She clutched his arm. "No. Don't go. I-I don't want to be alone."

"You have Mrs. Valder."

"I want *you*. Please stay."

He glanced at hearth. "I suppose I could make a pallet in here by the fire."

"Not here. I want you with me...in my bedroom...in my bed."

"I can't stay with you like that and not want to..."

"I know." She melted against him. "I need you, Preston. I need the comfort of your arms, of your body. Please say you'll stay."

****

Preston stopped on the second-floor landing. The faint glow of lamplight leaked from an open doorway at the end of the hall. Desire flared inside him. Meredith was in that bedroom, waiting for him. He'd gone out to see to his horse and to give her some time to prepare for bed. And think about what they were about to do. He wanted her to accept him willingly, with no second thoughts, no regrets.

He certainly had no regrets. He'd wanted her ever since he had set eyes on her...needed her, though he never would have admitted such a thing back then. What he *thought* he needed was just an illusion—a magic act orchestrated by his father's brainwashing propaganda. A soft ache filled him. That was all changed now. Meredith had helped him to see life differently. Made him see things as they should be seen, through his own eyes, through his own experiences. She was everything he wanted in life and more—*if* she would have him.

All was dark and quiet at the other end of the hallway where Meredith said Jana Valder slept. Good. If things got as heated as he hoped, he didn't want to disturb Meredith's friend—though he really didn't expect any interference or condemnation from that quarter. The reformed lady of the night would understand the needs of a man and a woman.

A clock gonging deep in the house urged him forward. He padded softly down the hall, the night-cooled boards chilling the soles of his bare feet. He'd left his boots, socks, and jacket by the back door. The less clothing he had to remove, the better. The flutter of undressing could easily make an inexperienced filly skittish.

He stopped in the doorway and took in the vision before him. She sat at a dressing table, clad in a thin, white robe and running a brush through silken locks. He itched to twine his fingers through that waterfall of spun honey and sink into her. He fisted his hands at his side and willed his heated blood to cool. Rushing would only spook her. He didn't want her bolting as she'd done before in his tent. This time he would go slow…let her decide how much and how far to let things between them proceed.

He moved into the room. Bedcovers had been pulled down, revealing inviting white sheets. A promising sign. Perhaps he wouldn't be visiting Dancer's Creek later to cool an unsated desire.

She stilled her brushing and spun around on the small bench. Her eyes were round as saucers, her breaths coming fast and shallow. She was nervous. That was to be expected. She had no experience in lovemaking. Her awkward responses to his kisses had been clearly virginal.

"Preston, you're back," she said in a breathless voice.

"I said I would return." He crossed to the vanity and held out a hand. "Let me do that for you."

She looked up at him, mouth agape and fingers strangling the brush handle. He gave a soft grunt. "What? Don't you think I know how to wield a hairbrush?"

"No. I-I just didn't…"

"You didn't expect such a thing from a man, especially a hardened trooper like me? Well, you will find there are a lot of things I'm quite adept at." *Many pleasurable things*. He waggled his fingers. "Brush, please."

She eyed his hand, and then set the brush in his palm. Fingers scraped his skin and pleasing tingles ricocheted up his arm. It wouldn't take much to turn him into a bonfire.

"Good." He prodded her shoulder. "Now turn around."

She slowly swiveled on the seat. Her wide-eyed gaze met his in the mirror's reflection. A pink tongue swept across her lips, sending fire racing in his loins.

"Did you get your horse settled? Was there room for him with Bessy? I know it's only a small building, more of a lean-to than a barn. Was there enough hay?"

She was rambling. Nothing soft words and gentle hands wouldn't cure. He pulled the brush bristles through her hair. "My horse is just fine. There was plenty of room and hay for him and your cow. They are both munching happily as we speak."

"I'm glad. I would have worried."

"I know you would have. That's who you are. You think about everyone and everything except yourself. Let me shoulder that worry for you. Just sit back and relax."

He concentrated on his brushing, going slowly, gently, letting each stroke quiet her. The tension went out of her shoulders, out of her face. She closed her eyes. Her soft moan curled around him, teasing banked embers to life. It took all his willpower to keep from hauling her from the bench and having her against the wall.

He leaned over, his head inches from hers. Her flowery smell invaded his senses. A longing came over him—the need to grab onto something that had eluded him for so long.

"Feels good, doesn't it?" he whispered into her hair.

Her eyelids slid open, revealing dark amethysts perfectly cut and shot through with flames. She was a rare gem. And she would soon be his.

"You're so beautiful. How is it that no man has claimed you?"

Throat muscles convulsed as she swallowed. She spun around on the bench. Her leg pressed against his, and longing leapt to hunger.

"Preston, I-I'm not sure…that is I know what should happen… I just don't know how…"

"Shhh." He set the brush on the vanity and drew her to her feet. "Don't worry about that. I'll show you all you need to know. But if you feel uncomfortable, or want to stop, all you have to do is say so. All right?"

She studied his face and apparently found her answer. Uncertainty faded from her eyes. A timid smile tugged at her lips, and she nodded.

He traced her cheek with a finger. Her skin was smooth and silky. The rest of her would be just as soft, the perfect arena for his lips. "May I kiss you?"

Her gaze shifted to his mouth and lingered there. "Yes, I'd like that."

He lowered his head and pressed his lips to hers. She tasted of peppermint and want. He coaxed her lips apart with his tongue. She stiffened at first and then softened, inviting him in. He slacked his thirst, savoring every drop. She was nectar and he the bee.

She stilled and drew away. He bit down on a curse. Rushing again. He'd best get a rein on his lust or this would be over before it got started.

"What is it, Meredith? Did I frighten you? Do you want to stop?"

"No. I'm fine. I…um… I just thought…" Her anxious gaze bolted to the bed. "Shouldn't we be doing this over there?"

"We can do whatever you want, wherever you want."

She fingered the sash belting her robe. "What about our clothes? Should we…undress?"

"Is that what you want?"

Her gaze inched downward to the hollow of his neck bared by the buttons he'd unfastened earlier. Her eyes darkened and she sucked in a breath.

"I want to feel you close to me..." Her words rushed on a breathless exhale. "With nothing between us. No clothes. No air. Nothing."

"Your wish is my command." He reached for the buttons on his shirt, but she stopped him with a gentle hand.

"Let me."

She unfastened each button, slowly, sensually, as if she were a practiced nightingale. His skin tingled and burned beneath her touch. Once all the buttons were undone, she slid her hands under the open folds and skimmed fingers over his flesh in a pleasing caress. She was learning fast. Her hands skated to his waist, and his groin tightened. *Too fast.* He couldn't stop a groan of pleasure.

She froze. "Did I do something wrong?"

"No, sweetheart. You didn't do anything wrong." He smiled down at her. "Quite the opposite."

"Oh. I wasn't sure."

"Don't be afraid. You can do whatever you want with me. Anything your heart desires. I'm all yours."

A nervous chuckle danced from her lips. "I've never had a man of my very own. A horse and a dog, yes. But never a man. Do you have any special needs I should be aware of?"

If he didn't know better, he would swear she was playing the coquette. "No special needs. Just to be fed, watered, and a given a good grooming now and again." *Preferably now.*

"I believe I can handle that. Let's get rid of this..."

She shoved the shirt off his shoulders. Cool air swirled around his bared chest. Her lips formed a perfect O that had him envisioning very unladylike things she could do with that mouth.

She trailed a finger over his chest, down his ribs, and halted at his waistband. Hunger paced inside him. He contained the beast with fisted hands and let her explore…let her gain the confidence she needed.

"Remarkable," she heaved out.

"What is, sweetheart?"

She lifted her gaze until their eyes met. A connection spread between them like the charge in the air before a skirmish. "You are. I don't think I could stand so still while you touched me like that. You are a patient man, Preston Booth. And I am a lucky lady."

"I'm the lucky one. My entire life has been devoted to following the path my father set for me. It has been a hard and often lonely journey, empty of emotion, which my father considers a weakness." The confession bubbled from him like a hot spring. He wanted her to understand what drove him, what had formed him—so she could appreciate how much she had changed him.

"What of your mother? Didn't she shower you with love and affection?"

"She may have wanted to, but my father wouldn't allow it. Said molly-coddling only weakened the soul. She, being the devoted wife, did as he bid." He closed his eyes against the past that still had the power to cut into him. "I never knew how to love, how to accept love. Until you."

He opened his eyes and poured his heart into his words. "Your love has shown me a new path to follow. I will be forever in your debt, Meredith Talbot."

"There's no debt to repay. I give my love freely."
She grazed a finger along his jaw. "That's the first time
you've really opened up about your past. Thank you,
Preston. Your trust means the world to me." Her lids
lowered to half-mast and her lips parted in sweet
invitation. "And thank you for letting me be bold and
daring without judgement."

"There's more where that came from. Much more.
If you want."

"Oh yes. I want." With a swipe of her hand, she
undid the sash holding her gown together. A brief shrug
and she was standing before him, a naked nymph ready
for a midnight swim. He was more than ready to join
her.

"Now you," she whispered. "I want to see all of
you."

Trousers and socks joined her dressing gown on
the floor. Meredith absorbed the intoxicating sight. He
was magnificent. Sleek and smooth with muscles in all
the right places—just as she imagined. An ache curled
inside her, a serpent seeking a warm spot to sun itself.
She wanted more, much more.

"Make love to me, Preston." She rested her hands
on his chest and his heat seared her palms. "Now.
Before I perish of want."

His hands cradled her waist, and he gently guided
her backward until her thighs met the bed. She reclined
onto the sheets, the cottony coolness bathing her skin.
Tiny shivers quivered through her as nervousness
warred with desire.

He hovered over her, his eyes flecked with fire.
"Are you sure this is what you want?" Gravel and heat
rasped in his voice. "I'm not sure I can stop if we go

much farther."

All her life, things had been forced on her—a new step-mother, her gift, and leaving her home. Being with Preston was *her* choice. *Her* decision to make. His gentle gaze poured over her, and all hesitation vanished. He was *exactly* what she wanted.

She grasped his arms and tugged him toward her. "There will be no stopping."

His body melded with hers, skin to skin, muscle to muscle, and heart to heart. Her head whirled. She couldn't think, couldn't talk. It was as if she were in the clutches of a vision except a hundred times more potent.

His lips and hands began to devour her. Every inch of skin flamed beneath his assault. Desire budded in that special place between her legs. She arched her hips, and his male hardness bucked against her thrust. He wanted her too.

He slipped a hand between them and stroked the small curls at the juncture of her thighs. Her insides flowered with pleasure. She gasped and pushed into his hand. He slid a finger inside her, and her body ignited into red hot flames.

"You're ready," he whispered.

Oh yes. She was starved. "Show me."

The fire in his eyes softened. "I'll try to be gentle, but this first time will hurt. Just keep still and the pain will pass."

Anything this pleasurable surely couldn't be painful. She wriggled beneath him. "Do it. Now."

Taking himself in hand, he guided his staff to her waiting cave. The warm tip throbbed and pulsed, stroking her folds, eager to enter. She was more than happy to welcome him. She lifted her hips, inviting him in.

He lowered his head and covered her mouth. His tongue stroked her lips, no less hot and eager than the staff between her legs. He was like an army, conducting forays on both fronts. She waved the white flag of surrender, ready to enjoy the submission.

He shifted and plunged inside. Pleasure turned to pain. She stiffened and cried out at the searing invasion.

His arms tightened around her. "Shhh," he whispered against her lips. "Keep still. The pain will subside in a few minutes."

She focused on the rise and fall of his chest, on the exquisite sensation of skin pressed to skin. Slowly, the pain receded. She relaxed and absorbed the fullness throbbing inside her. This conquest of her flesh was a pleasing mixture of strangeness and normalcy. He was part of her, yet he wasn't.

"Better?" At her nod, he clamped his arms around her waist and rolled over until she sat on top, straddling him. "You can move whenever you're ready. Go slow. Let your body get used to having me inside you."

He was letting her take charge, letting her be the one in command. She couldn't have loved him more. She rocked against him, slowly at first, then faster as pain turned to pleasure.

His fingers pressed into her buttocks. "Slower, sweetheart, or this will be over extremely fast."

She couldn't slow even if she wanted to. She bucked against his hold and rocked harder, searching for something elusive, something just out of reach. A vine of need twined through her body. It grew and grew until her insides exploded in pulsing heat. This time, she cried out with pleasure.

Preston thrust deep inside her. A ragged breath whistled through his clenched teeth, and a second later, liquid warmth spewed into her. She collapsed against him, spent. Never in her wildest dreams could she have imagined anything so wonderful.

He curled his arms around her and rolled her onto her side. Discomfort pricked at the sensitive area between her legs, and she stiffened.

His concerned gaze caressed her face. "I didn't hurt you too badly, did I?"

"No. All I feel is pleasure." She trailed a finger over his lips. He could do remarkable things with that mouth. "Will it always be that…amazing?"

He chuckled. "I'll do my best. Though I do intend to go slower next time; make the enjoyment last for much, much longer."

He wanted a next time with her. While the notion showered her with sunshine, gloomy thoughts intruded.

"Did you and Jana…um, did you ever seek her…um, her services?" She worried her teeth on her bottom lip, not sure if she wanted to hear his answer or not.

"Put your mind to rest, sweetheart. I never sought her out. This is the first time I've been inside this house."

A sigh of relief escaped. "I'm glad. If the two of you had been together…well, that would have been awkward." To say the least.

He chucked a finger under her chin. "You realize we skipped the courting part of our relationship. We'll just have to move up our future together."

"What do you mean?"

"I mean I love you, Meredith Talbot. I want to spend the rest of my life with you."

He loved her. It was as if someone had thrown open the door to winter and let in the spring. She palmed his cheek. "I love you, too, Preston. With all my heart."

"Then it's settled. We'll marry and you can come with me when I leave for my new assignment."

Sanity shoved a snowstorm into her springtime. "But I can't leave right now. Not until my aunt returns and the children are back together under one roof."

"We can still marry, and you can join me at Fort Sill once your aunt returns and the children have a new place to live. The separation will be hard, but I will manage knowing you will soon be by my side." He nuzzled her neck. "You'll make the perfect officer's wife."

She was not perfect. Far from it. She pushed out of his arms. "This is all so sudden, Preston. I never considered... I-I need some time to think about marriage."

"What is there to think about? We will have a wonderful life together, you and me and..." He smoothed a hand over her belly. "You could be with child. I refuse to leave Fort Dent without making you my wife."

Chapter Fourteen

The sun sat just over the tree tops, a glowing ball of warmth and light. All she felt was cold and dark. She'd let desire cloud her good judgement, and now she could be with child. She pressed a hand to her lower belly. *A daughter.* Her biggest fear could very well come to pass, and there wasn't a thing she could do about it…not anything she could live with doing. While Maddie most likely knew of a potion that could rid her of an unwanted babe, she couldn't intentionally harm an innocent. Nor could she carry the child to term and hand it over to someone else. That would be akin to cutting out a piece of her heart.

Preston wanted to marry her, wanted a life with her. The thought of being his wife filled her with exquisite joy. It was all she had ever dreamed of. It also filled her with great fear. She had no idea how he would react to her affliction. She could try to keep her gift hidden, but in her experience, secrets like that usually found a way out of their cage—at the most unfortunate of times. Besides, she didn't want their life together to start with lies and deceit. She would wait until Aunt Mildred returned and could advise her on how to handle the situation. Preston would just have to be patient and not push for an answer.

A pair of swallows swooped out of Jana's barn and lit on the clothes line. They sat, quiet and watchful, waiting for her to move. They appeared to know what the bowl in her hand meant. If only she had their fortitude. She'd lost count of the number of times she'd plowed out the door to retrieve the children, only to stop in the middle of the road, feet cold and heart sick. Charging headlong into the fray would only make the situation worse. She had to be patient, just as she expected Preston to be. She grimaced. Aristotle had it right, patience *was* bitter. It puckered her mouth like a green crabapple.

She upended the bowl of stale bread crumbs into the yard. *Wasteful.* Old bread made for delicious bread pudding. But with so few mouths to feed, baking seemed senseless. The bread would be going to mold soon anyway. Might as well let the birds enjoy a treat.

With a heavy heart, she retreated back through the doorway and closed the door. A deafening quiet enveloped the kitchen. She leaned against the counter and closed her eyes. Sadness sat like a sack of flour on her chest. Oh how she missed the quarrels over the last biscuit, the debates over whether honey or butter tasted better, and the races to see who could finish their milk first. She'd give anything to have all of it back. Anything.

"Meredith, where are you?"

Her pulse skipped just as it always did at the sound of Preston's voice. He'd left her bed before sunrise to attend to his military duties, and probably to avoid an awkward encounter with Jana. She hadn't expected him to return so soon...or at all for that matter. She had wounded his pride by not immediately accepting his marriage proposal. She saw it on his face and heard it in his voice. Knowing her indecision caused him pain nearly ripped her in two.

She slowly opened her eyes and set the bowl on the counter. "I'm in the kitchen, Preston."

"Come into the parlor. There's something I want to show you."

A sigh escaped from her lips. She just didn't have the energy for another skirmish. Last night, he'd gone on and on about how she would enjoy being a military wife until she put him off with claims of exhaustion, which hadn't been entirely a lie. She had been physically and mentally drained. Still was.

She undid the apron tied at her waist and set it on the counter. Best to just get this over with. Preston Booth was a most determined man.

As she made her way down the hall, a faint noise tickled her ear. It sounded like a child's giggle. She turned into the parlor, and her heart took flight. Mrs. Clement and the children stood around Preston, their smiling faces a balm to her raw nerves. Her knees gave way, and she sank to the floor. A second later, she was engulfed in a throng of loving arms. Tears spilled over and bathed her cheeks.

She kissed the top of each small head. Gabe pretended to gag. She gave him another just for good measure and then hugged the older girls. They all settled around her in a circle of love and happiness.

"Why are you crying, Miss Talbot? Are you sad?"

"Oh, no, my precious Anna. Those are happy tears. I'm so glad to have all of you here with me."

Anna smiled. "I knew you would get us back."

"It wasn't all my doing." She wiped away her tears and looked up at Preston. "How did you manage to get them released so quickly?"

"Major Allen and I had a long conversation this morning. We discussed Mrs. Valder's desire to turn her place into a boarding house and abandon her previous means of employment. As long as she abides by that plan, he agreed to allow the children to stay here until a new orphanage can be built. He even sent for a builder."

Encouraging, but there was still the matter of Harriet Allen. "What about Mrs. Allen? She has an unusual hold over her husband. What if she convinces him to change his mind?"

"That won't happen. Major Allen sends his apologies. He says he should never have allowed his wife's fanaticism to get so out of hand. He is sending her back east for a prolonged visit with her sister. I suspect to not only stop her activities, but to see if his stomach ailment improves with her absence. There will be no further trouble from her or the townsfolk she incites."

A weight lifted from her shoulders. "That's wonderful news. Isn't it children?"

Seven smiling nods answered her. Seven? Who was...of course, the intrepid explorer. "Where is Robbie?"

Preston turned in a circle, surveying the room and counting heads. "He was in the wagon. I thought he came in with the rest of the lot."

Becky shook her head. "He stopped to speak with that man."

"What man?" A nugget of worry sprouted in her stomach.

"The one who came to visit Mr. Hoggard at the jailhouse. He wanted to thank Robbie for stopping him from riding his horse when it was sick. Said he had a gift for him."

Preston's expression darkened and he bolted for the door. Meredith leapt to her feet and raced after him. "What is it, Preston? Why does Agent Finley talking with Robbie have you so concerned?"

He yanked open the front door and vaulted onto the porch. "Because Finley is supposed to be rotting in a jail cell right now."

"A jail cell? Whatever for?"

"For possibly being involved in the recent Indian attacks."

That nugget of worry blossomed into full blown fear. The Indian Agent had seemed disingenuous, but she never imagined he would be out and out evil. She charged down the steps and joined Preston at the wagon. There was no sign of Robbie. She cupped clammy hands to her mouth and called for the boy.

There was no answer. Not even the birds peeped a reply. Something tugged on her skirt, and she bent to see what it was. A tiny, whiskered creature clung to the hem. Her heart plummeted. *Oh, God no.*

She scooped up the mouse and cradled it in her palm. "Robbie wouldn't go anywhere without Petunia. Something must have happened to him. Something awful."

The children spilled onto the porch. "Did you find Robbie, Miss Talbot?" Becky called out.

"Not yet," she answered. "But we will." They had to. Robbie had suffered enough lately. They all had.

"Tell the children to stay on the porch," Preston said. "I'm going to see if I can pick up any tracks."

Cradling the mouse, she retraced her steps to the

stoop and stopped at the bottom of the stairs. "Becky, come down here for a moment. The rest of you stay on the porch until Lieutenant Booth says you can move. He's looking for tracks."

As Becky joined her, a quick glance confirmed that Preston was occupied with studying the ground around the wagon. Good. She didn't want him overhearing their conversation. He would have questions for which she couldn't give him any answers.

"What is it, Miss Talbot?"

She handed Becky the squirming mouse. "I found Petunia over by the wagon. Ask her what happened to Robbie. Did Mr. Finley take him?"

Becky cupped the mouse in her hands and briefly closed her eyes. After a moment, a frown creased the girl's brow. "Petunia says the foul-smelling man grabbed Robbie and took off with him. Robbie dropped her so she could tell us what happened."

Such a smart boy. Hopefully those wits would keep him alive. "Which way did they go?"

Becky focused on the mouse and then nodded. "She says the man rode away from the sun. Fast."

It was midmorning, so that meant Finley had headed toward the west. "Thank you, Becky. That helps a lot. You take care of Petunia until we get Robbie back. He would want you to look after her."

"You will get him back, won't you?"

"Of course we will." She tucked a stray curl behind the girl's ear. "Robbie will be back before you know it, pestering you and stealing tidbits from your plate for Petunia. I'll make sure of it."

After giving Becky one last encouraging look, Meredith walked to where Preston crouched near the wagon. Her mind whirled with all the possible scenarios of how to get him to search in a westward direction without revealing the why-fors.

She stopped behind him. "Can you tell which way Finley went?"

He lifted his hat and swiped sweat from his brow. "With all the comings and goings lately, the ground is pretty marked up. Hard to determine which prints came from Finley's horse and which didn't. I'll need to fan out. Check for fresher tracks leading away from the wagon. It's going to take some time."

Time Robbie might not have. "Try looking to the west first."

He squinted up at her. "Why west?"

Why indeed. The Shoehorn shimmered against the horizon, rugged and pocked with dark splotches where the sun couldn't reach. A thought emerged. Perhaps her nighttime forays into her father's collection of dime novels would pay off.

She pointed to the peak. "If I was on the run and needed a place to hide, that's where I'd go...into the mountains. Plenty of places up there to disappear into I'd wager."

"A sound observation. Can't hurt to try." He shoved on his hat and rose. Head bent, he moved away from the wagon in a westerly direction. He searched in a methodical manner, sweeping left to right, one step forward, then back right to left. No clue would escape his detection.

After what seemed like hours, he stopped at low spot just off the roadway and squatted. She hurried to his side. "Did you find something?"

He ran a hand over the sparse grass. "Fresh tracks.

Looks like Finley is indeed heading west. We ought to be able to track him from here."

A figure appeared on the road. It was Mr. Hoggard. He must have come to celebrate with them. Not much to rejoice right now.

"Can we come down now, Lieutenant?" Gabe asked.

Preston faced the porch. "Yes, you can come down now."

The children clattered down the stairs and raced toward the approaching handyman, all talking at once.

Joseph joined her and Preston at the army wagon. "The children say Robbie is missing. What happened, Miss Talbot?"

"Becky says she saw him talking with Agent Finley. When we came out to look for him, both he and Mr. Finley were gone." Meredith pointed to the mouse sitting on Becky's shoulder. "He left Petunia behind. Robbie wouldn't do that unless something bad had happened."

Joseph's face turned white as a rabbit's underbelly. "Dear Lord no. Did Agent Finley…did he take the boy?"

"We don't know for certain," Preston answered. "Finley was being detained as a possible suspect in the Indian attacks. He must have escaped somehow. Don't know why he would seek out Meredith or the children."

Joseph groaned and pressed a hand to his temple. "He did it because of me."

"You? How are you involved, Hoggard?"

"I saw Finley. At the orphanage…when he and his men were setting fire to it. They were garbed to look like Indians."

Meredith's stomach roiled. "Oh, Joseph. Why didn't you say so earlier?"

"Because the blackguard threatened to harm you and the children if I revealed what I saw. Remember that day at the jailhouse when he came to visit? You left to see to one of the children. That's when he confronted me." Joseph leaned back against the wagon, his expression tortured. "Dear Lord, what have I done? If only I had told the truth, none of this would have happened."

Her heart went out to the beleaguered man. As much as she wanted to criticize his decision, she understood why he had lied. "It's all right, Joseph. You only did what you thought was best at the time…to protect us. I would have done the same."

Preston's fist slammed the wagon bed, startling the mules and her. "It's not all right. What you did is unforgiveable, Hoggard. Now more people could die because of your cowardice."

She had never heard Preston speak so bitterly, or seen his face cratered with such contempt. Lies clearly set him on edge. "Preston, don't be so harsh. Joseph had good reason for withholding the truth."

"No, he's right, Miss Talbot." Joseph pushed away from the wagon and squared himself. "It was wrong to lie, no matter what the reason. I shall go to Major Allen and tell him of Finley's crime…as I should have done to begin with."

Preston footed the wagon cleat. "You do that. And while you're there, tell the major I'm gathering a squad to search for Finley and little Robbie."

Not without her he wasn't. She gathered a handful of skirt. "I'm going with you, Preston."

"No. It's too dangerous." He plopped onto the seat and gathered the reins. "Take the children inside and stay there until I get back."

"But I should go with you, Preston. Robbie might need me."

"What the boy needs is for you to stay here where it's safe. I'll make sure Robbie is returned to you unharmed."

He didn't wait for her to reply, merely whipped up the mules and rattled off down the road at a brisk pace. Meredith whirled for the house. She could not sit idle, worrying and fretting. It would drive her mad.

"Mrs. Clement, will you look after the children for a while?"

"Where are you going, dearie? The lieutenant said for everyone to stay here."

"I know, but there's something I have to do."

****

The bigger trees had been cleared for nearly a half mile outside of Mineral, for building materials and firewood. Over the years, undergrowth and stringy saplings had filled in the gaps. The small trees wouldn't do her much good. Their tap roots didn't reach deep enough. She'd have to go farther into the forest to find the gentle giants she needed.

The cottonwood growing near Dancer's Creek would be a good candidate. It had already provided a vision, even if it had been unsolicited. But getting to the tree would require journeying through the fort. She couldn't risk being seen and stopped by Preston. This trek, while exhausting and time-consuming, would have to serve.

Thorny branches scratched her arms. Vines

snatched at her boots. She pushed onward, her lungs burning with the effort. She wasn't about to stop. She had to find out where Finley had taken Robbie, before… No. She wouldn't think about what that awful man wanted with a young boy. They were going to get Robbie back safe and sound, just as Preston promised.

The overgrowth thinned, and the path opened to a deep gully that stretched for miles in either direction. She pulled to a gasping stop at the edge. On the other side of the chasm, the tops of several large trees reached for the clouds. Perfect. Just what she was looking for. All she had to do was cross a twenty-foot deep, rock-strewn deathtrap.

She pulled the bottom of her skirt between her legs and tucked it into her waistband, forming a sort of pantaloons. She'd done this many times back in Pennsylvania when she and Charles had gone exploring. It made navigating steep inclines much easier.

Easing over the lip, she worked her way down the slope, using imbedded rocks and protruding roots for hand and foot holds. It was slow going, but she didn't want to rush and end up with a broken leg or worse.

Halfway down, her foot slipped, and she scrambled for a purchase. Rocks and pebbles pinged on the boulders below. Her stomach and feet churning, she finally found a toehold and halted her plunging slide. She heaved out a relieved sigh. That was close.

As she resumed her descent, a frantic voice lifted up from the gully floor. "Is someone there? Help. Please help me."

It sounded like a child. Irrational hope surged inside her. It could be Robbie. She clambered the rest of the way down until her feet met solid ground. Boulders and scrub brush littered the bottom of the gully. The child could be anywhere in such a maze.

"Where are you?" she called out.

"Over here. By the big red rock."

The reply seemed to be coming from a large reddish-colored boulder about fifty yards away. She made her way to the rock, watching cautiously for snakes. This time, there would be no pistol or Preston to save her from a bite.

She rounded the boulder, and instead of Robbie, she found a boy about Gabe's age. His left foot disappeared in a crevice between two large rocks.

"My foot is stuck," he said. "Can you help me get out?"

"I'll try. What's your name, young man?"

"Pete. Pete Cavendish. My pa runs Cavendish General Store."

The rock-throwing, fist-tossing Pete. She ought to just leave him where he sat. It would serve him right. But she couldn't do that. Not to a child. Such cruelty went against everything she held dear.

She brushed dirt from her hands. "All right, Pete. Let's see about getting you out of there. Is your foot hurt? Are you able to move it?"

"It's not hurt—just trapped. And no, I can't move it. It's caught tight. I was jumping on the rocks and slipped. My boot got jammed in the gap."

Boys. Always getting into some disaster or other—usually of their own making. She moved behind him and slid her hands under his arms. "I'm going to pull while you push against the rock with your other foot. Ready?" At his nod, she barked, "Push."

She hauled on his arms with all her might. His wedged foot didn't budge. *Rooster's teeth.* She re-adjusted her grip and dug in her heels. "All right. Once more. Push."

He pushed, and she pulled. There was no movement. Not even a smidgen. His foot was lodged tighter than a fat rabbit in a hollow log. She'd have to find some other way to free the boy. If Gabe were here, he'd have the rocks moved in seconds. Wouldn't that just take the starch out of Pete Cavendish's britches?

The thought of shifting the rocks prodded an idea. "I'm going to look for a stout branch. Something I can wedge beneath one of these rocks and move it enough that you can slip your foot out."

He pointed to the other side of the ravine. "I saw a big branch lying over there by that thick clump of scrub brush."

"Perfect. I'll be right back."

Arms spread for balance, she crossed the uneven, rock-strewn ground and found the branch. It was of good size and solid, with no sign of rot. She picked up one end and dragged it back to Pete.

"I think this will work." She chocked one end under the smaller of the two boulders. "There. When I say push, you push as hard as you can. I'm going to put all my weight on this branch. With any luck, we'll move the rock enough that you can slip free. Ready?"

At his nod, she yelled, "Push," and leaned across the limb. Their groans clawed the air. Despite their labors, the rock held fast.

She shoveled the branch deeper. "All right. Try again, Pete. Push. Hard."

He grunted a response, and she bore down on the

branch. The rock shifted slightly. Pete strained, his face and ears turning red. The rock gave a sucking grumble, and the boy yanked his foot free.

"We did it," he yelped. "I'm out."

She let go of the branch and slumped against the rock. *We* sure did.

Pete shucked off his boot and rolled down his sock. The skin around his ankle was red, but not swollen.

"Try putting some weight on it," she suggested. "See if you can walk with no pain."

He took a few tentative steps and spun around. His face split into a wide grin. "It feels fine. I sure am grateful. What's your name, ma'am? I want to let my folks know who helped me."

"Miss Talbot. I look after the orphans from Seaton House."

His eyes widened, and he backed away from her. "The witch Talbot?"

"Pete—"

"I gotta go. My ma will be looking for me."

He shoved on his boot and took off up the incline, scaling it as effortlessly as a monkey climbing a tree. He certainly didn't have any lingering impairments from his ordeal.

She sighed and pushed upright. She still had a mission to accomplish, and this rescue had cost her precious time. Time Robbie might not have to spare.

She crossed to the far side of the gully. The gorge wall was steeper than the other side and had eroded to bare clay. Scaling it would be difficult, but she had no other choice.

Digging and clawing for each handhold, she moved slowly upward. Sweat trickled from beneath her bonnet and stung her eyes. Her breaths were coming in strained puffs. After what seemed like an eternity, she made it to the top. She hauled herself over the lip and paused to catch her breath.

To her left stood a thicket of pines, their branches elbowing each other as they reached for the sky. None of the trees were as grand as the oak at Seaton House or the cottonwood at Dancer's Creek, but they would have to do. She needed answers, and she needed them *now*.

Her breaths calming, she brushed mud from her hands and pushed to her feet. She crossed to the tallest tree and rested a palm on the trunk. The midmorning sun had penetrated the bark, turning it warm as toasted bread. She closed her eyes and gathered herself. She could do this.

She formed an image of Robbie in her head. Short-cropped curls, bleached almost white by the sun. Beaming blue eyes, and britches worn thin at the knees.

What do you see of him? Let me see.

There was no answer. Only a chattering squirrel interrupted the quiet. Perhaps being young in tree years, the pine required broader contact. She wrapped her arms around the trunk and pressed her cheek against the bark. Children needed hugs for encouragement, why not trees? She concentrated on connecting with the pine, on sending her thoughts deep into its heart.

Please, I need to see him.

The tree trembled beneath her embrace. Warmth bathed her arms and spread into her chest. Energy pulsed through her, welcoming her, connecting with her.

"Yes. That's it. Show me."

A low hum filled her ears. Her vision swirled with

white fog, dowsing the sunlight. A towering shelf of rocks stacked like books appeared. *Sitting Rock.* Aunt Mildred had mentioned the stone monolith located on the Creek Indian reservation where strange symbols had been etched into the rock face. Some claimed the markings were made by early Spanish settlers who had mined the mountains for gold.

"Is Robbie at Sitting Rock? Show me."

The mist swirled, and the image drifted downward, past rocks and scrub brush. The mouth of a cave emerged. Inside, silhouettes danced on the rock walls. One tall. One small and crouching. Faint sobs wafted from the opening.

Robbie. Fear throttled her throat. "Is he injured? Did that horrible man hurt him?"

A gunshot barked inside her head. And then another. The noise pierced her skull, making her stomach twist. She swallowed back a surge of bile and concentrated on the image. She would see this to the end no matter what the outcome.

The fog churned and rolled, revealing soldiers hunkered in the rocks below the cave. Gun smoke swirled around them. Slugs pinged into the hillside. One soldier stepped from behind a large, egg-shaped boulder. Another figure moved out of the shadows—a short, squat man, holding a short-barreled pistol. *Finley.* A shot rang out. The solider fell backward. Blood spread out in a circle, darkening his uniform.

Her heart crashed against her ribs. "Who is it? Who was shot?"

The image drew in on the injured soldier. He lay sprawled against the boulder. His gray-brown eyes were open but not seeing, his chest still as a frozen pond.

She dug her fingernails into the bark. "No, please. Not Preston."

A burst of light flashed, and then there was only inky blackness. She released the tree and slumped to the ground, head throbbing and mouth tasting of metal. The need to warn Preston battled the need to keep silent. The last time she told a non-believer about a vision, she'd been banished from her home.

Yet if she didn't tell him, Preston would die.

Chapter Fifteen

Meredith leaned against the newel post at the bottom of the porch steps and drew in several much-needed gulps of air. After navigating the gully and wading back through the undergrowth, she was quite winded...and sore. Muscles she didn't know existed screamed in protest. But she couldn't rest. Not until she found Preston.

A bay gelding tacked with a cavalry saddle stood tethered to Jana's porch railing. Preston must have dropped off the wagon and retrieved his horse. A combination of relief and dread swamped her. She would have to convince him to go against all he held sacred in order to save his life.

Footfalls sounded, and Private Greene rounded the corner of the house. Good. He would know where Preston was and save her the time of searching.

"Where is Lieutenant Booth? I need to speak with him."

Private Greene wagged his head. "He's not here, ma'am. The lieutenant rode off with a patrol to look for Agent Finley. He left me here to guard you and the children."

If it wasn't for bad luck, she'd have none. "How long ago did he leave?"

"'Bout an hour or so."

An hour. She'd never catch up to him on foot. She

crossed to the bay and freed the reins. "I need to borrow your horse."

"But Miss Talbot, the lieutenant said for everyone to remain here."

"It's vital that I reach Lieutenant Booth as quickly as I can." *Life and death vital.*

"He won't be none too happy to see you."

That was putting it mildly. Yet if it saved his life, she'd suffer his wrath. She tossed the reins over the gelding's head. "I'll deal with the lieutenant. Give me a leg up, if you would please."

Hesitancy twisted his face. He opened his mouth and apparently thinking better of arguing, propped his rifle against the porch and helped her onto the horse. She settled on the saddle and adjusted the stirrups to her shorter length. Cordelia would be aghast at her unladylike display...as would the good ladies of Mineral. If only they knew how adept and how often she had ridden astride, it would make their heads spin.

The trooper's withered expression clearly conveyed his concern. She was concerned, too, but she couldn't let doubts stop her from going after Preston. "Thank you, Private Greene. I appreciate your assistance. I need one more thing from you...how do I get to Sitting Rock?"

"Sitting Rock? That's on Creek reservation land. You shouldn't be going there by yourself."

"I won't be by myself. I'm going to meet up with Lieutenant Booth." She hoped.

"How do you know that's where he's headed?"

He wouldn't believe her if she told him. "I learned from a reliable source that's where Agent Finley went. Before you ask, I'd rather not reveal who my source is."

The trooper scratched his chin, mulling over her request. He was almost as mule-headed as his commander. Almost.

"Please. I don't have a lot of time, Private Greene. If you won't tell me, I'll just have to find the way on my own. And I'm running out of time."

His grumbling sigh scrubbed the air. "You remind me of my sister—strong-minded as the day is long. Reckon I have 'bout as much of a chance of stopping you as I did her." He pointed to the west. "Follow Dancer's Creek south. It runs along the base of the Shoehorn. After travelling a few miles, you should come to a gap in the ridge. That's Big Stoney Gap. Cross through that. On the other side, there'll be a wide mesa. Head west. Most of that will be Creek reservation land, so keep an eye out. They're a bit touchy 'bout trespassers. When you get to the oxbow lake, take the fork to the right. That'll lead you straight to the foot of Sitting Rock."

"Thank you, Private. You don't know how much this means to me."

He turned and retrieved his rifle. "Do you know how to shoot?"

She nodded. "Yes, I know how to handle a firearm." Quite well, in fact. When the fighting between the Union and Confederate armies had ventured close to the estate, her father had insisted she learn how to load and shoot both pistol and long guns. Even at an early age, she was a competent shot. It was one of the few times her father had been proud of her accomplishments.

"Is that a Sharps carbine?" She recognized the short-barreled weapon which had made shooting much easier for her smaller stature.

"It is. You know your firearms, ma'am." Private Greene slipped the carbine into the scabbard attached to the saddle. "The breech is loaded, and there's more ammunition in the saddlebag if you need it."

"Thank you again. I won't forget this."

She reined the horse around and nudged it into a steady lope. Nothing too strenuous. The animal needed to be fast, but not give out on her. She might be strong-minded, but she wasn't reckless.

It had been a while since she'd sat astride a horse, but it only took a few minutes for her body to remember the midnight rides she and Charles had stolen under the full moon. Her stepmother had accused her of inciting her son into wild and rebellious behavior. She had also accused her of causing his death.

Deep down, she knew that accusation was untrue. Charles' death had been an unfortunate accident. Yet a small tumor of uncertainty festered inside her. Perhaps if she had kept silent, her stepbrother might still be alive. Charles was not one to shy away from danger. In fact, he confronted it head-on, like the time he routed the copperhead from the chicken coop. Not an ounce of hesitation. She'd never know if he purposefully went into the pasture that day, or if fate had merely caught up with him.

Unease galloped in stomach, matching the horse's ground-eating stride. Preston was just as strong-minded as Charles, if not more. As much as she wanted to keep the details of her vision to herself, she didn't have a choice. She would have to tell Preston what she had seen. He would not sit idle while his men risked their lives—not without a sound reason.

Broaching the subject was another concern altogether. *I have a special talent. No. I have a gift. I can see things in the near future.* She groaned in frustration. Even to her, the words sounded fanciful and completely unhinged.

The horse stumbled, and she grabbed for the pommel. The path following Dancer's Creek had turned rocky and uneven. She slowed the gelding to a fast walk. Best stop her woolgathering and pay attention else she risked having her only mode of transportation come up lame. A half mile later, she reached the gap in the mountain ridge. Thankfully the owner of Shoehorn Silver Mine had suspended all operations until the renegades were captured. At times, the rumble of the mining blasts could be felt all the way to Seaton House. Riding so close to a blasting area would surely shake her right out of the saddle.

On the other side of the gap, a wide mesa spread out before her with another mountain ridge looming in the distance. Any other time, she would slow down and take in the wondrous sight. Right now, she had a mission to accomplish.

She set the horse to a slow canter. Little grew on the sparse butte. A few tufts of grass here and there and an occasional scraggly-looking bush. The Creek Indians sure did get the raw end of the treaty negotiation. She could almost sympathize with them for revolting.

After what seemed like hours, rolling hills replaced the flat terrain. In one low spot, rain water had collected in a shallow crater. She reined the horse to a stop and let him and her bottom have a quick breather. Unaccustomed to riding for such a long period, her bottom buzzed with discomfort.

She glanced skyward as the gelding nosed into the water. The sun had moved well past its zenith. She'd been riding for over an hour and was deep in reservation land. A trespasser. She prayed the Creeks would understand her need and not become provoked if they discovered her.

The gelding yanked his head up and sidled sideways. She yelped in surprise and scrambled to regain her seat. Once righted, she twisted around to see what had spooked the animal. Her heart leapt. Half a dozen riders approached at a fast clip, their dark-skinned faces and animal hide clothing unmistakable. She eased the Sharps out of the scabbard and onto her lap. She didn't want to use the rifle, but would if the Indians intended her harm.

They surrounded her, their ebony eyes taking her in, wary but not hostile. She held their gazes, refusing to show any fear. Maddie had once remarked that Indians respected honor and courage. She would be the American version of Joan of Arc.

One of the braves nudged his horse closer. A jagged scar raced across his cheek. It was distinctive and most unforgettable.

"I recognize you," she said. "You were part of the group arrested for attacking the homesteads."

"Wrongfully arrested. Your army commander realized this mistake. Set us free." Lines ploughed into his brow. "Why you on reservation land? White lady bring big trouble to Creeks."

He spoke passable English. That would make conveying her need much easier. Hopefully being freed had put him in an obliging mood.

"I'm sorry for trespassing on your land, but I have

to get to the place you call Sitting Rock as quickly as possible."

"What at Sitting Rock?"

"Lieutenant Booth has taken a patrol there. He's tracking Agent Finley who we believe has abducted a little boy. *My* little boy." Despite her attempt to be strong, her voice cracked.

The Indian's expression darkened. "Agent Finley is bad man. Very bad man."

Bad didn't come close to what Finley was. "Will you allow me to continue my search for Lieutenant Booth? I would be most grateful."

****

Preston motioned his patrol to a stop and dismounted. The trail of hoof prints ended at the base of a ridge the Indians called Sitting Rock. A couple of miles back, more tracks had joined Finley's. The man had reinforcements. They were most likely the men who had aided the agent with the recent raids and possibly with his escape from jail—and were most certainly armed.

A thick stand of trees ringed the bottom of the ridge and would conceal any approach. Yet once he and his men moved out of the tree line, the only protection would be a scattering of boulders and scrub brush. The muscles in his neck and shoulders pulled taut. They would be ideal targets. But it would have to be risked. A child's life could be in danger. He refused to return to Meredith with a blanket-wrapped body.

"What's the plan, sir?" Sergeant Reese asked.

Smart and a quick study, Jackson Reese was turning into a competent leader. The troopers liked and respected the non-com's *lead-by-example* approach.

The squad would be in capable hands when he left for Fort Sill at the end of the month—one less worry for him to shoulder.

"Have everyone check their weapons and ammo and assign someone to secure a picket for the horses." He slipped off his gloves and traded them for the spyglass stowed in his saddlebag. "I'm going to get closer and make an assessment of the situation."

"Yes, sir." Reese gathered his horse's reins. "I'll have Private Davis see to your mount, sir."

Preston left the glade and moved carefully through the thicket, using the larger trees for cover. He didn't want to alert Finley or his guards to their presence. Not until everyone was in place and primed to strike.

At the edge of the tree line, he stopped, extended the spyglass, and squinted through the eyepiece. A shelf of rocks that looked like a stack of books jutted from the top of the ridge. Below that, boulders and an occasional bush dotted the steep slope. Nothing moved in the barren terrain. He scoped to the left. A shadow twitched beside a large boulder. He focused in on the spot. The barest hint of a hat brim peeked around the rock. *Lookout Number One.* They'd take him out first.

He shifted the spyglass up a fraction and to the right. If this were his hideout, he'd post sentries at set intervals around the perimeter. He stilled his hand. That cluster of boulders looked textbook for a lookout.

After a few minutes, blue flashed among the sedimentary browns and grays. He smiled. *There you are, Number Two. You'll be next.*

He pointed the spyglass upward until the mouth of a cave came into view. It was the ideal hidey-hole to burrow in. Shadows drifted across the rock walls...two of them tall and slender, another short and stout. Three inside with two sentries outside. Five total. That tallied with the tracks they'd followed.

A smaller silhouette emerged and crouched on the cave floor. A soft sob drifted from the opening. *Little Robbie.* Preston fisted the spyglass. If Finley hurt one hair on that boy's head, he would pay for it—painfully.

Muffled thuds sounded behind him. He turned to discover a half-dozen Indians joining his troopers in the glade. It was Black Hawk and his scouting party. Hoggard must have convinced Major Allen of Finley's involvement in the Seaton House and possibly all the other raids, and the commander had set the Indians free. Black Hawk had apparently come across the patrol's tracks and trailed them here. Not that he could blame them. He'd want to investigate any incursion on his land too. Now that they were here, he could use their help in apprehending the real instigators of the attacks.

He pocketed the spyglass and started back. A lithe, gowned figure moved into view. He pulled up, heart bucking. What the hell was *she* doing here? She didn't appear to have been taken against her will. She moved through the warriors with ease, her head twisting from side to side as if looking for someone.

He stole back through the trees until he reached the glade. His men stood waiting for instructions, but he only had one person he wanted to school. Pain sliced him at the thought that she didn't trust him enough to bring Robbie back unharmed.

She spotted him and ran to his side. "Preston. Thank God, you're safe."

He steeled himself against the desire to pull her into his arms. She needed to know her disobedience was unacceptable. "What are you doing here, Meredith? I told you to stay at Mrs. Valder's."

The spark in her eyes dimmed. Perhaps he'd been too harsh, but dammit she should have obeyed his orders, should have trusted him to bring Robbie back safely. He didn't want to think about the dangers she could have encountered on her foolish jaunt. Damn woman was going to be the death of him.

She thrust up her chin in that defiant little gesture he had come to adore. "I came because of you and Robbie."

"I told you I would bring him back to you unharmed."

"I know you did. But I had to come. I had to find you."

"So you enlisted Black Hawk's help?"

The warrior stepped forward. "We found lady riding on Creek land. Said she was looking for you. That you tracked Agent Finley to Sitting Rock because he took her boy."

True, she had suggested the outlaw may have headed into the hills to hide, but she couldn't have known the exact location. Not unless she had inside knowledge. Yet the notion of Meredith in cahoots with Finley made about as much sense as glasses on a blind man.

"How did you know Finley had holed up here, Meredith?"

Color drained from her face. She opened her mouth to speak, but nothing came out. What was she afraid of? Him? After what they had shared, certainly she knew she could trust him.

"You have nothing to fear from me, Meredith. You

know that."

"I know. I want to tell you. I truly do. But…" Her throat convulsed as if she'd swallowed a nasty dose of castor oil.

"Just tell me, Meredith. Spit it out."

"I can't. It's not an easy tale to tell."

Unease wormed into his gut. What could she have to say that was so difficult?

"Question lady later," Black Hawk interrupted with an impatient slice of his hand. "We go after Agent Finley. Save boy."

The warrior was right. Defanging a nest of rattlesnakes and rescuing Robbie took precedence over any damn secret she might be harboring.

"We'll finish this conversation later. I need to brief Black Hawk on the situation." He skimmed her face for one last clue and only seeing mistrust and dread, turned to speak with the warrior. "I did a quick reconnaissance of the area. Finley has at least five men with him. Two lookouts are posted on each side of the ridge just above the tree line. The rest are hiding in a cave farther up."

"And the boy?"

"He may be with them inside the cave. I heard a child cry out."

The soft intake of breath spiked into him. He couldn't stop from looking at her, from wanting to ease her worry. "It's all right, Meredith. I'll make sure we get Robbie back to you unscathed."

Her hand snaked out and shackled his wrist. "You can't go up there, Preston. You'll be shot."

Just like at the creek when she thought the jailhouse had been on fire, her imagination went places it shouldn't. "You're merely upset by Robbie's abduction. I'll be fine, I promise."

Her fingers pressed into his skin. "You'll be killed. I saw it."

"Saw what? What the devil are you talking about?"

"Please." She inclined her head at nearby thicket. "Can we go over there where it's more private?"

He couldn't keep impatience from bruising his voice. "We don't have a lot of time, Meredith. Finley hasn't gotten wind of us yet, but he could at any minute."

"Please, Preston. This is important. It won't take long. I promise."

The knot in his shoulders pulled hangman tight. Whatever she needed to tell him must be truly earth-shaking if she was willing to delay Robbie's rescue for it. And based on the fear clouding those bright eyes, it wasn't going to be good.

****

Preston's hand on her arm should have put her at ease. But it didn't. The contact only heightened her awareness of him, of how much he meant to her. She had no idea how he would he react to her news. Disbelief, pity, revulsion—none seemed to fit the man she'd come to love. But she'd been wrong about people in the past. Dead wrong.

He gently tugged her to a stop in the grove and turned her to face him. "What is it, Meredith? What is so important that you need to delay this mission?"

She took a calming breath, heartened by the tenderness and concern shimmering in his eyes. She could do this. His life depended on it. "I care about you, Preston. With all my heart. But there is more to me than you know."

"What more is there to know?"

Enough to fill a lake—a very deep and murky lake. She scrubbed at her temple, searching for the right words. They were as elusive as a loose dollar bill on a windy day.

"Why all this fretting? You're acting like someone with something to hide. Are you in some kind of trouble?"

If only it were that simple. "No, I'm not in any trouble."

"Then what is going on? Tell me."

His frustration plowed into her. She twined her fingers into a tight ball, working to hold herself together. "You deserve to know the real reason why I asked for more time to consider your proposal of marriage."

"Yes, I know. Because of the children."

"That's part of it. But there's more. Something that may very well turn you against me."

Preston slid his hand down her arm in a slow caress that ended at her elbow in a gentle clasp. "There's nothing you can say that will turn me against you. Nothing."

She wanted to believe him. But uncertainty had its claws firmly clamped around her heart.

A hawk's screech pierced the air. She envisioned the bird riding the air currents, searching for prey. If it were a scavenger, it would find her the perfect meal, raw and bleeding and dying inside.

"Once you learn the truth, I fear that confidence will crumble."

His frown deepened. "Do you have so little faith in me that you think I would retreat at the least provocation?"

"I hope and pray with every fiber of my being that you won't."

"Then tell me. Let me show you how much I care."

A second screech joined the first. The hawk's mate. The pair hunted together, nested together, and raised their young together. The only thing that would separate them was death. If she couldn't find the courage to do this, Preston could be ripped from her forever.

"I am not...what I seem," she pushed out on a shaky breath. "I have a...a *gift*."

"You *are* gifted...with a kind and loyal heart."

"Not that kind of gift. It's a talent of sorts. An ability that stretches far beyond the average person." She fortified herself with another deep breath. No more dilly-dallying. It was time to bare all and let his judgment fall where it may.

"I can see visions. Visions of things to come...things in the near future."

There. The door was cracked. He didn't say anything. Didn't reject her announcement. Didn't condemn her. Just stared at her, his expression puzzled but still attentive.

She pushed the door wide open. "The visions come to me when I touch very old trees. I see images of things that are about to happen. When we first met, I had just seen a vision of soldiers, and then there you were. That day at Dancer's Creek, I saw a burning building and later realized it was Seaton House. The images are usually just fragments. Nothing specific that I can pinpoint or control."

"Visions, you say?" His hand dropped from her

arm. "Is that how you knew we tracked Finley to Sitting Rock?"

"Yes. I wanted to see where that horrid man had taken Robbie. I also saw you get shot." She pointed to the ridge beyond the tree line. Her finger trembled like a twig in a storm, and she balled her hand into a fist. She wanted to be strong and convincing, wanted him to believe in her.

"You were up there sheltered behind a large, egg-shaped boulder. When you moved out into the open, a man I believe to be Finley shot you with a short-barreled pistol. You were...you died, Preston." Just saying the words made her chest ache. Each heartbeat was a struggle—each breath forced.

"I'm not going to die. I promise."

A promise he may not be able to keep. "You have to trust me on this, Preston. Before I came to Seaton House, I saw a vision of my stepbrother getting gored by a bull. I told my father and stepmother, but they didn't believe me. I tried to push the tree for more details, but the elm wouldn't cooperate. Six hours later, our stud bull cornered Charles in the pasture. My stepbrother died right there, just as my vision foretold."

"Sounds like your stepbrother let his guard down and paid a heavy price for it. I plan to be extra vigilant. Always am."

"But that may not be enough. My stepmother said I caused Charles' death by *having* that vision. Maybe I did. Maybe I didn't. I just don't know for certain. This gift is so strange and uncontrollable."

"I've seen men get up and walk away after taking two or three bullets. Seen a drowned man breathe again. Both can be explained by the drive of the human spirit to survive." He shook his head. "But this vision thing…it's not explainable or logical."

"You can't rationalize it. Believe me, I've tried."

His lips collected into an impenetrable line, and he shifted his attention to the glade where the others were gathering. He was retreating from her, putting distance between him and her affliction. She felt as if she were standing in quicksand. Any moment, she would slip below the surface.

"You have to trust me, Preston. Let the others go after Finley."

He looked back at her, his eyes dark and unreadable. "Whether this vision thing is real or not, you know I can't shirk my duty. I won't."

"Please. You have to believe me." She grasped his arm. "Don't go up there."

"If you care about me half as much as you claim, you know I have to do this." He shrugged out of her grip and wheeled around.

She charged after him. "I can't let you, Preston. I won't."

He turned, his face etched with hard lines. "There's nothing you can do or say that will stop me from going. Stay here, Meredith. I don't need you causing a distraction and endangering my men or Robbie."

He gave her one last indecipherable look and stalked toward his waiting troopers.

Meredith sank to her knees, the will to go on leaking from her like blood from a fatal wound. He didn't believe her. Didn't trust her.

And now he was headed to his death.

Chapter Sixteen

She didn't know how long she sat. It could have been minutes or even hours. Dampness from the wet pine needles had seeped into her skirt. Even the bugs were treating her as part of the landscape. She didn't care. It was just as she feared, Preston had rejected her—didn't want his career stained by her taint.

Her head reeled. A whirring sound reverberated in her ears, and her stomach knotted as if she'd just had a vision. Except this time, she couldn't keep the sickness at bay. She leaned over and emptied her stomach, though there wasn't much to bring up. The most she'd consumed that day had been a slice of bread at breakfast and a few sips of water from Private Greene's canteen. Once Robbie went missing, food had been the last thing on her mind.

She swiped her mouth with the back of her hand. Only one trooper and the horses remained in the glade. Preston had gone with the others. She should have known his moral code wouldn't allow him to put credence in anything inexplicable or illogical. And if he did somehow believe her, he would never put his own life before those of his men. That was who he was. That was the man she loved.

She hung her head. Tears spilled from her eyes and wet her cheeks. She might one day fully understand her gift, might even be able to control it. But she would never be able to control how people responded to the warnings. That decision was theirs to make. Not hers.

"Meredith."

She lifted her head and blinked through a blur of tears right into familiar gray-brown eyes. Her heart lurched. "Preston…you came back."

He held out a hand. "I couldn't leave you like this, all sick with worry."

"But your men…the mission."

"The mission is proceeding as planned. Black Hawk and the others are moving into position as we speak. He and Sergeant Reese will lead everyone safely through the operation."

"I pray with all my heart that they do." She stretched out her arm and settled her hand in his. She wanted to believe all would be right between them, but the steely fingers chilling her skin said otherwise. "What made you change your mind, Preston?"

His grip on her hand tightened. "I won't deny that I wrestled with what you told me. I still am. But I realize there are things in this world that are just not explainable."

"You believe what I said? In what I can do?"

He drew her to her feet, his expression shuttered tighter than a window in a snowstorm. "After making sure everyone understood their assignments, I spoke with Black Hawk about Finley's escape. He said the agent had a visitor this morning who must have slipped him a weapon. When the morning meal was brought in, Finley drew a short-barreled pistol on the guard."

"Short-barreled. Just like from my vision."

"Exactly. I can't refute that or the fact that you knew I had tracked Finley here." His armor cracked.

Hurt and anger flooded into his face and graveled his voice. "What bothers me the most is that once we got close, once I opened up about my upbringing, you didn't do the same. You kept your past, your gift, a secret. You didn't trust me with the truth. That hurts more than any bullet, Meredith."

Her deception had cut him—deeply. She wanted to kiss away his pain as she did with the children. But the hard draw to his mouth told her doing so would just toss salt into his wound. She could only hope his hurt would lessen once he understood her reasons.

"I was afraid to tell you, Preston. Afraid you would cast me off, just as my father did. After Charles died, my stepmother insisted I be sent away before my gift caused anyone else's death. My father sided with *her*. He banished me from my home." The dark memories yanked the steadiness from under her voice. "Th-That's why I came here...to hide away with Aunt Mildred. That's why I couldn't tell you."

Her mouth tasted sour and somehow scalded. Her hands sagged to her sides, even their paltry weight too much to hold. She closed her eyes and stood at the edge of collapse, feeling the shakes, and knowing she either found her footing or plunged into the gorge.

"Are you going to be ill again, Meredith? Do you need to sit?"

His concerned tone pulled her back from the brink. She drew in a deep breath and another and opened her eyes. She locked her knees. She wanted to be strong. For him. For herself. "No. I don't need to sit."

"Very well. But if you start to feel poorly, let me know. As much as we need to have this conversation, I don't want to put your health in jeopardy."

He cared about her. That had to mean something. "I'm fine. Please go on."

His gaze drilled into her. "I understand how hurtful a rejection like that can be, and I'm sorry your father did that to you. But what I want from you, what I need from the woman I love is honesty."

Had she destroyed any chance at a life with him? It was hard to tell. He had wiped any trace of tenderness from his face. "I wanted to tell you so many times, but I couldn't. Most people have never understood or accepted my gift. I've kept it hidden for so long; I just don't know how to be open about it."

"I don't give a damn about your gift. You could turn rocks into gold for all I care. I just want us to be open and honest with each other."

"I never intended to hurt you, Preston. Never. I'm so very sorry. I promise to share everything I possibly can with you from now on."

"Everything you possibly can?" His irritation cut the air like a hatchet. "What kind of half-hearted pledge is that?"

She pressed a hand to her lower belly where a child could be growing—a daughter who would inherit the family misfortune. Preston deserved to know the *full* extent of her gift. Aunt Mildred would understand her need to reveal their secret.

"There are others with my ability." She met his incredulous stare head-on. "Aunt Mildred. My mother, God rest her soul, and all my grandmothers as far back as we know. The gift of sight is passed down the female line of the family. It's another reason I have been hesitant to marry. I don't want to saddle a daughter with such a horrible curse."

"It's a little too late to worry about having a daughter."

"Yes, it is. But I have no regrets about what we did. I love you, Preston, and I will love any child that results from our night together."

"Were you ever going to tell me the truth?"

His gaze probed her face, evaluating, testing her. It nearly killed her to think he would never believe a word from her lips. "I told the truth when I said I needed time to consider your proposal. I wanted to ask Aunt Mildred if she had ever revealed her gift to her husband and if so, how she went about it."

Footfalls strode into their conversation. Preston gave an exasperated groan and swung around to greet the approaching trooper.

"Pardon me, Lieutenant, but the horses are all secured to the picket line. Well, all except for Black Hawk's piebald. That one won't budge an inch."

Preston nodded. "Just leave the piebald where it is. The animal has probably been trained to stay in place. Go ahead and take up a position to the south. It won't be long before the main assault begins."

As the trooper trotted toward his assignment, Preston clasped her elbow and urged her forward. "Come. We can wait in that grove near the tree line. It'll give us a clear view of the slope without being out in the open."

She fell into step beside him, her gait slightly gimpy from where the saddle had rubbed her skin raw. If her efforts saved Preston and Robbie, she would gladly endure any suffering the journey had inflicted.

Only the faint thud of their footfalls broke the quiet. Not even her bleeding heart made a sound.

"What about the children?" he finally said. "Were the accusations of them conducting witchcraft true?"

The man could put two and two together faster than a fox sniffed out a rabbit. Denying the truth would only widen his wound. She had trusted him with her secret; she could certainly trust him with the children's.

"We don't consider our talents as witchcraft, but yes, each of the children has a gift of some sort. That piebald your trooper was having trouble with... Robbie could probably get it to cooperate. He can converse with the animals. Literally. He hears their thoughts in his head and they can hear his."

"Holy cow."

Meredith couldn't help but smile at his quip. "His sister, Becky, has the same gift. Mildred rescued them from a town in Ohio. They had been orphaned by a fire which they escaped with the help of the town mongrel. The townsfolk were none too receptive to their abnormal abilities and refused them shelter."

"And the others?"

"Gabe can move small objects with his mind. Remember that day at Seaton House in the parlor when you tripped over the footstool?"

His eyebrows shot skyward. "That footstool *did* move. I knew it had."

"Gabe was trying to stop you from stomping Robbie's pet mouse."

"That little scamp." He wagged his head. "I knew there was something unusual about your orphans; I just didn't know how *very* unusual."

"Well now you know. Mildred established the orphanage specifically for children with special talents just as our ancestor Mistress Seaton. She teaches them to control and conceal their gifts so they can assimilate into society without fear of being discovered and persecuted. It's a secret we all share and work hard to preserve."

"You won't have to worry about me revealing your secrets. You have my word."

His hand grazing her arm gave her hope. She might have assuaged some of his pain by opening up to him, but it would be a long, hard road to fully earn back his trust.

The echo of gunshots shattered the stillness. She jumped at the sound, a gasp escaping her lips. The rescue had begun.

Preston unholstered his pistol and motioned to a nearby thicket. "There's more protection over by that cluster of pines. You'll be safer there. And don't worry about Robbie. He'll be just fine. Finley's reign of terror will soon be over."

If only she had his confidence. Maybe her insides wouldn't be so twisted with worry.

She moved to the base of a large pine tree and sank to the ground. Sunlight dribbled through the canopy and speckled the carpeting of pine needles. It reminded her of that day seemingly an eternity ago—one that had changed her life forever. She'd been sitting under the big elm near the barn, waving her hand through the sunbeams and watching as they sparkled like magic on her skin. It had been a lovely afternoon, full of chirping birds and lazy breezes. Until a tortured scream shattered the tranquility. She'd raced to the pasture but arrived too late. Charles lay silent and still on the grass, outlined in a glistening puddle of red.

She'd knelt beside him and touched his face, letting

her sisterly love go out of her and into his cooling skin. She wept with her hand on his cheek, wept for what she had done to him, for not being able to save him, for not being there to hold him when he left the world. She'd wondered if he had looked down on her, stunned and confused, while the birds sang and the sun speared her with magical beams.

The snapping of a branch stabbed into her thoughts. Preston had shifted closer to her, watchful and protective. A searing breath scorched her throat. Thankfully his death would not be a haunting regret.

The gunfire slowed and finally ceased. She rolled up on her knees and peeked around the tree. *Please let it be over. Please let Robbie be safe.*

A flash of tweed caught her eye. A man slithered from behind a cluster of rocks—a short, squat, snake of a man toting a short-barreled pistol. *Finley.* Even from a distance, she could see the fear pocking his blubbery face. He should be afraid. If she had a gun, she'd shoot the serpent herself.

"I'm going after him," Preston whispered. "Stay here and don't move."

Fear robbed her of a breath. "Preston…you can't."

He looked down at her, his gaze soft and reassuring. "I know what to expect now. Finley won't get the drop on me."

If she ever wanted him back in her life, she had to trust him—without reservation. She nodded. "Be careful."

He left the grove and crept along the tree line, angling for the far side of the slope ahead of the escaping serpent. A hundred heartbeats later, Preston traded the protection of the trees for a large egg-shaped boulder—exactly like the one in her vision. She held her breath, waiting, watching. Tension filled the air, thick and dark, like smoke from a coal fire.

Finley drew within twenty yards of Preston's hiding spot and slowed, his pistol hoisted. She wanted to call out, wanted to warn Preston of the danger. She held her tongue. She had to believe in him as she wanted him to believe in her. This was what he had trained to do. He would keep himself safe.

A movement at the top of the boulder caught her eye. Instead of moving around the rock and into the open as she'd seen in her vision, Preston was going over it, using the rock as a shield. His head and upper body came into view. Finley also caught sight of him and skidded to a halt, pistol pointing upward.

A gunshot barked out.

Finley's pistol clattered to the ground. The agent staggered backward, howling and clutching his shoulder. Preston surged over the rock and dropped to the ground. He reached Finley in three strides and kicked aside the dropped weapon.

Her heart started pumping again, her lungs drawing air. She slumped in relief. Preston was alive. Her vision had been thwarted.

The crunch of footfalls sounded, and Black Hawk and his warriors emerged from the other side of the slope, herding three rope-bound men in front of them. Preston's troopers trailed them, one of them toting Robbie.

The boy wriggled free and raced toward her. She gathered him in her arms and gave him a quick squeeze before pushing him out to arm's length. He appeared to be unharmed. No blood, no bruising. But that didn't mean there weren't other injuries hidden beneath his clothing or worse…deep inside.

"Are you all right? Did that rotten man hurt you?"

Robbie wagged his head. "Finley only hit me once. It didn't hurt for long."

She glared across the glade at the agent who staggered and moaned like he was on death's doorstep. Evil, maggoty man. Lucky for him, Preston had only shot to disable. Another four inches to the left and Satan would be celebrating a new arrival in hell.

Robbie wriggled out of her grasp. "Did you find Petunia? I dropped her when that mean old goat grabbed me. I told her to let you know what happened."

Leave it to him to think of his pet rather than himself. Meredith smoothed down a lock that stuck out from behind his ear. "Petunia told us everything. She's doing fine. Becky is looking after her for you."

"Good. I was worried. She doesn't like to be alone."

Preston joined her and Robbie in the grove. "Is the boy all right?"

"He's fine. Just a little shook up as anyone would be after such an ordeal. What on earth did that man want with you?"

"Ummm. I can't say." Robbie cut a glance at Preston and lowered his voice. "It's about my gift."

"That's all right. The lieutenant knows all about us. He's promised to keep our gifts a secret."

The boy beamed up at Preston. "We won't have to hide things from you no more."

"Any more. And no you won't, son. Not around me. What did Finley want with you?"

"He somehow figured out I could talk to animals.

When we got to Mrs. Valder's, he came up to the wagon and said he wanted to give me something for helping save his horse. That's when he grabbed me."

Such a brave young man. Putting on a courageous face when he had to be scared to death. She certainly would have been. She was. "You must have been so very frightened."

"I was a little scared. He put a knife to my neck and said he'd cut me if I told his horse to act up or if I tried to call any critters to help me. Once we got to this place, he ordered me to talk to the animals. Find out where the gold mines were hidden."

"Gold mines?" she asked.

Preston wagged his head. "Of course. I should have seen through all the smoke. It's rumored that Spanish settlers found gold in these hills centuries ago. The Creeks have had a lot of trouble keeping trespassers off their lands. It's probably the reason Finley started staging raids to look like the work of the Indians. He wanted the army to move the tribe to another reservation. Then he would have easy access to the mountains and could search for the gold mines. I wish I would have figured it out sooner."

"If it helps any, sir. I learned where they are."

"Where what are?"

"The mines. A nice fox said he chased a chipmunk into a cave one day. Said there were strange markings all over the walls. I didn't tell that polecat Mr. Finley where they were. But I will tell you if you want."

Preston patted Robbie on the shoulder. "You can tell Black Hawk. These are his people's lands. They are the ones who should decide what to do with the information."

****

At the garrison gate, the troopers guarding Finley and his cohorts peeled off and headed in the direction of the jailhouse. A large splotch of red stained the agent's jacket. The bandage Sergeant Reese had applied had stopped the bleeding, and much to the relief of Preston's ears, the sniveler had abandoned his caterwauling. Finley hunched over in the saddle, head bobbing and jowls sagging. The man knew there would be no escape from where he was going. Not this time. And if convicted of his crimes, he'd soon be trading a jail cell for a fire pit in hell—a more fitting place he couldn't imagine.

Preston guided his horse onto the main thoroughfare leading through town. Darkness had settled in during the ride from the reservation, sending folks into the comfort of their homes. Only small pockets of lamplight spilling from the windows lit the deserted roadway.

He reined in beside Meredith's mount. A shaft of golden light outlined the weariness tugging at her eyes. Yet her lips held a contented smile. She had her children back. All of them. She would do anything to keep her charges safe, even risk her own life. Hell, he'd have done the same if it kept his troopers from harm.

However, what he couldn't abide, what ate at him the most, was her reluctance to open up about herself and her gift. If she could keep something that important from him, what else might she hide? With lives depending on his judgement, he needed a wife he could trust and depend on. As much as he loved her, he wasn't sure he could do that. To make matters worse, she could be with child. His child.

He clenched his teeth around a curse. He could marry her. Give her his name, but not share a life with her. He could rescind his offer of marriage, but that would leave his child a bastard. Two options, each a bullet to his moral code. How the hell had it come to this?

The boy sitting on his lap squirmed as if sensing his disquiet. He'd offered to let Robbie ride back with him. Meredith was clearly exhausted and if her limp was any indication, saddle sore too. She didn't need the added burden of a fidgety child.

Robbie had jumped at the opportunity and chattered non-stop most of the way, asking about army life and chasing down outlaws and rogue Indians. The boy had a vigorous mind that was for certain—most likely made all the more intense by his magical gift.

The rascal could converse with the animals. That morning when he'd gone to fetch the dawdling youngster as they were vacating the jailhouse, he'd thought the boy was having a one-sided conversation with the cow. *Apparently not*. Robbie had questioned him about whether he could talk to his horse. He chuckled under his breath. On days when his mount decided to spook at the least little provocation, he could sure use such a talent. But then again, hearing every miniscule thought, whether animal or human, could get tiresome. Robbie's gift would definitely be a double-edged sword.

"You know what, Miss Talbot?" the boy said after a spell of uncharacteristic quiet.

She laughed softly, the sound tinkling like a soothing waterfall. "With you, Robert Edmunds, one never knows *what*."

Robbie tipped his head back and peered at her from beneath the slouch hat's wide brim. The boy had remarked it was the *niftiest* hat he'd ever seen. From the appreciative gleam in the boy's eyes, he took that to mean something good, so he'd offered to let the boy wear it. If the hat made the child feel special, so be it. Robbie deserved some joy after what he had bravely endured, even if the thing did nearly swallow him whole.

"I've decided I'm gonna be an army officer when I grow up, just like the lieutenant."

"Are you now?" Meredith cut a glance his way, a coquettish glint slanting her eyes. "Girls just adore men in uniform. You'll have them falling at your feet."

The slouch hat wobbled with the boy's wagging head. "Girls. Ugh. I just wanna ride around the country and protect folks from bad people."

That tune would change in about ten years, once adolescence kicked in and pretty lips and rounded backsides beckoned. "Work hard at your studies," he said. "Keep out of trouble, and maybe you can go to West Point Academy."

"What's that?"

"It's a school back east that teaches young men academics and military leadership. President Grant graduated from there."

"Did you?"

"I did." Memories of his school years bombarded him. The comradery. The feeling of belonging, of being a member of the Long Gray Line—and later, of joining the brotherhood of fighting men. He thought that's all he wanted from life. Until Meredith Talbot.

Robbie thumped the hat brim. "Then that's where

I'm going. West Point Academy. Just like President Grant and Lieutenant Booth."

A warm, fuzzy feeling washed over him. Was this how it felt to have someone want to follow in your footsteps? To leave behind a legacy when you left the world? It made his father's uncompromising fanaticism toward his education almost understandable. Almost.

If he took the assignment at Fort Sill, he would surrender any chance of guiding young Robbie toward achieving a career in the military. He wouldn't be able to help any of the orphans attain their goals. His gut clenched. Or be in the life of any child he and Meredith might have created.

She feared passing her curse to a daughter. He understood her worry. People were contrary beasts. Anything strange or mysterious frightened them and that fright caused them to act out. He'd seen such a thing firsthand at the academy with one of his older classmates. Andrew Sawyer had been exceptionally gifted in mathematics. He could tally troop assessments and distances within seconds. For that exceptionalism, he was ostracized by the other plebes. No one wanted to befriend a freak of nature.

He hadn't really considered how her *gift* might affect his career. While he wanted to be there for his daughter or son; it also meant he had to make a decision about their mother—about what he wanted with her. Right now, he just didn't know.

The door to the General Store opened, spilling lamplight into the street. A man stepped onto the boardwalk. "Is that you, Miss Talbot? Did you find the boy? Is he safe?"

Meredith slowed her mount. "We did, Mr.

Cavendish. He's right here riding with Lieutenant Booth, safe and sound."

"That's very good news indeed. We heard about his abduction and were worried…worried about you too." A woman joined Cavendish on the boardwalk, and the store owner draped an arm around her waist. "The missus and I want to thank you for rescuing our Pete earlier. The boy gets himself into the darndest spots."

"It was nothing. I'm glad I could help."

"We're sorry about the harassing of you and the children. We got caught up in the frenzy with the rest of the folks. It was wrong. We should have been better Christians. Rest assured it won't happen again. I'll see to it that someone comes by first thing to replace Mrs. Valder's window."

Preston grunted under his breath. Well, well. The good folks of Mineral were finally seeing the error of their ways. Too bad it took a child's abduction and the discovery of the real wrongdoers to open their eyes and their hearts.

Meredith dipped her head. "Thank you, Mr. Cavendish; your kindness is much appreciated."

As the pair disappeared back inside, Robbie twisted to look at Meredith. "You helped that polecat Pete Cavendish?"

"Of course I did. He needed my help. That's what decent folks do; we show compassion even when it may not be reciprocated."

"Well, I wouldn't have done it."

Preston nodded. He wasn't so sure he could have shown such compassion either. Meredith certainly was a bewildering mixture of softness and strength.

The road darkened as they left the more populated

section of town. Mrs. Valder's house loomed ahead, every window glowing with lamplight. Images surfaced of the night he and Meredith had shared there. It had been perfect. She was perfect. Like a multi-faceted gem. No matter which way he looked at her, she sparkled and shined.

Preston reined up in front of the house and handed the boy to the ground. As Robbie raced for the house, he dismounted and went to help Meredith from her horse. She leaned into his hands and heat shot through his veins. His body certainly had no lingering doubts.

Once on the ground, she rested a hand on his arm and turned that sunny smile on him. "Thank you, Preston. For bringing Robbie safely back home. I want you to know I never doubted you would."

"I'm glad everything turned out so well."

Her smile faded. "Did it? We never really settled things between us. I know I hurt you by keeping my gift a secret, but I'd like the chance to make it up to you. I can only hope you find it in your heart to forgive me."

Could he? That was a question he'd tossed back and forth in his mind ever since she'd blindsided him with her confession.

The front door blasted open and lamplight and children spilled onto the porch and down the steps. The orphans surrounded them, their questions peppering the air. A month ago, he would have cringed at the noise. Now, it was a musical symphony—and it added another facet to an already complicated decision.

****

The children whirred around her like excited bees, all buzzing at once. While pleasing, the commotion was tiring, and she was already drawing on the last reserves in her pantry. Thank goodness Preston had offered to let Robbie ride with him back to town. She didn't think she could have handled a squirming child. Preston had no doubt seen her weariness. He cared for her, cared for her welfare and that of any child she might be carrying. She could only hope it was enough to get him past his doubts.

There had been no opportunity to talk during the ride home. He'd stayed well behind her and only moved closer when they reached Mineral. She thought she saw warmth spread into his eyes when he lifted her from her horse. But that faded as soon as the children had surged from the house. Perhaps he just needed some time to digest the vast amount he had been forced to consume.

"Let's go inside children," Meredith urged, giving the more spirited heads a containing hand. "It's getting late, and Robbie needs to rest."

"Aw, Miss Talbot," Gabe whined. "We want to hear more. What happened to that rat-faced Finley? Did he get shot? He should have. Right between his beady black eyes."

"Gabriel Hunt, such violent talk. You know better than that."

"Sorry, Miss Talbot. I just wanted to hear what happened."

"You can hear all about it inside. The milder version, only. Do you hear me, Gabe?" She didn't need to be up all night calming nightmare-plagued youngsters. At his nod, she shooed them with a sweep of her hand. "Go then, all of you."

As the children dashed toward the porch, Robbie remained behind, holding out the slouch hat that Preston had allowed him to wear. It had been a kind gesture. One she was certain the boy would never forget. Neither would she.

"Here's your hat, Lieutenant." Robbie's face glowed with adulation. "I 'preciate you letting me wear it."

Preston waved a dismissive hand. "You keep it, son. I'd be honored to have a brave young man like you taking care of my hat."

"Don't you need it?"

"I can purchase another at the Sutler's store. You go on inside now like Miss Talbot said."

The boy gave an excited yelp and rushed up the stairs, waving the hat like a victory flag. Meredith smiled at the display. Preston had come a long way since that first encounter in the foyer at Seaton House. So stiff and stodgy and full of rules on how children should behave. He had softened a great deal. He might even enjoy being around them if that amused glint in his eyes was any hint.

Private Greene emerged from the side of the house and joined them. Lines of relief fanned out from the corners of his eyes. "Lieutenant. Miss Talbot. I see you got the boy back unharmed."

Meredith nodded. "Everyone made it back safely. Well, everyone except Finley and two of his thugs who were shot during the rescue. With the help of Black Hawk and his warriors, Lieutenant Booth and his patrol were able to capture the outlaws. You'll never believe what that despicable Indian Agent was up to."

Private Greene's face bunched in bewilderment. Preston handed the trooper the reins of her horse. "I'll explain on the ride back to the fort. Mount up. I'll join you shortly."

The trooper led the gelding a discreet distance away before mounting. He was giving them space to say their goodbyes. She only hoped it wasn't a forever farewell.

Excited voices drifted from the house. Preston shook his head. "Sounds like the children are back to their normal selves."

"You're welcome to come in and join us. I'm sure they would be fascinated by your account of the mission…if you can get a word in around Robbie and Gabe."

He gathered his horse's reins. "Thank you for the offer, but I should go. Major Allen will be expecting a report, and I want to make sure Finley is locked up good and tight this time."

Disappointing, but not unexpected. Duty came first for Preston. It was what drove him, what made him the man she loved. It might also keep him from forgiving her.

"I hope you'll come back. There's so much more I want to say."

Indecision clouded his eyes. "You've said all there is to say. It's up to me to decide what I can and can't accept."

A tiny figure moved out of the shadows, interrupting their conversation. Lamplight shimmered on brown curls pulled back with a lace-trimmed ribbon worn only on special occasions, like church services or weddings. The child might have a long wait for the latter ceremony, if there was going to be one at all.

"What is it, Sally?" she asked. "Do you need something?"

The girl stopped in front of Preston and held out a

flower. It was a daisy she'd plucked from Mrs. Valder's flower garden. Sally was forever puttering in the soil, turning puny, wilted plants into vibrant foliage. Perhaps she could communicate with them. She'd already shown an aptitude for sending mental messages. It was not out of the realm of possibilities.

Preston squatted. "Is this for me?" At the girl's nod, he took the flower. "Sure is pretty. Thank you, Miss Sally."

"It's for saving Robbie."

Meredith gasped and took a step back. "She talked. Oh, my goodness. Sally, you talked."

Sally smiled and shrugged. "It was time."

"I suppose it was." She laughed and shook her head. "Preston, you should be honored. Sally hasn't spoken a word since she arrived at the orphanage. Yet she talked. *To you*. It's a miracle."

"Miracles happen every day," a familiar voice called from the porch. "Even when you least expect them."

Her heart leapt, and she whirled around. There was no mistaking the tall, slender woman with violet eyes and blonde hair fading to white at the temples. "Aunt Mildred," she cried out. "You're back!"

Chapter Seventeen

Preston dismounted and led his mount into a stall. Lanterns hanging from the wall posts provided just enough light to see by. Yet he would have welcomed the gloom. It mirrored his misery.

He'd almost turned around three times during the ride from Mrs. Valder's house. The hurt and disappointment shadowing Meredith's eyes haunted him. He was breaking her heart, but he couldn't help himself. She wanted forgiveness and an acceptance he wasn't sure he could give.

He loved her. There was no denying that. Believing in her, in what she claimed she could do? That was a mule of an entirely different color. How did any sane person grapple with such a thing as having visions of the future? He trusted in what he could see and touch and control. Yes, Finley had tried to ambush him at Standing Rock just as she had foreseen. But any snake on the run would have done the same. On the other hand, she knew where Finley had taken the boy. That couldn't be explained with logic or reasoning. What a quagmire.

"You sure you don't want me to take care of your horse, Lieutenant?" Private Greene said from the adjacent stall. "It's late. You must be awful tired after chasing down Finley and his gang."

He unfastened the girth strap and let it swing

beneath his horse's belly. Though his striker usually saw to his mount, he wanted...he needed...the physical exertion. With all the thoughts warring inside his head, sleep would be as elusive as a royal flush at a poker table.

"No. I'll do it. I'm too wound up to sleep anyway."

Private Greene grunted. "I can understand that. All the vile things Finley has done overwhelms the mind. And all for a rumor of gold."

He'd given the trooper a brief account of Finley's activities. Thankfully the agent's villainy was at an end. He'd made sure of that with a stop at the jailhouse before heading to the stables. Finley and his cohorts had been placed in separate cells with three soldiers assigned as guards. He'd instructed the men to limit visitors to Dr. Troutman for medical purposes and Reverend Scott for heavenly healing—neither of which the varmints merited. Pain and fire pits were all they deserved.

He slid the saddle and blanket off his horse and onto the stall door. Entering the jailhouse had stirred troubling thoughts. At the table where the guards played cards, the children had sat doing their schoolwork and eating their meals. Mundane activities. Yet, according to Meredith, the Seaton House orphans were anything but ordinary.

"I'm glad you got the boy back safe," Private Green said, breaking the quiet. "Miss Talbot, too. That is one determined lady."

Determined didn't come close to describing her. He picked up a currycomb and attacked the gelding's dust-coated hide. "She is perplexing; that's for certain."

Greene chuckled. "If I wasn't already shackled, I

might just set my sights on her. She'd definitely make a fascinating companion. Around her, life would never be dull."

Indeed. Meredith Talbot was anything but dull. More like a blinding summer sun.

Preston moved to the horse's other side. Until meeting her, he hadn't known anything was missing. He'd thought his life was full and rich and filled with a sense of duty that carried him from day to day. Some days were better than others, but when you loved something that much, you had to accept the good with the bad. Was he looking at Meredith from the wrong angle?

"Not that I'd have much of a chance," Greene added with a grunt. "Miss Talbot has eyes for only one man."

He stilled his currying. What if she did find another man? Someone who could look past her odd ability and accept her for who she was? Another man who would be sharing her life and her bed. A pang stabbed his heart. He might as well let Finley take a shot at him as to let that happen.

"You gonna ask her to marry you, Lieutenant? I don't mean to meddle, but I seen too many of my mates lose something good 'cause they couldn't get out of their own way. Don't think on it over-much. Just do it."

Just do it. Preston shook his head and resumed grooming his horse. "When did you trade your kerchief for a priest's collar, Private Greene?"

The trooper's head bobbed over the stall door. "Truth be told, I'd much rather be a lawman. Can't abide law-breakers. People like Agent Finley need to be brought to justice, though he probably won't be an agent for much longer. Not after what he did. Those poor Creek Indians. They deserve better than Finley."

Yes, they did. Preston smiled for the first time that evening. He knew exactly what he needed...*wanted*...to do.

****

The creek ran low after a span of no rain and hot weather. Water coursing over exposed rocks embroidered the air with a soft burbling. Waning sunlight dappled orange shafts across the polished surface. It was the perfect time for a swim.

A pair of shiny black boots sat on the bank below. Uniform trousers and a white shirt decorated a nearby bush. Farther out in the shallows, water rippled around a muscular back dotted with droplets that glistened like diamonds on sun-kissed skin. Her pulse danced a polka.

It was also the perfect time for carrying out her mission.

Mildred had offered sage advice about earning forgiveness. She'd said that we all do thoughtless things, break promises, or simply make bad choices. The best thing to do was to let Preston know how deeply she regretted her behavior. Let him know that actions spoke louder than words and from now on, her actions would match her promise. She squared herself. That was exactly what she had come to do.

She kicked off her shoes and toed them aside. Private Greene informed her that Preston had gone for a swim. She knew exactly where to find him. Preston had pointed out the ideal spot for swimming that day of the rattlesnake debacle. Hopefully the location would evoke fond memories of their first kiss and not one of the secret she had withheld.

She began unfastening the buttons lining the front of her dress. Preston would be surprised to see her. Would he be pleased? In the two days since Robbie's rescue, he hadn't come by to see her, hadn't even sent a missive explaining his absence. Worrisome thoughts gnawed at her. Had he reconsidered his offer of marriage? Felt he couldn't trust her enough to allow her to share his life?

She tugged loose the last button. *There was only one way to find out.*

Dress clutched closed, she eased down the well-worn path winding through the sawgrass growing on the embankment. It was indeed a popular spot to swim. With any luck, filling empty bellies would trump the desire for a dip, and she and Preston would remain undisturbed.

She moved slowly, being careful with the placement of her feet. A wrenched ankle would not help her cause. At the bottom, she paused and dug her toes into the cool silt lining the bank. She was stalling. She'd rehearsed her pitch over and over, selecting and discarding various renditions. Now that the time was at hand, fear of his response throttled her throat.

He could send her away without hearing her out. He could take what she offered and then dismiss her. Or her prayers could be answered and he would accept her back into his arms, back into his life. As Lily's tarot cards had foretold, he had a choice to make. Her breath hitched. *Please let it be me.*

She must have made a noise because Preston spun around, his expression leaping from alarm to surprise in the time it took a hummingbird to flit from danger. "Meredith. What are you doing here?"

No more delaying. She had to do this. For both of their sakes. She wriggled out of the dress and let it dribble into a puddle at her feet. Cool air coiled around her bared flesh. She shivered and fought the urge to cover herself. She'd forgone the layers of petticoats and drawers normally worn beneath her skirts. What she intended required as few garments as possible.

"I came to see you..." She spread her arms wide, welcoming the air, welcoming his fiery stare. "To show you that I have nothing to hide. That I will always be open and honest with you."

His mouth opened and closed like a fish tossed onto a river bank. She had him off balance. Good. At least he wasn't completely shutting her out.

She reached up and removed the combs, letting her hair tumble around her shoulders. "I want to be your wife, in every sense of the word. If you'll have me, I give myself to you freely, with no pretense, no conditions."

His strangled moan shot across the water. "Right here? Now?"

"If that is what you want, yes."

He mashed a hand through his wet locks and pitched a fretful glance at the embankment. "There's not much privacy. What if someone happens upon us?"

"It's near sundown. Most folks will be in their homes, having supper. And mess call sounded not ten minutes ago at the fort. No one will be out and about."

"Even so, this is not exactly Eden. There's mud and sawgrass and insects. You know how much you detest spiders."

He was hedging. He didn't want her—not as his wife, not even as a lover. She dropped her hands to her sides, defeated. A breeze whipped through the glen, making the tall blades wave back and forth as if applauding her downfall.

"I can see you don't want me...don't trust me enough to get that close again. I understand." She bent and retrieved her dress. Picking up the pieces of her heart would require a shovel. "I'll just go and let you have your swim in peace."

"Stop." His command thundered through the air. "Don't you go anywhere."

He pushed through the water and three ragged heartbeats later had her wrapped in his arms. His heat surrounded her, lapping at every cove in her body. "I do want you. More than anything in this world."

His intense gaze raked her face, and then he lowered his mouth to hers, possessing her, demanding she respond. And she did. She swiped a greedy tongue across his lips and dipped inside. He tasted of whiskey. He'd been drinking. Because of her? Because of what she had done to him?

She pulled away and studied his face. There was no hardness there. No hurt. Just puzzled concern. "Did that kiss mean you have forgiven me, Preston? That you believe in me and trust that I will be honest with you from now on?"

His hands slid down and cradled her hips, fingertips pressing gentle fire into her skin. "While your betrayal hurt, I understand why you withheld the truth. It wasn't out of cruelty or selfishness. You were protecting yourself. I get that. The only thing I ask is that you trust me...as your husband...to keep your secret safe. Trust me to be your protector." He brushed a hand over her lower belly. "And to protect our child, should we be so blessed."

Her body quivered beneath his touch. She ached to have him, not just now, but forever. She reached up and ran a finger along his jaw. So strong. Yet gentle and loving when it came to her and the orphans.

"I trust you with my life, Preston. With our child's life. I want nothing more than to be your wife, to be loved, honored, and protected by you. There won't be any need for a separation. Aunt Mildred raised enough funds on her trip to rebuild, and Jana decided she would rather help care for the children than run a boarding house. So I am free to go with you when you leave for your new assignment."

"You'll be my wife, but you won't be coming with me."

He wanted to marry her not because he loved her, but out of obligation. Hurt carved thick, rounded slices out of her heart. Not even her father's rejection had cut so deeply. She closed her eyes, battling tears that threatened to spill out. If his name was all he could give her, then she would accept. It was the least she could do after the pain she had inflicted.

"Very well. If you want me to stay behind, I won't fight you. I'll be the obedient wife you need me to be."

His warm breath caressed her lips. "You're not coming with me, my sweet, talented Miss Talbot, because I'm not going to any new assignment."

She opened her eyes and met the warmth of his gaze. "Wh-what do you mean? Are you staying here at Fort Dent?"

"Not in the manner you think. I haven't called on you the past few days because I've been busy with paperwork and handling the details of my resignation."

"Your resignation? From the army?"

"My period of service is coming to an end, and I decided not to renew."

She didn't know whether to shout for joy or cry for his loss. "But Preston, the army is your life. It's everything you ever wanted."

"*You* are everything I want, Meredith."

She wanted to believe him, but doubt hovered over her like a thundercloud. "What will you do instead? All your training and education has been for the sole purpose of serving this country as your father and grandfather did."

"And I will. Major Allen and I had a long discussion. We decided that I should take over Finley's position as Indian Agent. I can still honor my duty to country, but in a different fashion. The Creeks need a strong advocate to voice their interests in Washington. That has been much lacking lately."

Sweet words that could sour with time. "Are you certain this is what you want? I fear you would wake up one day full of regrets."

"I'm certain. We will have a lifetime full of love and happiness. There will be no regrets." He gathered her hand and pressed a tender kiss to her fingers. "Will you marry me, Meredith Talbot? Be my wife, the love of my life?"

Sunshine burst inside her and scattered the clouds of doubt. "Yes, yes, yes. A thousand times yes. I will marry you, Preston Booth. I couldn't ask for a more perfect husband and father for our children."

"Children? What about your fear of having a daughter? Of passing on your gift?"

She rested a hand on his chest, treasuring the solid

heartbeat thudding beneath her fingertips. "Because of your love and support, I no longer fear passing on my gift. You taught me that I can embrace my ability and be all the stronger for it. We can do that for our daughter too."

"Smart as well as beautiful. It's no wonder I fell under your spell."

She smiled at his jest. "I love you, Preston. With all my heart."

"And I love you, my beautiful, bewitching nymph." He scooped her up and carried her into the water. "I've envisioned doing this ever since I laid eyes on you."

She twisted and wrapped her legs around his waist. "Is this what you envisioned?"

Epilogue

The oak trembled beneath her fingertips. Warmth spread from its trunk and pooled in her palm. Energy pulsed through her, inviting her, welcoming her. She smiled. It was good to be back.

She formed an image in her head of a dark-haired girl dressed in brown muslin and running from a torch-bearing mob. *Show me what you see. Let me see her.*

A low hum bathed her ears. Her vision swirled with white fog, cloaking the sunlight. Her body tingled with awareness. A new effect—strange but not unpleasant. It was like plunging into a cool river after a long hot day.

The fog parted, and a man appeared, his gait angry and purposeful. He toted a rifle in one hand and a flaming torch in the other. Firelight scrubbed over his face and revealed the heated bent to his eyes and mouth. More torch-bearing men emerged. Her skull echoed with the thud of their footsteps. She waited for the recoil in her stomach. It never came.

Where is the girl? I want to see her.

The vision shifted to a small, thatched house silhouetted by the light of a full moon. The windows were dark. The door shut tight. Nothing moved in the cabin or in the clearing around it. All was quiet. Graveyard quiet.

Firelight danced in the surrounding woods,

splattering the trees with burnt gold. The faint echo of shouts and crashing brush buzzed in her head. A pale glow stained the window, and then the silhouette of a girl emerged.

Closer. Move closer so I can see her.

The image drew in on the window, revealing a young girl of no more than fourteen or fifteen. Dark hair framed a pale, oval face. Despite the courageous tilt to her chin, her almond-shaped eyes flickered with fear.

The torch-bearing mob broke through the woods and encircled the house. One of the men holding a coiled length of rope and a Bible stepped forward. "Witches of Satan come out and meet your judgment."

"We have done nothing wrong," came the girl's confident reply.

"Moira Devlin, what you do is evil. You have bewitched the good folks of Willoughby. Little Jimmy Thacker died at your hands."

"We did all we could for Mr. Thacker's son. The boy could not be saved."

The man jabbed his Bible skyward. "Come out. Or we'll burn you out of that accursed hovel."

The girl's chin rose higher. "If you believe us guilty, then have the sheriff arrest us. Let a judge of this fair state determine our guilt or innocence."

"We are the only law in Texas."

"Burn them," someone yelled. "Send them to hell where they belong."

The mob began chanting the word "burn." One after another, they tossed their torches at the house. The thatch caught fire, and flames engulfed the roof. Black smoke billowed skyward. The silhouette at the window disappeared.

Take me inside. I want to see her.

The fog swirled and darkened, and then parted, exposing the inside of the hut. The young girl, Moira, knelt beside an elderly woman lying on a cot. Smoke eddied around them. Moira tugged on the older woman's arm—to no avail. The woman didn't budge. There was a loud splintering, and the roof gave way. Fire and ash enveloped the room. An agonizing scream made the hairs on the back of Meredith's neck stand on end. She stiffened. She couldn't allow such a horrible thing come to pass. She wouldn't.

The tree shuddered beneath her touch. It probably recalled its own horror at the hands of fire. A burst of light flashed, and the vision went dark. Her head spun, and her knees wobbled beneath her. She leaned back and anchored herself on the firm body that had been shielding her from curious eyes.

"Steady now." Preston wrapped his arms around her. "I have you."

She stood in his embrace, drawing on his strength. The spinning subsided. Her legs grew stout as tree trunks. It was a much quicker recovery than ever before.

"Are you all right, sweetheart?"

"I'm fine." She twisted around. "Perfect, in fact."

"Were you able to see any more of your aunt's vision?"

Earlier that week, Mildred had been scrying for gifted children in need of help. She'd been given a vision of a dark-haired girl being driven out of town amid cries of witchery. Unable to coax any more details from the tree, she'd urged Meredith to try. Said the older she got, the less productive her visions were. Meredith suspected it was a ploy to get her to practice her gift.

"I saw a house in the woods surrounded by an angry mob. They were going to burn the girl and an elderly woman alive." She grasped his arm. "We have to find them, Preston. Save them from those evil people."

"Don't worry. We will. Where was this happening, could you tell?"

"They mentioned Texas and a town called Willoughby."

"In east Texas. I'm familiar with it. How much time do we have?"

"I saw a full moon. Last night's moon was more than three quarter full." Her vision had provided her with more details and pushed much farther into the future than ever before—which was a good thing. It gave her a chance to change the outcome.

"We'll have to hurry," he said. "But we should be able to make it in time. How do you feel about taking a trip? A belated honeymoon so to speak. With the rebuilding of the orphanage and my new position, we haven't had a chance to properly celebrate our wedding. We can take the train to east Texas. Enjoy the trip in a private railcar."

"Will you be able to leave your duties for that long?"

"Things have settled down at the reservation now that negotiations with the railroad are over. I should be able to leave for a few days. How about you?" His fingers grazed over her rounded belly. "Will you and our little one be up to a trip?"

"We should be just fine. The episodes of morning sickness have subsided. Our little butterfly should stay nice and comfy in her cocoon another four or five months."

His eyes widened. "*Her* cocoon? Did you see something in your visions that says we're having a daughter?"

"No. But Nel spoke with my mother who hinted about seeing her granddaughter soon."

"Your *deceased* mother." He wagged his head. "I don't know if I'll ever get used to such goings-on."

"You're doing just fine. Let's go tell Aunt Mildred about our plans."

She tucked her hand in his crooked arm and fell into step beside him. Activity around the orphanage had ceased while the workers broke for dinner. Construction was nearly done, thanks to the efforts of volunteers from Mineral and from Fort Dent. The abrupt reversal in attitude toward the orphans was quite astonishing. Mayor Wood had awarded Robbie a medal of honor for his bravery, and Major Allen made him an honorary trooper. The commander had recovered quite nicely in the absence of his wife and was no longer plagued by painful stomach ailments. It was sad that a woman who espoused God's word had poisoned the man she vowed before Him to love.

Thankfully Harriet's fanaticism had no residual hold on the townsfolk. Gifts of money, clothing, and toys had poured in from all over the territory. Even the Indians had contributed, supplying building materials using the gold they mined from the cave Robbie told them about. Seaton House had risen from the ashes like a bird of paradise.

And not a moment too soon. Earlier that morning, the children had arrived for their first look at their new home. Their exuberant shouts and clattering feet had christened the building with joy and love.

As she and Preston approached the house, little Anna rose from the porch steps where she'd been playing with her kitten. She didn't appear to be alarmed by Preston's presence. Quite the opposite. Her face blossomed with a cheerful smile.

"Good afternoon, Anna," Meredith greeted. "Does Daisy like her new home?"

"Daisy likes her new home very much. We even have our own bed." Anna peered up at Preston and held out her hand. "Would you like to see it, Mr. Booth?"

Surprise puckered his brow. "You want me to take your hand?"

Anna nodded. "So I can show you where my bedroom is."

"Very well." Preston snuggled the child's hand in his. "Lead on, Miss Anna."

Meredith's heart swelled. She had her children and the love of a man who accepted her for who she was. Her world was complete.

A word about the author...

Donna Dalton lives in central Virginia with her husband, two sons, and a grandson. An avid reader of historical romances, Donna uses the rich history of the "Old Dominion" State for many of her story settings. You can visit her at www.donndalton.net or on Facebook at DonnaDaltonbooks.

www.ingramcontent.com/pod-product-compliance
Lightning Source LLC
Chambersburg PA
CBHW051520260626
47170CB00003B/701